Portal 37

One-One-Seven

by

Sherie L. Howard

Matter is neither

created nor destroyed –

Antoine Laurent Lavoisier, 1785

One

"Will I sleep forever?" Anastasia looked into the penetrating brown eyes that hovered over her playful blue ones. "Goldie is still sleeping."

"Who's Goldie?" Dr. Allison Starr was good with kids, even though she was forty-two years old, childless, and hadn't given much thought to her declining fertility. Hell, who am I kidding? Her basket probably didn't contain any eggs, but that was okay. It was by choice. One she had made at an early age.

"Goldie was my fish." A small tear pooled in the corner of the five-year-old girl's left blue eye reminding Allison of Azure Lake, the location of Allison's weekend hiking trip in the North Cascades National Park last summer. She would have enjoyed it had it not been for the company she kept – an obnoxious forty-something man she had met at her Seattle apartment complex. Not only did he misrepresent himself – still legally married, and did I mention he had four kids? – but he gave off a bad vibe Allison still couldn't shake. "Goldie went to sleep forever."

"Goldie?" Allison asked as she snapped back to her life as a single medical professional, taking her eyes away from the child's hypnotizing blue ones that held her captive.

"My fish," the child reminded her.

"Well, Anastasia, I promise that will not happen to you." Starr had just started her fifth year as a cardiovascular anesthesiologist at the Swedish Medical Center's Cherry Hill Campus in Seattle, Washington. Confidently, the forty-two-year-old anesthesiologist reassured her young patient. "You will wake up feeling much better, and I will visit you when you do." It was a promise Allison would keep, even if it meant staying late, past her regular shift at the hospital. "I need you to trust me." She instructed. "Begin counting backward, just as we talked about."

Allison Starr listened as five-year-old Anastasia avoided using her vocal cords full-force. Each word came out in a slow, delicate whisper. *Three. Seven. One.* The young patient's eyes fluttered before her lips could correct the sequence Allison hoped for – Three. Two. One.

Dr. Starr knew paralysis had taken over the small body and that the surgery needed to repair the young girl's septal wall would be painless, while Dr. Ben Gerhart, Chief of Surgery, used robotics to patch the small hole in the child's heart. There would be no human-made incisions. Over the last five years, surgical robotics had taken over the movements of endoscopic instruments. Dr. Gerhart's role was to use the Mind-Controlled Communication Device (MCCD) to communicate with the thin robotic arm. After placing the black-colored band around his forehead, any chit-chat in the small surgical room ended, and complete silence filled the sterile operating chamber. Aside from Dr. Gerhart, the chief surgeon, and Dr. Starr, the anesthesiologist, only one other human medical professional was in the tiny space. His name was Dr. Holm. He is a renowned MCE, or Motions Computer Expert, whose job it was to monitor and troubleshoot any technical problems with Dr. Gerhart's MCCD and the bionic arm, the latter of which the staff at Swedish Medical Center referred to as Dr. Chrome.

Allison Starr watched Dr. Chrome respond to Dr. Gerhart's silent thoughts. Occasionally, she would notice Gerhart shake his head up and down, signaling his agreeance with the robotic arm. Sometimes, even though less often, she would catch Gerhart moving his head in a slight side-to-side motion, signaling a difference of opinion with the bionic arm. Their discrepancy would dissolve after a matrix of computer chips and software analyzed the probable outcomes. This procedure takes place after examining both Gerhart's thoughts and the robotic arm's central processing unit (CPU). Rarely, Allison Starr imagined, did Gerhart's suggestion override Dr. Chrome's. There hadn't been any errors since Dr. Starr joined the team almost five years ago.

The team took just under ten minutes to complete the surgery. First, Dr. Chrome cut a one-fourth of an inch opening into the skin on the young girl's chest's right side, then a one-inch square of pericardial tissue was cut and retrieved internally. Finally, with minutes to spare, the created patch was placed between the young girl's right and left atrium, repairing the tiny hole in her heart. Starr watched Anastasia's body. Her tender age magnified her angelic appearance, which seemed to separate itself from the bright lights and white walls. Analgesia had protected the young child from any agony. Her petite body had been sedated and given appropriate pain meds. She was without pain, an outcome that Dr. Starr tried to maintain in her career, dating life, and private life, all of which had caused excruciating pain in the past, a feeling that Allison believed children and animals should be spared and not have to experience. Her compassion for young children and critters was unlimited.

Smiling at the tiny angel, she gently used her gloved finger to tuck a small strand of Anastasia's hair behind the sleeping child's ear. The adjustment uncovered a small birthmark just below the young girl's left earlobe; Allison studied the shape. *Butterfly?* The question consumed Allison's thoughts. *No.* She was sure the form was different after allowing her medical mind to compare the birthmark's shape to that of a thyroid gland, an organ whose shape resembled a butterfly. The small birthmark had too many curves. *It's not a butterfly,* Allison concluded but sustained her observation.

Before her thoughts prevailed, she watched Dr. Gerhart remove the MCCD from his head and walk out of the operating room. As usual, he did not give any type of recognition or acknowledgment to his team for a job well done. People didn't expect or look for that sort of thing in 2037, although Allison felt it would be nice. Still, she knew times had changed. The expectation was that people would do their jobs correctly. Rewards were self-given and internal, at least for the human species.

"Nice job Dr. Chrome." Those were the only words spoken postoperative. Dr. Holm smiled at his compliment's intended recipient – a bionic arm. Dr. Allison Starr continued to monitor her sleeping patient, even after the Patient Transport Personnel (PTP) entered the room, whose job it was to transport the minor child to recovery. Starr followed, not because it was medically necessary but because she felt compelled to do so. Her shift had ended. Typically, she would be making her way through the hospital's main annex and boarding the Seattle Center Monorail. It was a straight shot to her small Seattle apartment, where she would spend her evening watching Wall-T.V., drinking a glass of Bordeaux, and curling up with her cat – Pumpkin. Single life, and one without a car.

Driving an automobile was a memory. Since Allison's thirty-seventh birthday, she hadn't owned or operated a vehicle, following a law passed in 2032. It was a law banning an automobile's operation unless the car had a GFS (Global Friendly Sticker), and the driver had earned a special vacation pass or worked in a field where a GFS vehicle was required. Non-private trucks or cars, such as fire trucks, ambulances, police cars, and DME (Dining Made Easy) autos, had been converted to operate on hemp fuel. The conversion to hemp fuel created a clean burn and was a low threat to the environment. Every operational vehicle had to have a workers' permit sticker, or the driver was fined and given jail time.

Each state was allowed to maintain and operate a certain number of box trucks and semi-trucks. The allotment depended on the state's population. The state government was responsible for making sure that GFS guidelines were followed. The top priority was to ensure that all operational vehicles had been converted to perform using hemp fuel.

In Allison's world and other large cities in the United States, the free twenty-four-hour monorail system was used to travel from point A to B. Locations reached outside city limits were accessible by hemp-fueled locomotives. Bicycles were free for public use and were kept in parking garages throughout every major city. In rural areas, people had returned to horse and buggy usage or off-road ATVs, the latter of which also operated on hemp fuel.

The official POTUS since 2032, Pearl Thornburg, awarded the gainfully employed a vacation pass each year, which included free car services and unlimited hemp fuel. Of course, all loaner vehicles had the correctly displayed GFS. As a result, the environment had improved. Global warming had become non-existent. The government purchased the surplus of unused automobiles, stripped the wheels and engines, refurbished them inside and out, and placed them in Automobile Community Zones (ACZ). There, the local government agencies arranged them like tiny homes for anyone who needed shelter. Allison remembered seeing people sleeping on the streets and under bridges in Seattle and throughout most cities up and down the west coast, remembered seeing tents that fought the cold weather and lost, and remembered seeing large cardboard boxes that functioned as one-room homes. Now, the ACZ areas stood surrounded by flowers, fruit trees, and vegetable gardens, a colorful display that Allison routinely studied as she rode the monorail to work each morning. People who would otherwise be homeless seemed to take pride in their tiny gardens – tilling, pulling weeds, pruning, and even making and hanging wooden or metal birdhouses.

Still, Allison felt that parts of her world had grown excessively sterile, both inside and outside the operating room. In her opinion, the world had lost its authenticity and genuineness but had gained a different sense of being authentic – validity. Hardly anyone lied anymore, but it was a double-edged sword creating a world full of uninspired humans. Empty. People didn't share their inner feelings. Most people were loners. Marriage wasn't respected or encouraged. Children became limited, not by law, but by desire. Workplaces had taken on a very formal and impersonal atmosphere. Nothing questioned. Expectations both in and out of people's work lives seemed preestablished. Individuality had disappeared.

A nanosecond before the five-year-old child's eyes had closed after being administered anesthesia, and again after opening in the recovery room, Dr. Allison Starr felt an awareness she couldn't shake. A familiar spirit lived inside the mesmerizing blue eyes of Anastasia Elpis – an unadulterated human with wings.

Two

"Mommy, Do I have it on my face?" Anastasia held her mother's hand when Dr. Starr walked into the recovery room and overheard her question. Searching the bed tray in front of her minor patient, she expected to see ice cream or pudding, probably chocolate, and was surprised when she only saw water within reach of the five-year-old.

"Nothing is on your face except my lipstick," the single mother replied. Anastasia was her only child, unplanned, following a late summer, almost fall, fling with a man Karen Elpis met on the coast of Washington state. The romance was short-lived and didn't last more than two weeks, but the unexpected result was something Karen wanted and loved from the moment she found out she was pregnant, even though the father had demanded an abortion. Choosing to keep the baby, Karen struggled through pregnancy and raising a young child alone.

Allison observed while her mind processed their relationship. *Fatherless is okay as long as you have a good mother.* Dr. Starr's thought was true, at least based on her own experience. She remained a few steps back, admiring the mother-daughter moment and giving them their space while studying her young patient's captivating, nearly reflective deep-set eyes.

"No, Mommy. It's not lipstick." The five-year-old voice sounded disoriented and confused, still waking from anesthesia.

"What do you think is on your face?" The mother asked the question just as Dr. Starr moved a few steps closer to check the young patient's vitals, displaying them on the monitor near the head of the young child's hospital bed.

"Mud." The one-word answer brought a smile to Karen Elpis' face. She knew her daughter was groggy. Anastasia probably recalled their recent mother-daughter afternoon when they planted a garden last Thursday, just as Seattle's August rain began its constant drizzle, quickly muddying the ground around their new home. Anastasia had seemed upset that she was getting muddy. *Girly*, her mother thought, but the child stayed determined. She finished a row of carrots and a row of tomatoes around the shiny black 2019 Ram Pro-Master Conversion Van, a step-up from the 2015 Nissan Versa they had been living in – a reward Karen Elpis received from the government after securing steady work as a hairstylist at a company called Wind Blown, the business, located in a rehabbed luxury RV, a Monaco Dynasty 45P, where Karen cut and styled hair in the pull-out section. Now, the anxious mother looked into the face of the attending anesthesiologist for an explanation.

"It's called postoperative delirium." Dr. Starr explained. "She recalls a time she played outside and got dirty." The explanation confirmed the mother's thoughts, eliminating some of the young mother's tension. Stress had caused Karen's idle hands to twist her daughter's hair into a bun, something she found comforting and something she often did, probably because she loved styling hair.

Now, Karen politely moved aside after giving her daughter a new doo, allowing Dr. Starr extra room to conduct her examination. Allison studied Anastasia's magnetic blue eyes. "She'll be back to normal in another hour," the doctor reassured the mother before reaching for and lightly squeezing the child's right hand. "I told you I would check on you." She paused, long enough to search the young girl's neck, cleared of curly strands, for the birthmark she had noticed on her young patient earlier when she had prepped the child for surgery —*the wrong side.* Remembering the birthmark was below the child's left earlobe, she kept her attempt to search and analyze private, choosing to listen to Anastasia's incessant babble instead.

"Mud. Run. Fast." The series of words didn't make sense, not to Karen Elpis, but Dr. Allison Starr visualized the young girl in a game of tag. *Playing.*

"I'll revisit you in the morning." Dr. Starr studied her patient's expression before continuing to speak. The young child's light brown brows moved closer together above the bridge of her small nose, and the curvature of her girly lips worked into an upside-down U. *Confusion,* Starr concluded. "You get some rest." Then after smiling at her young patient, Dr. Starr extended her left fist, gently bumping the fist of Anastasia's mother. It was a gesture that replaced most handshakes following the 2019 coronavirus and replaced all handshakes following the 2023 strand. "Very nice to meet you, Ms. Elpis."

"You too. That was so nice of you to check on Anastasia."

Allison Starr smiled at the five-year-old one more time before exiting the recovery room, carefully making her way down the hall while simultaneously studying her watch – *8:20 p.m.* The Seattle Center Monorail (SCM) would load patrons at the hospital's sky bridge entrance, off 16th Avenue, in five minutes. The ride home to Allison's small apartment in south Seattle would only take twenty minutes. It wouldn't offer the same well-lit view she had experienced during the 6-a.m. sunrise on her monorail ride into work. Nevertheless, it would be a chance to study and identify as many automobiles as she could remember from her twenties and thirties before the average American wasn't permitted to own one. She had memorized the first row of vehicles in the ACZ, an area that fifteen years earlier had displayed rows of low-income houses, most shingled in dark gray or ash-blue, weathered by years and poverty,

condemned or in significant need of repair, now torn down and
replaced with rows of automobiles that the city had refurbished into
tiny homes: a silver Kia Forte, a dark gray Ford Focus, a bright red
Mazda 3, a black Honda Civic, a maroon Hyundai Accent, and her
favorite one in the first row of make-shift housing, a gold Kia Soul,
the one she imagined would offer the most head and leg-room inside
the small living quarters, its body shaped like a boxy station wagon,
a vehicle similar to one her mother had owned and had shown her a
photo of when she was a child – a 1995 Buick Roadmaster Wagon.
She smiled, thinking of her deceased mother, after boarding the nine-
p.m. monorail and after settling into an aerodynamic swivel chair,
where she opted to face the nearly dark Seattle sky instead of the
drop-down television monitor that had electronically lowered to her
scanned eye-level. Boarding just in time to watch the last two
minutes of the sunset, Allison witnessed vibrant orange and
cadmium red drown the August sun in the Pacific, leaving her world
black and empty. *No chance to see the cars and their colors now,*
she thought, as her mind accepted her eyes' loss to the darkness.

It wasn't until Allison Starr placed her left index finger on
the print scanner by her apartment door that she allowed herself to

see color again. Greeted by an apricot hue, Pumpkin, her Kurilian

Bobtail, followed her to the living room sofa, where her body settled

into dark-gray oversized cushions. Pumpkin jumped on her lap,

positioning himself so that his broad chest faced her, and his walnut-

shaped eyes looked into her almond-shaped ones demanding

attention.

"I love you, Pumpkin," she said before brushing his soft coat

with her fingers while listening to his purr, which seemed to

intensify with each stroke of Allison's hand. Her brown eyes studied

the Wall-T.V. located just above Pumpkin's head. Then she quickly

focused in another direction after she remembered that staring at the

Wall-T.V. longer than thirty seconds would automatically turn it on.

Allowing her brown eyes to follow the hallway to an area just inside

her bedroom, she noticed broken pieces of bright blue stoneware,

dark potting soil, and her uprooted fairy castle cactus lying on the

bedroom's hardwood floor. "Pumpkin, did you knock over my

cactus?" He answered by jumping down and leaving the proof all

over the pant legs of Allison's white scrubs. *Guilty,* she thought,

after looking down at her lap and studying the damning evidence he

had left behind – dirty paw prints. *That's it!* She felt as if she had solved a puzzle. *An upside-down heart with four ovals above it.* She closed her eyes, trying to picture Anastasia's tiny birthmark. *Cat paw.*

Exhausted, she made her way into the bedroom, where she stepped out of her scrubs and into the automated shower. But not before instructing her voice-activated Robotic Cleaning System (RCS) to collect the scattered bits of broken pottery and soil, which it would automatically place in the clear plastic discard bin. Without differentiating her instructions, she knew her RCS would collect and store the fairy castle cactus in the system's oxygen bin until retrieved and replanted.

Tomorrow morning, she would get up an extra hour early to replant her fairy castle cactus and in time to confirm the shape of Anastasia Elpis' birthmark before starting her shift. *Cat Paw.*

Three

"Three more days, and we'll be on the road." Allison chatted with Pumpkin while busying her hands during the early morning hours on the twelfth of August, 2037. "Your first road trip, Pumpkin." It was a much-needed break. Allison worked as a cardiovascular anesthesiologist at Swedish Medical for five years without taking a vacation. She was approved to take a five-week road trip starting on the fifteenth of August. "What do you think about heading down to Santa Monica for a few days and then cutting over to Arizona,

Pumpkin?" After realizing she thought of Arizona, she giggled to herself, remembering how much her mother liked cacti and that she was ironically replanting one. Pumpkin watched her hands, working diligently to rehome the fairy castle cactus into an empty unglazed clay pot, a spare that she kept in her small area of gardening supplies. Spires and turrets, ranging in different heights, appeared to appreciate the mix of potting soil and perlite. "You're lucky this cactus is non-toxic to animals." She looked at Pumpkin, wondering if he had tried to eat any of it.

Thirty minutes before she needed to leave for her shift, she hurried to tidy and put up her supplies before placing the delicate replanted cactus on the sill of her highest bedroom window, one where the full sun would hit it most of the day. "Stay away from it, Pumpkin." She reached to scratch the top of Pumpkin's bright orange head before heading out the door. Simple. Not like the old days, when she had to remember her purse, make sure she had money, check for her ID, and grab her keys.

Boarding a monorail? Scan index finger. Stopping for food at a neighborhood market or walk-up window? Scan index finger. Entering a restricted hallway at work? Scan index finger. Everything that required entry or payment needed the scan of an authorized print. Supermarkets were small, most housed in luxury RVs or like-sized buildings. A few larger grocery stores were in refurbished retail buildings. Walmart, Target, and Costco survived the last fifteen-plus years of economic ups and downs by offering everything from fresh produce, meat, and dairy, to clothing and gardening supplies. People didn't travel outside their communities. Big-brother scanned individual items as people exited hardware stores, grocery stores, clothing stores, and pet stores. Select. Place items in your reusable bag. Exit building through the scanner, which in most businesses would address the customer by name. "Thank you for buying cat food today, Dr. Starr." Allison smiled at the robotic voice every week. The system replaced the need for cashiers when the electronic scanning process began debiting paychecks automatically. The POTUS had developed a new system that even accommodated people on pensions or approved medical disabilities-act. SCAN. PRINT. DEDUCT.

"Good morning," she said as she took a seat on the crowded monorail beside another hospital employee Allison recognized, and one she found herself secretively attracted to. Men hadn't been one of Allison's strengths. It was a fact that even she would admit, after

dating a series of losers in high school, after losing the love of her

life before starting college, and after dating several men in med-

school who were more focused on arm candy than a quality

relationship. Even the man in her apartment complex, the one she

had gone on several short outings with, including the hiking trip in

the Cascades, had put another blemish on her track record for dating.

Over the summer, she had seen his photo on her Wall-T.V., listened

to the news reporter announce that the police wanted him for

swindling several older adults out of their savings, and even watched

the Seattle Police arrest him in the center of the apartment's

courtyard. Now, she wanted someone good in her life—a redo.

"Good morning Allison." The voice came from a man in his

mid-forties, with blond hair, contrasting Allison's dark brown, and

his blue eyes were strikingly different from Allison's chocolate

browns. His smile was genuine, something that seemed rare in 2037.

"Playing in the dirt this morning?" His question was simultaneous

with his actions, as he swiped his left fingertips across Allison's

right brow-line, wiping off black dirt that looked out of place on her milky complexion. After showing Allison the tip of his index and middle fingers, he said, "I'll analyze this when I get to the lab."

Embarrassed, although wishing he had touched her longer, she giggled after looking at his fingertips before speaking.

"I'll save you some time, doctor." She laughed. "It is potting soil mixed with a little volcanic glass." Her smile lingered, and without thinking, she quickly grabbed his fingers, brushing off the tips with hers. "There," she said, "all clean." She felt embarrassed a second time after realizing that she hadn't let go of his hand right away but then caught her morning reflection in his blue eyes long enough to assess whether she had violated his boundaries. She hadn't. "I don't want to become another specimen." She joked. "How's the lab anyway?"

"Busy." He couldn't take his blue eyes off her smile. "I'm ironing out some environmental concerns." He had wanted to ask her out for over a year now but hadn't worked up the courage. *Ask her out.* His mind interrupted his train of thought, slowing his dialogue. "I've been analyzing the food and water in the ACZ areas." *Maybe I should ask her out.* He kept his thoughts private, for now.

"Well, Dr. Jeffery Linus, the world needs more men like you." Allison knew Dr. Linus was responsible for the ACZ areas' clean water and thriving gardens, something Karen and Anastasia Elpis needed to survive. *I'm happy about Karen's job at Wind Blown,* Allison privately thought. *Karen is now authorized to shop in the market to add extra protein to their meals,* she thought, remembering the law required paychecks or pensions for scanning and deduction. No cash in 2037. None. No pan-handlers. None. The world had changed. "I, for one, appreciate you." There, she said it. In her world, recognition was allowed. She knew Dr. Linus had spent years helping several large automobile companies convert vehicles to operate on hemp fuel. It was work that relied on his expertise in chemistry. She also knew he and some other molecular biologists helped stop the most recent spread of COVID (Coronavirus Disease 2031) and knew he had earned his Ph.D. in Biochemistry and Molecular Biology in Seattle. He was respected coast-to-coast for his expertise, but Allison saw a different side to him. He was precise, caring, open-minded, and thought a bigger picture of the universe existed than most people did.

"Thanks, Dr. Allison Starr." Then, at the risk of sounding corny, "The world has a chance with you in it." He smiled as he stood to exit before taking her arm to ensure she kept her balance as the monorail came to a stop in front of the hospital. "Same time tomorrow?" He asked while he was still holding her arm and walking into Swedish Medical Center.

"You got it, Jeffery." She liked the way his name came out of her mouth.

"It's a date." That was as close as he could come for now. "Thanks for making me smile, Allison." That was a little better. He watched her walk toward the cardiac unit, his heart needing the attention she could give him. Her slender figure disappeared into the seven-story hospital, which functioned as Providence Seattle Medical Center thirty-seven years earlier. Still, the building whose color reminded Allison of Florida sand was in excellent condition.

Dr. Allison Starr made her way to the Recovery Unit, then a beeline to Anastasia Elpis' room. The child was still sleeping. *Good,* she thought, *a chance to look at the birthmark I am obsessed with.* Allison studied the pattern just below the girl's left earlobe. Her hair was neatly tucked into a bun, giving Allison a clear view. The birthmark looked like an upside-down heart-shaped nose underneath four ovals. *That's unique*, she thought. *It does look like a cat's paw print.* Without waking Anastasia, she made her way to the cardiac unit, scanning her fingerprint to access an area with large digital boards. *Perfect,* she thought, *my first patient is scheduled for anesthesia at 10 a.m., enough time to grab a coffee and enough time to do a little research on birthmarks.* She knew almost eighty-five percent of all babies were born with birthmarks and knew that the birthmarks faded over time, but she had always been curious about the many different shapes. She recalled a woman in college obsessed with butterflies, and ironically enough, the woman had a small spot on her right shoulder blade that looked like a butterfly. Allison thought about her birthmark, one she had into her teenage years, one located on the left side of her forehead, one her mother always said was beautiful, and one that her mother always thought looked like a crescent moon. It had faded by the time Allison turned seventeen.

Sipping a Kona Peaberry coffee, one Dr. Allison Starr had ordered from a gourmet coffee machine in the doctors' lounge, she sat in front of the 40-inch HP ENVY screen and spoke the following words: **the meaning of birthmarks**. In less than one second, a full page of results popped up. Allison started at the top of the list, clicking, clicking, clicking, and reading. First: *The Etiology of Birthmarks*. Second: *The Connection Between Birthmarks and Reincarnation*. And, third: *What Birthmarks Reveal About Death*. Transfixed, Allison spent most of her time reading. First, about how birthmarks reveal hints about a person's previous life. More precisely, the birthmark might even be a clue as to how the person died. Cold chills traveled down Allison's spine. *That's interesting.* She told herself, before instructing the computer: **Clear screen**. Allison made her way to the forty-year-old man who was waiting for general anesthesia.

"Mr. DuPuy, I'm Dr. Allison Starr." She smiled down at her patient. He couldn't hide the fact that he was nervous. "I promise to take good care of you." He nodded. For a moment, Allison wondered if he spoke English, but then he whispered a request.

"If I don't make it, tell my wife I love everything about her, and tell her that I'm sorry I've been hiding bags of chocolate-covered macadamia nuts in the frozen cauliflower." All Allison seemed to hear was *married*. She thought about the definition of marriage when she was a kid: *the state of being united spiritually and physically to a person.* It was an outdated and unacceptable definition in 2037. Looking into the worried hazel eyes, she tried to think of a description that would fit the world of 2037. She imagined a realistic definition: *The legal union between two people where all entitlements are surrendered to secure larger housing accommodations from the government. Pointless. Empty. Sterile.*

"You're going to be just fine, Mr. DuPuy." She answered his request with her standard reassurance. "You'll see your wife again soon." She watched her patient's eyes flutter. His breathing became shallow. His muscles became paralyzed. His blood pressure dropped slightly.

"All systems are operational," announced Dr. Holm, after checking the bionic arm and connecting monitors, part of his job as the Motions Computer Expert (MCE).

"Let's begin," Dr. Ben Gerhart said as he placed the MCCD around his forehead. Now, the only communication was between Dr. Gerhart and Dr. Chrome. It was a silent communication that filled the room.

Four

Dr. Ben Gerhart shook his head from side to side rapidly and repeatedly.

"No!" Gerhart's one-word exploded, breaking the silence in the small surgical room. "It will cause the channel to rupture!"

"Ben, would you like me to override Dr. Chrome?" The question came from Dr. Steven Holm, MCE, who saw the look of panic on Gerhart's face. He had known Ben for years, and even though it was somewhat unethical, he would override Chrome for

Gerhart if needed.

"Yes, immediately." Overriding the bionic arm was a

decision that was nearly unheard of and one that would result in both

Dr. Holm and Dr. Gerhart losing their licenses to practice medicine

if the decision caused injury to the patient.

"Sorry, Ben, the internal system has already proceeded."

Then, with regret, "There's no way I can stop it."

Dr. Allison Starr watched Randall DuPuy's vitals on the

monitor. His breathing had slowed, and his heart rate had weakened

dramatically. She stood over her patient, feeling for a pulse. Weak.

"Goddammit." Dr. Gerhart directed his anger at Dr. Chrome,

a bionic arm whose internal computer network had decided to cut the

aorta's inner layer. "Fucking Chrome." Gerhart's anger and emotions

filled the operating room. He knew the aorta had ruptured, causing it

to dissect. "It's too fucking late," Gerhart added. "There's no way to

save him."

Dr. Starr noticed her patient's change in color. Pale skin. It

was the first death *during* a surgery Allison had witnessed in her

five-year career. Patients had experienced complications after surgery, and a small percentage of those patients died of related causes during her career at Swedish. Still, no one had ever died *during* a surgery performed by the fantastic foursome: Gerhart, Chrome, Holm, and Starr.

"Time of death, 10:07 a.m." Dr. Allison Starr called the time of death with a lump in her throat. Her gloved fingers were still holding the cold blue fingers of Mr. Randall DuPuy, forty-seven years old and married. She thought of his wife as she looked down at the bright gold wedding ring that glared back at her. *If I don't make it, tell my wife* – her mind worked to remember the rest of his words – *love everything, chocolate covered,* and *cauliflower.*

Dr. Gerhart removed the MCCD from his forehead and left the room without speaking. Dr. Holm powered down the bionic arm. Today he would leave the tiny operating room without giving a compliment to Dr. Chrome.

Dr. Allison Starr stayed behind with her patient once again. This time she waited for the PTP to transport Mr. DuPuy to the refrigerated morgue. She knew they wouldn't be as prompt as they usually were for transfers to recovery because being dead is not a priority, so she sat with Randall DuPuy, thinking about his soul. *Was his soul in another dimension? Will he be reincarnated? Will he have a small heart-shaped tattoo on his body in his next life, signifying that he had died during heart surgery?* There were no answers. Only tears. Allison cried for Randall DuPuy. Uncontrollable sobbing filled the sterile room.

"Allison, are you okay?" The familiar voice came up behind her. It was Jeffery Linus. She wiped her eyes quickly, then turned to face him.

"Jeffery, I'm sorry you walked in on that." She knew she couldn't hide the fact that she had been crying. Okay, bawling.

"Don't be sorry for showing you're human." He pulled up the stool Dr. Holm had used earlier and placed it beside her before taking a seat, his eyes level with hers. "I overhead Gerhart in the doctors' lounge ranting and raving about how doctors can't always trust technology." He shook his head in agreeance. "I knew I'd find you here."

"What made you think I'd still be in here?"

"You're the most compassionate person I know, Allison." He smiled. "I knew you wouldn't leave your patient."

"I feel bad for his family." She formed her concern into a question. "Do you know if anyone has told his wife?"

"I'm pretty sure the woman pacing the waiting room down the hall is Mrs. DuPuy, and if so, then she hasn't been told." He sensed the silent prayers, a rare and outdated gesture, and recognized her hopeful eyes when he had walked by the waiting room.

"I need to tell her," Allison said as she attempted to find strength in her voice. "Randall wanted me to," she added.

"Would you like me to stay here with Randall?" Jeffery knew Allison didn't want her patient to be alone, so he didn't wait for her to answer. "Go talk to the wife," he said. "She shouldn't have to wait any longer." Then he added, "do and say what feels right."

Allison stood. Her legs felt weak and her heart tender before placing her hand on Jeffery's shoulder. "Thanks, Jeffery," she looked down into eyes that reminded her of the ocean, and she felt him look at her the same way – bobbing and weaving like a sailboat surrounded by seagulls. He stared deep into her brown ones as she continued speaking. "Please don't leave Mr. DuPuy before the PTP gets here.

"Understood, Doctor." He smiled, trying to give her a little more strength.

Dr. Allison Starr noticed the tears in Victoria DuPuy's eyes as she approached. Starr could read the woman's fear before she exchanged words, so she proceeded carefully. Slowly.

"Mrs. DuPuy?"

"Please call me Victoria."

"I'm so sorry." After Allison saw the excessive worry flow across Victoria DuPuy's face, the words came out – a combination of honesty and straightforwardness.

"I felt him leave me."

"Can we sit down?" Allison's question simultaneously occurred with the placement of her arm around the woman's shoulders. Dr. Starr's actions directed the grieving woman to a small sofa in the corner of the family' waiting room. "Randall's aorta separated, causing severe blood loss." She took Victoria's hand. "There was no way to save him." And then again, "I'm so sorry."

"Where is he now?" Allison wanted to tell her the truth. She wanted to tell her she didn't know. She wanted to tell her his soul was waiting in another dimension, and wanted to tell her he would be reborn, possibly as another human, or maybe a rainbow, a butterfly, a flower, or raging water rapid. She wanted to let Victoria DuPuy know that her husband would never truly be gone, but she couldn't; instead, Dr. Allison Starr's answer was unimaginative.

"Your husband is being taken care of by my colleague, Dr. Linus, who will stay with him until a PTP transports his body to the morgue downstairs." Allison watched the light go out in Victoria's eyes. Shattered pieces of hope leaked down the side of the wife's face. Twenty-five years of marriage had ended. The world felt colder. Unbearable. *Do and say what feels right.* Allison recalled Jeffery's words as she held the weeping widow's hand, a gesture that had become taboo in 2037. "Mrs. DuPuy, would you like to see your husband before he's transported to the morgue?"

"Yes, please." The woman's face pleaded. It was a procedure that wasn't allowed, but one Allison felt would bring peace to the grieving widow, enough of a reason to break a hospital policy.

"Come with me." Within minutes they were standing in front of the surgical door. "Wait here until I come back for you," Allison instructed.

Jeffery had heard the directive and was already on his feet, making sure Randall's body was displayed properly, with fresh white linen over his chest and abdomen. Allison smiled at Jeffery without speaking when she caught him tucking the clean linen around her patient's lifeless body and thanked him with her silent brown eyes.

Both doctors moved aside after giving Mrs. DuPuy instructions to enter. She moved slowly to her deceased husband's side, soaking the fresh white linen with her tears.

"I love you," Victoria spoke the words to her husband's face.

"He left me with instructions before I administered his anesthesia," Allison spoke to the husbandless woman that had just planted a single kiss on Randall's forehead before she turned to face Dr. Starr. "Randall wanted me to tell you that he loves everything about you and that he's sorry he's been hiding bags of chocolate-covered macadamia nuts in the frozen cauliflower."

Victoria DuPuy broke into a mixture of laughter and tears. "Randy thought I didn't know," she took Allison's hand, a gesture that she wanted to reciprocate. "He wasn't supposed to be eating them, you know, but I couldn't take everything away." Allison smiled at Victoria's painful sense of humor. "Chocolate-covered macadamia nuts were his weakness."

Dr. Jeffery Linus walked near Mrs. DuPuy, reached for her empty hand, and dropped Randall DuPuy's shiny gold wedding band inside. "He's part of the universe now." The comment put a much-needed sparkle back in Victoria's eyes.

Mrs. DuPuy thanked both doctors before walking out and before leaving her husband's body behind. The small surgical room no longer felt sterile. Allison stepped close to Jeffery, and then without wasting another minute, she kissed him. Deeply. Passionately. Her soul felt it had known him several lifetimes. Their lips melted into each other, and their bodies floated amongst moons, asteroids, and billions of stars as they drifted endlessly on the sea.

Five

"How are you feeling?" Dr. Starr visited Anastasia Elpis' room before the end of the day.

"Good." The five-year-old answered in one word. Expected. Allison had forgotten she needed to ask questions that would require longer answers, especially for that age bracket.

"What do you miss most about being home?"

"My dog." *Two words*, Allison thought.

"Tell me about the last time the two of you were together." Then, to make sure she got a longer answer, she added, "What did the two of you do?"

"We ran from the mud." *Better, five words,* Allison thought.

Before Dr. Starr could think about how to word her next question, Karen Elpis walked in. She had just come from Dr. Gerhart's office.

"Dr. Starr, I'm glad you're here." Karen Elpis was happy to see that her daughter was being taken care of in her absence. "I just found out Anastasia gets to go home tomorrow."

"Perfect." Dr. Starr smiled at the child's mother. "Thursday is going to be a special day." Allison was thinking of herself too. It was the last day she had surgery scheduled for the week. Friday, she would attend a medical seminar at the hospital, and Saturday was the first day of her five-week vacation. *I can't wait to stick my toes in the hot white sand on Santa Monica Beach,* Allison thought. *Then I'm going to stand in Arizona's Canyon de Chelly so that I can overlook spider rock.* Allison thought about the magazine photo she kept in her bottom dresser drawer. Red sandstone and colorful cliff walls held her captive for hours before she decided to cut the image from *Traveler's Delight* and tuck it away. But not before promising herself that someday she would see the spiraling 800-foot spider-shaped legs that proudly stood in the belly of Canyon de Chelly's desert floor.

Of course, driving anywhere was a vacation within itself. Allison had spent endless hours romanticizing about how it would feel to be behind the wheel of a vehicle on a long coastal and desert road trip, solo. After the government had taken away the privilege of owning and operating a car, she fantasized even more.

Now, in less than seventy-two hours, she would be gripping a steering wheel, making her way down I-5, and stopping as needed for unlimited hemp fuel. It would be her first vacation in five years, since starting at the hospital, and since Pearl Thornburg had become POTUS. Allison had voted for her. Thornburg had a fresh face with ideas on how to help the environment. She was the youngest candidate to ever run for president. She was only twenty-nine years old when she was sworn in, after the minimum age for serving changed to twenty-five, and after the twenty-second amendment was rewritten, allowing presidents to serve up to two full terms of ten years each. Now, halfway through her first term, Thornburg, 34 years old, had eliminated global warning, created a free health care system for all, provided free college education to students maintaining Cs or better, had created ACZ areas to eradicate homelessness, and had created incentive programs, such as the GFS automobile program for employed personnel. *Five weeks.* It had taken Allison five years to save up that much time, and on Saturday morning, she would start spending it.

"Mommy, where's my dog?"

"You don't have a dog."

"Yes, I do, Mommy."

"Sweety, we've never owned a dog."

Dr. Allison Starr listened to the friendly banter before weighing in. "Anastasia was just telling me how she was running from the mud with her dog." She studied Karen's face. *Embarrassment?*

"I thought she'd grow out of it by now." Karen rolled her eyes.

"What's that?" Dr. Starr was confused.

"Having an imaginary dog." Then Karen added, "The only pet we've ever had was a goldfish named Goldie."

"I guess she likes animals." Suddenly, Starr felt comfortable enough to share her discovery. "I even noticed she has a small birthmark below her left earlobe." Then continuing, "to me, it looks like a cat paw."

"It's a dog paw print. Cats retract their claws when they make a print." The mother corrected as she leaned toward her daughter and pointed at the small birthmark. "See, it has nails." Allison Starr leaned in, examining the birthmark once again, and realized the mother was correct. Dog paw print. Karen was right. Cats don't walk with their nails extended.

"She's probably heard you tell people about her birthmark," Dr. Starr concluded. "That's why she believes she has a dog."

"I guess." Karen Elpis chuckled. "She has even named it."

"That's okay." Dr. Starr knew it was customary for kids that age to have imaginary friends, even pet friends. "What's your doggie's name, Anastasia?"

"Miles." The five-year-old voice said.

Allison Starr felt her blood turn cold.

An hour later, Allison Starr sat beside Jeffery Linus on the monorail. Speechless.

"I know you're still upset about losing Randall DuPuy, but I can say this, you handled things perfectly with Victoria DuPuy." He searched her face. Still nothing. "Talk to me, Allison."

"Jeffery, you told Victoria DuPuy that Randall was part of the universe now. What did you mean by that?"

"I believe life continues after death."

"Do you believe in God?"

"No, Allison, I don't, but I do believe in the human spirit and consciousness."

"So, do you believe Randall DuPuy is a spirit now?"

"I believe he's in an unknown form."

"Like energy?"

"Yes, he'll come back in nature or as a new person."

"You believe in reincarnation?"

"I think the human body decomposes, but the energy will show up again in other people, plants, or even an animal." He put his arm around her, pulling her close. "My Ph.D. is in Biochemistry and Molecular Biology." He whispered into the side of her face. "My favorite professor was a Quantum Physicist. He believed, and I do too, that there is a field of energy inside the human body that is indestructible." He pulled away, just enough to turn his head and plant a gentle kiss on the side of her face.

"Are you talking about the conscious part of a soul?"

"Yes, my professor called it the Conscious Dimension." He took Allison's hand in his own. "We both know from studying science that energy can't be created or destroyed. We also know that energy transforms." Allison was absorbing every fiber of Jeffery Linus. "That means the human soul is timeless."

"I stopped to revisit Anastasia Elpis today." She turned to face Jeffery. "She has a small birthmark just below her left ear in the pattern of a dog print." At the risk of sounding crazy, Allison continued. "Anastasia has an imaginary dog companion she calls Miles."

"Allison, where is this going?"

"My mother had a dog named Miles."

"Coincidence?" Jeffery asked her dark brown eyes, which at the moment looked focused and precise, holding secrets like the deepest depths of the Atlantic Ocean.

"Following surgery, the child thought she had mud on her face, which I chalked up to postoperative delirium."

"I would agree with that, Allison."

"But even the following day, when Anastasia was coherent, she talked about mud and running fast."

"Tell me what you're getting at?"

"I think Anastasia Elpis is my mother." Jeffery Linus stared at her without speaking. He knew he loved Allison, something he hadn't admitted out loud. He also knew he would never dismiss her thoughts and concerns, no matter how far-fetched.

"How does the mention of mud factor into that?"

"My mother died in a mudslide in Alaska."

Jeffery Linus realized two things – one, he wasn't about to let Allison toss and turn throughout the night alone, and two, he had missed his stop. He stood to exit the monorail, his hand holding hers, a human touch he missed, with his heart in his throat.

"Do you have coffee?"

"Where?"

"In your apartment?"

"Yes," she laughed after realizing that they had gotten off the monorail together, a short walk from her apartment.

"I'm going to need lots of it," Jeffery said.

"Deal." Allison squeezed his hand. An unannounced secret surfaced.

She was falling in love with Dr. Jeffery Linus.

Six

"Imagine Dr. Chrome, Allison." Jeffery took a long sip of black coffee with one hand and reached to scratch the top of Pumpkin's head with his other. "Chrome's microchips upload data and store information, just like a single brain cell stores years and years of memories." Allison listened while taking a sip of her coffee, two cremes, no sugar, her desired formula for as long as she could remember. "The stored information is a form of energy." He leaned in. "And, what do we know about energy from physics?"

"It can't be created or destroyed."

"Exactly. Your answer is right there, Allison."

"Jeffery, you're saying reincarnation is possible?" She wanted to hear him say the three-letter word – yes.

"Absolutely." She'd take the ten-letter word instead.

"You believe Anastasia could be my mother?" It was a question – one that needed affirmation.

"I believe it's possible." Jeffery took her hand. "Tell me more about your mother."

"She was adventurous, kind, loving, compassionate, humorous." He smiled without interrupting and continued to listen. "It was the year of the three quakes and the three tsunamis, 2019." Allison didn't spend too much of her life looking back anymore and found it difficult to share, but not with Jeffery. "My mother had made it to the top of Alaska by car with her dog Miles and had made the trip back down the Dalton Highway, despite the dangerous road conditions, a pipeline explosion, and limited gasoline." She smiled at her mother's perseverance. "I was able to talk with an elderly couple who owned a place called Harry's Hubcaps, a sweet old couple, that had housed my mother for several hours after the quake and during a volcanic eruption." She wiped tears with her free hand. "Making it toward Fairbanks after leaving them, she pulled over, probably to walk Miles." She swallowed. "The mudslide came out of nowhere. She didn't have time to clear its path." Remembering back seventeen years, she pieced together details. "The world was a mess at that time. Three earthquakes and three tsunamis had taken many lives. Electrical outages and gas shortages remained a problem for months. Crime skyrocketed. People killed other human beings to take their food and gasoline, and sometimes just for pleasure." It was a significant turning point in Allison's life. "I was dealing with not knowing, not knowing if my mother was okay, not knowing if my brother had been affected by the quake and tsunami that hit Africa where he had been living, and not knowing where to get food or clean drinking water." She was trying not to ramble. "Survival was a daily challenge with three dogs, a black and white cat, a six-year-old child, her yellow lab named Buttons, and my fiancé." Allison noticed Jeffery's smile fade, so she took the time to explain. "We were both in our early twenties. We never got married." She didn't want to elaborate further about Reese Kabula, not now, so she focused on the little girl. "The child was found in an RV park, a six-year-old surviving alone after her mother had OD'd." Allison stopped talking for a moment, remembering the young child, recalling the significance of the child's name. "The child's name, Hope, was ironically enough something my mom always believed in." *Were you already giving me a sign, Mom?* "After the west coast started to heal, we were able to locate the child's aunt and uncle." She smiled. "I kept in touch with that family for many years. The last thing I remember was getting a letter after Hope had started high school. Buttons had died as an old, happy dog. Hell, even my dogs had died old and happy by that point."

Jeffery Linus didn't want her to stop talking. He wanted to know more. It was the first time she had shared her past. He had spent hours chatting with Allison on the monorail about *his* life on the east coast. He was twenty-seven years old when the earthquakes and tsunamis changed parts of the world forever. The east coast was unaffected, except for a spike in gas prices and the two or three people he knew who lived in the small Maryland community where he had just completed his undergraduate degree. The lives of several people he knew writhed in sorrow after the world disasters turned their family members' lives upside down. He saw the pain in their eyes as he listened to them talk about how the Pacific Northwest was in dire need of help, both in the medical field and for scientists who could improve the quality of life. That's when Jeffery decided to make his way to the center of Hell. Seattle was overpopulated, polluted, and crime-ridden when he arrived in 2020. Most people with Jeffery Linus' intellect would have run in the other direction, but Jeffery settled in Seattle, dove into medical school head first, finished at the top of his class, and helped bring Seattle back to life.

"Allison, tell me more."

"My mother's body wasn't recovered for two months." Details of the police report still haunted Allison. "Her skeletal remains were found next to Miles' skeletal remains." Allison's fingers caressed a small pendant that hung around her neck. "I had both of their remains cremated together and spread off the coast of Seattle, except for this." Allison showed Jeffery a jewelry urn pendant shaped like a lotus flower, which her mother always thought symbolled rebirth. The significance of the word hit Allison hard. *Rebirth.* She started to cry. *Maybe, just maybe, my mother knew.*

"She's out there, Allison." Jeffery held her close, whispering into the side of her wet face. It was two a.m., late, but there was still enough time to grab a few hours of sleep. He led her into her room and helped her to bed. "I'll grab some sleep on the living room sofa."

"No." She looked at him. "I want you here." Moving over, she made room. Dr. Jeffery Linus held her. Nothing more. Pumpkin stayed at their feet, purring until the alarm went off three hours later.

Thursday five a.m. came early. Allison showered while Jeffery made coffee and bagels. Jeffery stepped in the shower while Allison made the bed and fed Pumpkin. They could have saved time by showering together, but Allison didn't want that first experience rushed and knew Jeffery didn't either. *Two more shifts.* Allison's thought remained private as they boarded the morning monorail.

"So, what happened to your black and white cat?"

"Serenity lived through my four years of medical school before passing away." She smiled, remembering the tuxedo cat. "I found Pumpkin wandering around Seattle a few months later," she said. "We needed each other."

"I don't have any animals." Jeffery had always wanted one but knew he spent too much time at the lab. "I can see how easy it must be to fall in love with one."

"Falling in love with an animal is easy," Allison smiled, thinking of Pumpkin.

"Falling in love with you is easy too." The words left Jeffery before he had a chance to stop them.

"Dr. Linus, you're stepping up your game." It was Allison's non-committal attempt to bring humor into a delicate situation.

"I guess that was too much," he said, almost embarrassed.

"No, it wasn't," and then, "I feel the same way about you." Allison's reply was as close as she could come right now. There was still too much he didn't know about her.

Jeffery Linus took Allison's hand, silently allowing the sunrise to fill their view of the eastern sky. Another day at Swedish, another chance to save a life, and often another opportunity to save a community.

The community had been something Jeffery Linus had started saving in 2020. During his seventeen years in Seattle, Jeffery had dedicated himself to his education. He had researched procedures that decreased environmental hazards, had been one of the leading scientists to discover the antidote for the most threatening strand of the coronavirus, the COVID-31, and had helped make homelessness obsolete. There had been a lot of changes in Dr. Linus' world.

There had been just as many changes in the world of Dr. Allison Starr. Changes she never verbally shared. Allison had been born Allison Narducci and was called Allie by her mother. Allie's mother, Enola May Starks, died in a mudslide in 2019. It was a significant turning point for Allison. Her world felt smaller. Being close to anyone wasn't worth the risk. Her heart shied away from Reese Kabula. Allison needed to be alone. Seattle was a place she could hide. Reese would never look for her there. Not in the city. It was a city where Allison could become someone else. Starting over was something that ran in her mother's blood, and it was something that ran in her blood too. Changing her name was part of her new life. It was her idea to adopt her mother's last name – Starks, legally. It was the surname of her mother's biological father, or so she thought. But after researching more about the grandfather she never met and the biological father her mother only briefly knew, she uncovered deeper roots in his ancestral tree, her ancestral tree.

Grover Starks' great-great-great-grandparents had the last name of Starr, one that they felt forced to change to Starks in the

1700s. It was common practice that Native American's adopt European names, a practice that usually happened when children on the reservation started in the educational system. The process of being forced to take a particular surname sickened Allison. Before graduating with her undergraduate degree, she legally changed her last name to Starr, honoring both the grandfather she never met and her mother. Enola would have been proud of her daughter's tenacity.

By August 2021, Allison Starr came to life. Now, Dr. Jeffery Linus placed his hand on the small on her back, making sure she could exit the monorail in front of him safely.

"You just made my whole world brighter." Jeffery smiled at Allison, thinking of her last words, *I feel the same way about you.*

"I'm stepping up my game too." She smiled. "What about coming over around seven tonight? I'll make dinner."

"I'll bring a razor and clean clothing this time," he answered, still glowing.

"Oh my, once again. The good doctor shoots. He scores." Allison laughed out loud as she made her way down the hospital hallway. "Don't forget your toothbrush, Doctor."

Seven

"Good morning, Anastasia." Allison smiled at the young child, secretively wondering if her mother's soul was somehow inside the five-year-old. "Are you excited that you go home tomorrow?"

"Yes." Another one-word answer.

"Tell me more about Miles." Allison realized it was a good time to chat with the child about her imaginary dog while Karen Elpis was at work and before Allison's next scheduled surgery at ten-a.m. "What does he look like?"

"He's funny," Anastasia whispered, leaving Allison Starr wondering what that had to do with looks.

"He looks funny?" Dr. Starr wanted more information. Something.

"Yes." *Anything but one word*, Allison thought.

"Why does he look funny?"

"His tail is crooked."

Allison Starr teared up, almost unable to breathe. Her mother's dog, Miles, had a broken tail. It was more than a coincidence in Allison's opinion; although, she was trying to remain reasonable. *Don't overreact.* Starr reminded herself that a lot of dogs have crooked tails. *Stay scientific.*

"Tell me about the time you played in the mud together." Allison knew the young child's answer would pull her back to reality. She imagined that the five-year-old would recall playing with her imaginary dog in the ACZ residential area.

"We couldn't get away from the mud." Anastasia's eyes widened. "It got in our throats, and it knocked us down." *Don't let your mind go there. All children play in the mud with their dogs. Don't distort the truth to reinforce a scientific theory.* Allison Starr slowed her interrogation, trying to think of a question that was not leading the patient's imagination. She wanted to be careful that she wasn't using the child's creative mind to support her fairytale beliefs. *Think.*

"I've played in the mud before with dogs I used to have." No question. Just chit-chat. Easy.

"Where are your dogs, now?"

"They all died of old age," and then, to make sure she didn't scare the child, "They were all happy."

"My dog died with me when the mud got in our throats." Dr. Allison Starr felt her arms tremble. Speechless, she studied the child's light blue eyes, similar to her mother's; although, she knew *that* was coincidental, even if reincarnation had occurred. Trying to control her emotions was futile, as she could feel several tears sliding down her left cheek. "Don't cry," Anastasia added. "It makes the moon look sad."

"What moon?"

"That one." Anastasia Elpis touched the left side of Dr. Allison Starr's forehead, directly above her brow-line. It was the exact spot where she used to have a small crescent moon birthmark, one that disappeared when she was around seventeen years old and one that no one ever said looked like a crescent moon – except Allison's mother – Enola May Starks.

By nine-a.m., Allison was in front of the 40-inch HP ENVY screen in a small research room for medical personnel. She spoke clearly to the voice-activated research system: **Meaning of crescent moon birthmark**. Within seconds an article appeared. Allison quickly read it, deciphering information and forming a consensus. *I have a solid connection to the cosmos.* Again, she spoke to the HP ENVY: **Clear screen**.

She stood, studying her forehead in the mirrored wall above the computer. Nothing. Not even a faint mark. *How did Anastasia see my childhood birthmark?* The probable answer gave Dr. Starr chills. She hurried down the hall, quickly entered the small operating room, and greeted her patient that a PTP had just brought into the small surgical room. *Focus.*

"Good morning, Walter."

"Hey, Doc." The seventy-three-year-old smiled up at Dr. Allison Starr. "I guess it's been a long time coming." Allison knew he was referring to the problem he was having with blood flow. She knew he was alluding to the fact that his clogged artery could have ended his life. Walter Jacob considered himself lucky. He had made it to age seventy-three without having a heart attack, even though his left anterior descending (LAD) artery had a blockage. His doctor discovered the blockage after Walter's recent bout of dizziness and pressure in his chest. A lucky catch.

"The stent placement in your LAD should only take about twenty minutes, Walter." She smiled down at her patient. "You'll feel like a new man in no time." Dr. Starr reassured her patient while watching his eyes grow heavy, a sign that the combination, one of inhaled gas and intravenous medication, a preference for his age group, was working to sedate her patient.

"Sounds good, Doc." Those were the last words spoken in the sterile operating room before Dr. Holm signaled Dr. Gerhart, letting him know that Dr. Chrome had been programmed to complete an angioplasty and stent placement and was ready to begin. Ben Gerhart placed the MCCD band around his forehead. Ready.

Within moments, Dr. Chrome made a tiny incision in Walter's sterilized arm. Gerhart nodded his approval. Chrome continued. His long robotic arm effortlessly and proficiently guided a tube to Mr. Jacob's LAD. Dr. Chrome didn't need dye to reveal the blockage; instead, the bionic arm was programmed to locate the blockage and was able to reach the confined area within minutes. Dr. Gerhart watched Chrome's every move, and Dr. Steven Holm, the MCE, was on high alert: interpreting Gerhart's facial expressions and ready to react if instructed. Ben Gerhart was satisfied as he watched the bionic arm inflate the blocked area, then nodded in agreement. Chrome continued, placing a wire stent in the area that he had robotically widened. Satisfied, Gerhart privately instructed Chrome to exit the site and apply pressure to the patient's arm, a discomfort that Walter Jacob was unable to feel. The operation was complete.

Dr. Gerhart gave a rare smile in Holm and Starr's direction before removing his MCCD and leaving the small surgical room. Dr. Holm spoke to Chrome after Gerhart cleared the room. "Good job, Dr. Chrome." No other words were exchanged.

Allison Starr looked down into the face of seventy-three-year-old Walter Jacobs, remembering that he was a person and reminding herself that just because the world had grown cold, she didn't have to. She remained by her patient's side until the PTP wheeled Walter to recovery. Allison would check in on him in a few hours. First, she would make her way back to Anastasia Elpis.

"How are you feeling, Anastasia?" Her question was direct after scanning the room. No one.

"Good." One-word again.

"I wanted to say hello again before your mom gets here and before you leave the hospital today." She kept her real motive to herself but quickly maneuvered the conversation to reach her goal. "How did you know I used to have a crescent moon birthmark on my forehead?" Dr. Starr pointed to the area that five-year-old Anastasia Elpis had pointed to earlier.

"I can see it on you." The child giggled slightly.

"Do you know you have a birthmark shaped like a dog's paw print below your earlobe?" Maybe the question was too much for the minor child to process, as she looked at Dr. Starr for several long moments without speaking. Speechless.

"That's Miles' paw." Anastasia smiled while touching below her left earlobe.

"Where is Miles now?" Like a seasoned attorney, she felt she had caught the child in a lie. She remembered how the child had asked her mother about Miles' whereabouts, a conversation she had in front of Dr. Starr, and remembered that the child had explained that Miles had died. Gone. *It can't be both ways,* Allison Starr thought. *Is her imaginary dog a thing of the past, or is he still here?*

"He's right beside you."

Allison Starr slowly turned her head. There was nothing, aside from her bright blue medical Style-mate clipboard, something Allison had placed on the small table at the foot of Anastasia's hospital bed, and something she often carried around with her while completing hospital rounds. *Imagination. Nothing more.* Allison's mind accepted the fact that the child had a vivid imagination.

"Hi, Miles." As she reached for her medical clipboard, Dr. Starr spoke to the imaginary dog, then she talked to Anastasia one last time, just as Karen Elpis entered the small room. "I'm so happy I was able to meet you." And then to the child's mother, "Please let me know if there's anything I can do for you in the future." Smiling, she turned to exit the room, but not before fist-bumping Ms. Elpis' closed hand and not before hearing the child's last comment.

"Miles looks funny as a cat." Karen Elpis laughed, shaking her head at Anastasia's babble.

Unfazed, Dr. Allison Starr hurried to Walter Jacobs' room in time to witness the seventy-three-year-old sitting up in his hospital bed and give him the postoperative instruction form she had clipped to the top of her medical clipboard. It was a document listing signs of infection and general care instructions. She pulled the paper's top edge out from under the bright metal clip and handed it to Walter.

"Make sure you read this, Walter." She watched the older man's eyes as they seemed to stare past the postoperative instruction sheet and look directly at the clipboard she still held in her arm. Still, she continued speaking. "I'm sure you won't have any problems with infection. Just keep the area clean." She watched him smile. His eyes remained focused on the back of her medical clipboard. "You should be out of here by tomorrow morning." Engrossed on Dr. Starr's clipboard, Walter wasn't focusing, at least not on the directions given by Dr. Starr.

"That's a beautiful cat, Doc." The older adult grinned.

Allison had forgotten about the 5x7 photo of Pumpkin, one she had laminated to the back of her medical clipboard during her second year at Swedish Medical. *Miles looks funny as a cat.* She recalled Anastasia Elpis' words before forming her private thought.

She was referring to Pumpkin. Allison felt satisfied having solved another mystery, then redirected her medical advice and conversation to Mr. Jacobs.

"Thanks, Walter," she said. "Just keep your surgical opening clean and covered." Then to be friendly, "That's Pumpkin, my cat." She didn't allow herself to interpret Anastasia's comments further or give any more thought to Pumpkin's photo. Instead, Allison wished Mr. Jacobs a speedy recovery and exited the room.

It wasn't until she was on the monorail home, sitting next to Jeffery Linus, that she permitted herself to entertain such a far-fetched and almost ridiculous question, one she only felt safe asking around Jeffery.

"Can animals be reincarnated too?"

Eight

"I believe animals have souls," Jeffery spoke after swallowing a small bite of Kobe filet, seasoned in kosher salt and one he had stabbed concurrently with a piece of roasted asparagus.

Allison chuckled as she realized how bizarre her thoughts were after calculating the probability of Miles living reincarnated. In the scientific world, she knew the odds exceeded a trillion-to-one that Miles reincarnated as a cat and the odds then multiplied by infinity that he had entered her life, the daughter of his previous owner.

"Reincarnation has never been proven in the scientific world." Allison's polite banter followed her last bite and a full swallow of Domaine Leroy Richebourg. A vintage red wine Jeffery Linus had been saving for a special occasion. And one that the two of them were polishing off over dinner in her small apartment. Studying the label, Allison processed the year *1961*. Her mother's birth year. *Another coincidence,* she imagined. *She would have turned seventy-six years old last week.*

"You know, as well as I do, that scientific proof requires a measurable outcome that duplicates by testing method and results." He swirled his wine around in his glass, intensifying the aroma, and took a small sip. "That rarely happens with anything involving astrology or reincarnation."

"I've read about people who claim reincarnation. I attended a neurobehavioral scientists' seminar last year. I remember the speaker, a doctor of clinical hypnotherapy, claimed that he used hypnosis with patients to support reincarnation claims." Allison had another long sip of red wine. "But I also know how badly I want my mother to be out there." Allison paused, fighting tears, then shaking her head. "Now I'm trying to convince myself that Pumpkin is Miles reincarnated." Even after polishing off her third glass of vintage red wine, she could still hear herself being ridiculous. "I don't know, Jeffery."

"You don't have to know Allison. It's perfectly okay to be an excellent doctor, to support and believe science, and to question the possibilities." Following her lead, Jeffery drank down the last of his 1961 Richebourg. Taking her hand, he led her into the master bathroom. This time he wouldn't be showering alone.

Friday morning came too early. Pumpkin watched them share another bagel, just as he had watched them share a night of love-making—their first one with each other, since eyeing each other discreetly over the last five years at Swedish Medical.

The monorail ride to the hospital was quiet. Jeffery knew Allison would be leaving in less than twenty-four hours for a five-week road trip, knew she needed her sleep tonight, and knew he was deeply and madly in love with Dr. Allison Starr, so he used every moment on the monorail wisely: first, by holding Allison's hand, an act that seemed so rare and precious in the world they were living in, and next by soaking in the early morning sun's reflection as it glistened off her face.

"Enjoy Gerhart's seminar, Allison." Jeffery knew she was attending the all-day seminar, but he wasn't sure what topic Gerhart had scheduled, just like Allison. Both doctors knew that Dr. Ben Gerhart liked to change things up, addressing an issue that seemed to spark controversy.

"I'll stop in the lab to see you before I go home today." She smiled back at him.

"You better," he said. "I already miss you."

The available seating in the hospital conference center was already dwindling when Allison entered. She sat near the back but in reasonable viewing distance of Dr. Ben Gerhart, who was already on stage. Allison scanned the room, locating the digital ACUMEN-Wizard, an advanced interactive display that stated Gerhart's topic: The finality of death. *That's ironic,* she thought, as she tried not to laugh out loud.

"Welcome, colleagues and students from the University of Washington and Pima Medical Institute. I am Dr. Ben Gerhart, Chief of Cardiac Surgery at Swedish Medical Center. I'm glad you're here.

Please sit back. Relax. Take notes. I will be taking you on a journey. A dead-end journey." Chuckles filled the small auditorium. "Please hold all questions until the lecture portion of the seminar has concluded." Dr. Allison Starr sat back, her left hand gripping a Kona Peaberry coffee, her mind open. "Let me start by reviewing the laws of our universe." Allison watched the digital display change: Universal Laws.

Three hours passed. Allison listened to every word. She listened as Gerhart talked about the law of physics. She listened as he reminded the mixed audience, consisting of forty-five medical professionals and students, that human consciousness would have to exist separately from the human body for post-partum survival to be possible. Finally, she listened as he explained that human particles do not survive death. Taking her last sip of Kona Peaberry, she let the room temperature liquid slowly work down the back of her throat. Her mind tried to accept Gerhart's words without hesitation, dismissing any Cinderella make-believe bullshit she had been desperately trying to believe about reincarnation.

"The Quantum Field Theory or QFT is proof that all particles have a separate field. There have been numerous tests on the quantum field to detect the existence of unknown particles, or what some physicists or cosmologists call spirit particles, and to date, well, they simply don't exist."

Hands raised simultaneously, filling the next two hours with questions, which Gerhart answered one at a time.

"Dr. Gerhart, are you saying that the only particles found in the human body are hydrogen, carbon, nitrogen, and oxygen?" The question came from a first-year medical student.

"Yes, ninety-nine percent of your body is made up of those particles."

The first-year medical student watched several hands around him go down. Satisfied. Something the twenty-one-year-old from Pima Medical Institute was not.

"Dr. Gerhart, if I may ask a follow-up question, what is the other one percent?"

"Mostly antimatter." Six other hands went down, leaving the Pima Med student's arm raised in an otherwise satisfied room. Even though Ben Gerhart appreciated thoroughness, he had lectured, explained, and answered questions for almost six hours. *Five*

Minutes Remain flashed in red across the ACUMEN-Wizard. Now, Gerhart was anxious to exit the room.

"Dr. Gerhart, isn't it true that antimatter converts into energy?"

"If you are referring to Einstein's $E=mc^2$ the answer is yes."

Then without raising his hand, Ely Davidson asked one more question. "So, isn't it possible that the very essence of a human soul is found in this matter, Doctor?"

"That's highly unlikely." Gerhart walked off stage, leaving the room satisfied, except for Ely Davidson. And, except for Dr. Allison Starr.

Making her way to The Department of Molecular Biology on the fourth floor, Allison Starr composed her thoughts. *Highly unlikely does not mean no.*

"How was your seminar, Doctor?" Before smiling at Allison, Jeffery's line of vision left the Cell-Detect 5000, one he had been using to study a cell sample from a patient with a rare type of cancer.

"It left me with more unanswered questions." Allison smiled back, all the while walking toward the man who she found herself loving.

"That's science." Jeffery laughed. "Was the topic interesting?"

"Are you ready for this?" She finally permitted herself to laugh at the topic, although slightly. "The finality of death."

"Ouch." Jeffery could tell her head was spinning. "Let me guess, Gerhart does not believe in possibilities?"

"Highly unlikely." She restated. "He was drilled a little bit at the end by a Pima med student."

"What about?" Jeffery Linus knew Dr. Ben Gerhart was excellent in his field, but he also knew the good doctor wasn't open to the suggested theories about reincarnation and the human soul."

"Gerhart doesn't believe that the one percent of antimatter in the human body could contain a soul." Allison Starr hoped Jeffery would put a Band-Aid on her disappointment.

"Essentially, it can't." The answer was quick, leaving Allison feeling hopeless. Jeffery violently ripped a Band-Aid off Allison's emotions instead of gently applying one. "But it can happen in dark matter." Allison felt the color come back to her cheeks.

"Dark matter?"

"A portion of the one-percent Gerhart failed to mention is dark matter. Since 2020, NASA has made tremendous progress photographing dark matter in several newly discovered galaxies. Once thought to be invisible, today, dark matter is photographed using the ROSAT36 Satellite System that NASA has had in orbit for over a year. The photographs are amazing, Allison. The ones I've seen show such a variation of blue, bright white, and pale red." Jeffery pulled Allison close. "As a promotion, NASA created four handheld versions of their 450-ton ROSAT36 and awarded them to the top four Molecular Biology Departments in the country." He chuckled, thinking about the quarter of a million dollars that NASA spent to design each two-pound handheld replica, a one-million-dollar total price tag to create four devices that seemed to work best for PR relations. "They didn't think about the fact that the top four Molecular Biology Departments exist in big cities. Cities where finding a high dark area is next to impossible." Jeffery made numerous attempts from the hospital's main annex. He tried the top of its seventh-floor rooftop, one that towered above the city of Seattle, after factoring in the location of the hospital, built high on a hilltop in an old neighborhood where cars once parked on the surrounding streets, each with an emergency brake engaged to prevent the automobiles from rolling toward the Pacific, and where people mowed their tiny front yards with push mowers that worked shoulder, neck, and leg muscles with every uphill cut. Even so, testing the ROSAT 36-Mini numerous times in the dark of night and under clear skies, Jeffery was still unable to photograph dark matter around the Milky Way with the handheld device. Nothing.

"Did your department receive one?" Allison assumed that his familiarity with the small handheld device probably meant he had at least seen one.

"Yes, Swedish Medical Center was given one to honor our work."

"You mean your work." It wasn't a question. Allison knew Jeffery had received numerous awards.

"Don't make me blush, Doctor," he said, getting up long enough to walk across the lab, unlock a wall safe, and remove a black case. For the next hour, Jeffery showed Allison how to assemble the ROSAT36-Mini.

"If I wasn't living and working in the middle of Seattle, I could record and transmit small photographs showing the existence of dark matter." Allison watched his eyes sparkle when he talked about the controversial dark matter and the galaxies that hid its secrets. "It's made up of particles that we still have very little information on. What I know, and what science proves, is that a portion of dark matter exists in each human being, but it can't be studied when the person is alive, only after death, and what makes it extra mysterious is that after death, it simply disappears." He studied Allison's deep brown eyes. They were endless in thought. "Scientists don't know where it goes." He looked at her with magic in his eyes. He placed his hand on the back of her neck, pulling her in, then whispered, "It's like a ghost."

Allison Starr felt her feet leave earth. She floated above two trillion galaxies. Below her, she saw twirling periwinkle, marmalade stirred by a honey-dipped spoon, swirling sapphire, and ivory that pirouetted over stars.

Nine

Dear Allison,

I feel like we've been in each other's lives forever and made love a million times; still, I crave a million more. You told me my eyes sparkle when I talk about stars, the vibrant colors of the Milky Way dust, the light that dances between them, and the mysterious clusters of dark matter. My eyes only sparkle because I'm talking to you. Five weeks is a long time. Take the ROSAT36-Mini with you. Maybe when you're looking up at the dark sky from a mountain top or while you're standing in the middle of a desert, you'll be able to see what I see when I look at you. All my love, Jeffery.

Allison Starr folded the note previously taped to the black case lying on the front passenger seat in the GFS automobile. She smiled. Dr. Jeffery Linus had discreetly upped his game once again. He stopped at Allison's apartment building early Saturday morning in time to approach the GFS delivery driver. He offered a substantial tip as he held his iPhone XXXVII in hand, his fingers quickly maneuvering two clicks, which permitted Cash-Right-Now to transfer two hundred dollars from his account to the delivery driver's private account. Done. The well-orchestrated deal allowed the well-known doctor to leave the black case and note on the front passenger seat of Allison's GFS loaner car.

At first, Allison overlooked the black protective case. It wasn't until she had loaded a suitcase of clothing, her cosmetic bag, several blankets, a sleeping bag, a propane stove, a supply of soup, and Pumpkin (who immediately went for the top of the dashboard) that she recognized the impact-resistant protective case. It was the same one Allison had watched Jeffery open in the lab, its insides lined with cubed foam and the outside boasting a large silver latch and a mixture of bold letters and numbers: **ROSAT36-Mini.**

Leaving the satellite case beside her, she pressed the gas pedal in the 2035 cyan-colored Nissan like a silent passenger. It was her first time in five years to sit behind the wheel of a vehicle. She could have requested a 2037 Tesla, which operates on auto-pilot, solely. The Tesla has a built-in bar stocked with Alize Vodka and Last Drop Whiskey and has a heated back seat that folds flat, one where she could have stretched out her slender 5'5" frame, leaving her hands free for photo ops or her body free to grab a nap. Simultaneously, the automobile would have self-piloted over mountains and through reinvented cities, but she had requested the 2035 Nissan. Purposeful. No automated driving capability. No alcohol, except for an occasional glass of wine. It did come standard with an area that accommodates sleep, unfolding a memory mattress that detects and controls body temperature. That was enough to make the trip comfortable. Autopilot was something Allison didn't want or need. She had her mind and heart set on being in control, both inside and outside the vehicle.

Interstate 5 South from Seattle wasn't like Allison last remembered. Memories of 2031's winter bumper-to-bumper traffic were just that – memories. The four lanes heading south on I-5 made Allison's world feel empty. Aside from one Alaska Marine semi-truck, one Fed Ex semi-truck, and one Amazon Prime, Allison hadn't passed any other vehicles during the first two hours of her journey. They were hours that allowed memories to become visions. She could see herself driving her thirteen-year-old baby-blue Ford Focus RS, its windows down – the car she had owned through undergraduate school, medical college, and her hospital residency. It was a December day when Allison pulled out of Seattle's Pike Place Market. That was the same year she had turned thirty-six. And the same year, she had graduated with her Ph.D. in Cardiothoracic Anesthesia, giving her an excuse to buy a hundred-dollar cut of fresh Copper River king salmon and a pound of Yamashita spinach.

A few days later, that same week in December, the snowy Seattle sky hung low. Each nimbostratus cloud darkened due to a combined result of light snow and ozone pollutants, both of which magnified the coastal city's dreary mindset, as the Pacific coastal city received the same news as every other city and town in America – the declaration of war with COVID-31.

Allison had first heard the acronym in her mid-twenties. During the early spring of 2020, COVID-19 made its way from Wuhan, China, to every country worldwide. Then again, in 2025, when several large congregations reported similar cases after COVID attacked Southern Nigeria following their large Christmas gatherings in churches built for fifty but attended by crowds of 300 or more. By Easter, several Christian Nigerians had made their way to several large churches in Houston, Texas. The media didn't hold back cruel headlines after uncovering the celebrations that far exceeded the recommended size limits for a church gathering. *God Let COVID Kill 4,102 Men, Women, and Children in His House* Allison still visualized the dark bold words. Then, in 2031, Allison heard the acronym again. *This strand of COVID has the potential to be far more devastating,* Allison recalled the health officials stating. They were right.

COVID-31 was a different strand. None of the previously developed vaccines responded to the newest strand. It hadn't originated in China or in overcrowded churches where people felt their faith would protect them. No. This one grew in the good ole USA. There was no way to get around the accusations. Middle America took the blame for COVID-31 after the virus was traced back to an egg farmer in Kansas. It was common practice to raise chickens on a cattle farm. What wasn't standard was one chicken's dinner: a sizeable bug from the cow-pie of a sick Hereford, which contaminated that chicken's eggs, which infected the farmer, his wife, and their three children following Sunday breakfast, prompting them to seek medical care and much-needed pharmaceutical supplies from downtown, errands that quickly spread the unknown virus, first throughout their state, then from coast to coast. Fast. Every cough, sneeze, and contaminated surface filled America's hospital beds with critically ill patients within two weeks.

The new POTUS, Pearl Thornburg, wanted to make sure COVID-history didn't repeat itself. Therefore, less than a month later, when she took office in January 2032, she immediately enforced *stay-at-home* orders in every state in the United States of America, flattening the curve and allowing Dr. Jeffery Linus and others like him to eliminate the threat of COVID-31.

That was the turning point for America. During the shutdown, a lifestyle that nurtured people and the environment flourished. Large stores immediately shut down. Going to church was wholly banned until refigured safe restrictions became law. All restaurants, including fast-food chains, permanently eliminated inside dining and followed the simultaneously enforced automobile regulations. The sound of busy two-lane roads through even the tiniest neighborhoods ceased as automobile travel reinvented itself, and hemp fuel's implementation took priority. Driving was no longer a privilege to be enjoyed by the masses.

Instead, homelessness became the priority. Government agencies converted automobiles to an inoperable status, using them for shelter. The homeless were given refurbished 2-door and 4-door autos as housing but were allowed to move into a van or box truck after securing employment. As a result, unemployment reached an all-time low. More than two million Americans worked on hemp farms and other critical farming areas, some through the state and some through individual counties.

Following Dr. Jeffery Linus' suggestion, individual counties strategically placed each automobile used as a housing unit on a small plot of government-provided land routinely weeded and tilled by county workers. In addition, individual counties supplied vegetable seeds, a water source, and a new breed of healthy brown-egged bearing chickens. The USFA (United States Farmers' Association) established essential produce plants and two chickens for each ACZ owner. The process supplied the needy with a limited protein source until they secured employment. At that time, income could be added to the owner's print-identification system, allowing the ACZ resident to shop at small markets for fish, meat, dairy, and other essentials.

Although micro-managed, the new system of today's American government had proven worthy. Now, after just five years, Allison couldn't help but notice how America had benefited. The saying *less is more* had taken on a new meaning. She listened to a slight whistle in the empty August Seattle air as she hung her left arm out of the two-year-old teal-blue Nissan. Her eyes studied the sky; there wasn't a plane anywhere around her. Unobstructed. She breathed deeply, allowing her body to take in as much oxygen as possible. Simultaneously, her chocolate brown eyes searched the right-hand side of I-5, catching a glimpse of a familiar building –

The Emerald Queen Casino. She thought about how she and Reese would stop to play slots in the building whose entrance remained adorned with seven golden flags, although most of the sparkly paint had faded. Allison couldn't help but remember the eight thousand dollars they had won, enough to put down on a good size piece of property. It was a goal that backfired and quickly became the beginning of the end. Even so, she couldn't help but recall their last year together. It wasn't a memory she cherished, and certainly not one she wanted to have on her vacation, so she tried to refocus on the stretch of road in front of her. **Port of Tacoma. One mile.** Noticing a large ACZ on her right, she exited. A weathered green sign read: **Tolmie State Park.**

The road narrowed as she slowly passed her first sighting of two other passenger automobiles. She smiled and waved as she privately acknowledged their correctly displayed GFS stickers, one on each vehicle as it approached her line of vision and one on the rear of each car as it left her rearview mirror. Her world had changed indeed. For the next two hours, she walked a small pebbled beach. Pumpkin followed her like he was a small dog. They glanced at the inlet, which flirted with the mouth of the Pacific Ocean. Off in the far distance, she could see a freight-liner. Allison had read that even the large tankers operate by using hemp fuel. The ship's massive, darkened outline made her think of her brother, Mitch. She wished she knew how to contact him, although remembering the last time they spoke on the phone, almost eighteen years ago, she expected it wouldn't be worth her time. At that time, standing on opposite sides of the United States, she told him there had been several family emergencies in his absence.

First, the death of Aunt Dixie. Cancer. Only fifty-eight years old. Then, the uncertainty of their mother's fate. *Mudslide. Still missing.* Remembering those words, the exact words she used on the phone with her brother, followed by *I need your support* and *come quick.* She felt her stomach harden, even now, after recalling his reaction. Two words. *I can't.* That's when he decided to get back on the tanker ship. That's when he decided Africa was his home. That's when he decided to sever all contact. It wasn't *can't*; it was *won't.*

After making her way back on I-5, Allison cleared Tacoma's city limits, passing old motels now renovated into apartments for those working white-collar jobs. Next, she saw Harbor Freight, a business that remained strong in the new world, before passing one more GFS-auto and one more semi-truck. *Head south,* Allison reminded herself, embracing her freedom. Pumpkin napped under the overcast sky until the first raindrop hit the front passenger window waking him. Even the rain smelled different in 2037. Cleaner. Allison continued to drive, allowing her driver's window to stay down so her left arm could absorb the uncontaminated rain.

"I love you, Dr. Starr." Jeffery's voice filled the still-new cyan-colored Nissan after a generic female voice gently and delicately announced his incoming call and patched him through. It all happened without Allison touching a button; automation is considered standard in the 2035 model, allowing the driver to keep both hands on the wheel at all times. Of course, Allison had the option of switching the automation to the off-position.

"Do you miss me already, Dr. Linus?" She asked as her voice vibrated in the afternoon air – an incoming airstream that worshipped the left side of her face.

"I do." He laughed. "My ride on the monorail this morning felt exceptionally long."

"Maybe that's because you left your apartment, traveled to the front of my apartment building, and planted a mysterious black case in the car I'm driving before traveling toward Swedish Medical."

"Maybe." He chuckled. "Do you remember how to use it?"

"I'm a doctor." Her tone was matter-of-fact. "I remember everything."

"I'm writing that down." Jeffery controlled his chuckle. "Note to self: remembers everything." He knew her memories of driving on open road had never left her, knew she had dreamed about this trip for five years, and knew before he spotted the 2035 teal-blue Nissan in the early light that she would choose a vehicle that did not have autopilot.

"I don't want to let go. I just want to feel the wheel in my hands forever." Euphoria filled Allison's voice as she approached the Mount Rainer and Mount St. Helen's exits, both stretches of interstate that were often bottlenecks of bumper-to-bumper traffic in her memories, but not in 2037. She let her eyes soak in the various green shades of towering sequoias, cottonwood, spruce, and hemlock. She could see an ACZ area off to her right, but this one consisted of refurbished box trucks, each placed like a shoebox on a small plot of land, which included a well-cared-for garden and small chicken coop. She imagined the inside of each unit: *equipped with running water and a small bathroom.* The county had given make-overs to the outside of each truck. Old company logos hid under the home's new paint job – bright apple red, crisp grass green, sky blue, and honeysuckle yellow. Bits of the past were no longer identifiable. Most had side windows installed, several of which displayed a potted plant or two and assorted curtains. Allison watched plaids and brightly colored flowery patterns keep pace with her driver's window.

"I want to feel you in my hands forever." It came out cornier than Jeffery expected, but Allison laughed a slight girlish giggle, letting him off the hook.

"You will again. I promise."

"Good," and then, "I'm only a phone call away." He didn't want to keep her on the hands-free communication device any longer. Picturing her, hands on the wheel, with a smile on her face, was all he needed right now. "Soak up the freedom, Allison." He understood the hunger she had inside of her.

"I plan on it." She needed her space, but she also needed to hear his voice. "I'll try to call you tonight, Dr. Linus."

Jeffery grinned ear to ear.

It wasn't until he received a stat lab analysis request, one for possible bacteria or a parasite, that his smile faded. He recognized the name immediately – Anastasia Elpis.

Ten

"Staphylococcal food poisoning," Dr. Jeffery Linus spoke to the back of Dr. Gerhart's head as he entered the doctors' lounge, his feet moving as fast as the worry spreading across his face. "Anastasia's blood sample is loaded with round clusters."

"Goddammit." Ben was on his feet as soon as he heard Linus' announcement. "Could it have been caused by contaminated surgical equipment?" The question waited for an answer, one that would refuel the anger Gerhart still harbored for Dr. Chrome's careless maneuver during the Randall DuPuy' surgery if answered with a *yes*. The decision made by the bionic arm cost a forty-seven-year-old patient his life. Ben suspected Dr. Chrome was somehow responsible; it would be just like Dr. Chrome to have a malfunction in the built-in disinfection and sterilization process triggered to occur before and after every procedure. *Maybe, there was an improper release of combined steam and fumigation in the computer-controlled system,* Ben thought.

"I just spoke with Karen Elpis," Jeffery was shaking his head as he answered. "Her daughter was throwing up and complaining of stomach pain after playing outside."

"I know. That information is on the intake form," Ben interrupted.

"Exactly," Jeffery sputtered, not allowing Ben to get in another word. "I read the fucking intake form, and what surprised me was that no one asked the mother follow-up questions. What was Anastasis' first symptom? Her second symptom? Did she have any other symptoms? What was your child doing thirty minutes before the onset of symptoms? What was your child doing two hours before? What was your fucking child doing six hours before?"

Jeffery Linus wasn't trying to contain his anger. "I asked the mother those questions," Jeffery took a deep breath before rattling off the grocery list of answers. "Nausea. Vomiting. Severe stomach cramps. Playing outside with her imaginary dog. Feeding her imaginary dog and herself an uncooked chicken egg. Washing runny yellow yolk off her five-year-old hands when she entered the conversion van," Jeffery's jaw tensed. "Now, because of wasted time, we've got a five-year-old admitted to intensive care," Jeffery's voice met Ben's face. "Most patients recover from staph caused by food poisoning. Unfortunately, in this case, several strands of bacteria have already spread to her blood. Maybe you should be concerned about the bacteria that could be attaching to the lining of Anastasia Elpis' heart instead of sitting in the fucking doctors' lounge while trying to think of how to pin something else on Dr. Chrome." Ben Gerhart took a step back after realizing that the man at the other end of the increasingly loud and angry voice looked like he wanted to take a swing at him. Ben stood. Emotionless.

"Do you suspect endocarditis?" Dr. Ben Gerhart followed Linus' train of thought so he didn't continue to lose face. "If bacteria exist in Anastasia's bloodstream, her heart is the target."

"It's probably already there," Jeffery didn't feel like sparing Ben's feelings. "She won't survive sepsis." Dr. Jeffery Linus knew Anastasia Elpis' five-year-old immune system wasn't strong enough to remove the bacteria independently. He also knew the child's chances of surviving damage to her heart valves were slim to none. A round of antibiotics wasn't going to cut it. Another surgery was her only option. Maybe then, Dr. Chrome, the bionic arm that Gerhart had grown to hate, would be able to determine if AHT – Advanced Hemodialysis Treatment would work for the young patient. Just maybe. Out with the contaminated blood and in with the new.

"I'll schedule surgery as soon as she's strong enough." Dr. Gerhart needed Dr. Chrome once again.

"Don't wait too long." Dr. Linus wasn't a surgeon, but he knew the young child's blood had clumps of various types of bacteria, and he imagined the worse for her – seizure, embolism, kidney damage, and even complete heart failure. "I'll stay at the lab late in case you need other tests," Jeffery's tone became a bit calmer. "She's a priority, Ben." He thought about how Allison was going to be devastated to hear the news. Allison wouldn't be able to fathom a five-year-old dying.

Dr. Jeffery Linus broke eye contact with Ben, long enough to read an incoming text message on his iPhone XXXVII – *I downloaded your fingerprint to my apartment's authorization system. Please stop by and water my fairy castle cactus occasionally. Just a few sprinkles of water will do. I love you.* A part of him smiled, and another part of him wondered how Allison had acquired his fingerprint. However, he knew her investigative skills exceeded the norm, skills that she had once joked came from her mother – a Virgo who paid attention to details and analyzed everything.

Jeffery excused himself from Ben's presence and placed a call to the 2035 Nissan's Bluetooth system. It had only been six hours since he had spoken with Allison, only been seven hours since he had placed the Rosat36-Mini on her front passenger seat, and hadn't even been one full day since he last laid eyes on her. Still, it was one of the most challenging days Dr. Jeffery Linus had experienced in five years. Maybe that's because today was the first day in five years that he hadn't at least caught a glimpse of Allison

Starr in a hallway or on the monorail. Every fiber in his soul missed her.

"You have an incoming call, Dr. Allison Starr," the generic female voice filled the inside of Allison's Nissan.

"Thanks, Flo," Allison snickered as she thought about how the nickname, one she had come up with impromptu, and one the doctor knew fit the 2035 Nissan she was driving, matched its looks and personality. Its teal-blue exterior and female voice reminded her of the 1957 GM Motorama, a talking car in a Disney movie she had watched as a young girl, and one where the blue-teal paint job glistened on the full-figured wife. The husband, Ramone, proudly came to life as a 1951 Impala low-rider. Allie was only eleven when the 2006 movie was released, an age when she imagined automobiles, like people, could have feelings and be married to each other. Time had altered her beliefs on both authentic emotions and the sanctity of marriage. Still, time didn't erase her memories of watching the Disney movie with her brother, Mitch, and her mother, Enola.

"Who's Flo?" After hearing Allison's voice inadvertently, Jeffery smiled as his mind noted the 2035 Bluetooth system's number one feature – promptness. "You're not thinking of the movie, *Cars,* are you?" Jeffery's smile widened as he thought of her childlike spirit – another reason he loved her. When the movie was released, Jeffery was fourteen, a little too old to publicly admit he enjoyed Disney magic. Even so, Jeffery could still remember owning the die-cast set of Disney Pixar cars. Jeffery would never forget how his fingers felt alive as he raced Lightning McQueen over ant-piles in the front yard of his Maryland home as a boy and could still remember how it felt watching the red race car take down an entire ant colony. "After all, that car you're driving has the same paint job – a bright cyan." Jeffery's attention to detail was just one of the many reasons that Allison loved him.

"Cyan, Doctor?" Allison found it impressive when a man recognized various shades of color, right down to the precise tone created by light and wavelengths. "And, yes," Allison laughed, "Flo."

Jeffery realized he was still smiling after discovering that they shared a common bond in Disney history, but he quickly refocused, causing his smile to fade. He knew that he couldn't put off talking to Allison about the hospital's youngest ICU patient.

"Allison, I have some bad news," he started, although a part of him wanted to hold the news captive for five more weeks, giving Allison a chance to enjoy every moment of her vacation. *Maybe Anastasia will pull through. Perhaps I should let Allison enjoy her trip.* Their relationship did not exist on maybes, and neither did Anastasia's fate. It wasn't good. He had to tell her. Now. "Anastasia Elpis is back in Swedish," he kept going. "ICU. Staphylococcal food poisoning."

"How?" Allison's watery eyes blurred her view of I-5 South and the long stretch of BNSF tracks. *Trains? Are they still operable?* Her attempt to think of something else besides the life of a five-year-old was unsuccessful. Instead, she could see the child's blue eyes staring up at her.

Truth, Jeffery reminded himself. *Full disclosure.* "Anastasia was feeding her imaginary dog raw egg and herself."

"No big deal unless you're five years old and only a few days into recovery following septal wall repair," Allison announced knowingly.

"Exactly," Jeffery wasn't about to sugar-coat things. "Bacteria clusters are in her blood. Several types."

"Dammit." Jeffery could hear the pain in Allison's voice, pain for a five-year-old, pain for a living, breathing soul, a soul that kept Allison questioning her belief in reincarnation. *My mother.* Allison shook off the thought. *How did Anastasia know about my crescent moon birthmark? Why did she have flashbacks about mud getting in her throat? About dying with her dog, Miles? How did she know Miles had an orange tint to his fur, just like Pumpkin?* She recalled Anastasia's comment about how her dog was near, recalled how the child noticed the photo on the back of her medical clipboard and remembered how Jeffery hadn't shut down the possibility of animals being able to reincarnate. *Is Pumpkin, Miles?* Allison took her eyes off I-5 long enough to stare at Pumpkin's glossy apricot coat, stretched under the 3-p.m. sun that had grown cooler since crossing into Oregon. The sixty-eight-degree temperature filled the mid-August air, turning the front window dash into a canvas that welcomed Pumpkin's nose. Its outline replicated on the vinyl dash like a well-done painting created by condensation and was something that caught Allison's attention when he raised his head to look at her. She had always seen Pumpkin's dog traits – affectionate and playful during the day, and as Allison had learned since morning, he likes car rides. "I don't want to lose her, Jeffery."

"I know," he answered. "I'm going to do everything I can." Next, he thought about the necessary surgery. "Gerhart will operate as soon as she's strong enough. I'm hoping she'll be able to undergo AHT. During a couple of recent trials conducted in the United States, doctors successfully filtered a patient's blood through a dialyzer removing everything from cancerous cells to blood clots. It's a procedure that could remove all types of deadly bacteria from the blood." Then, to lighten the conversation, "How did you get my fingerprint, Doctor Starr?"

"My keyless entry system automatically scans and saves the print of anyone that enters my apartment," she informed him. "You should be more careful, Doctor." Jeffery listened to a slight giggle accompany her playful suggestion.

"I guess I should. I think you might frame me," Jeffery joked.

"Yes, I could," Allison answered playfully. He had taken some of the worries out of her heavy heart. Still, he could tell she was concerned, even after another twenty minutes of babble and another twenty-five miles on Interstate 5.

"I love you, Allison." Jeffery wanted to add on a supportive statement about how Anastasia was going to be alright. Still, he didn't want to make a promise he couldn't keep, so he left the well-being of five-year-old Anastasia where it had ended – unknown.

"I love you too," her voice was steady, a contrast to her dark-brown eyes that were darting from one side of Interstate 5 to the other as she made her way into the middle of Oregon.

Everything had changed.

Eleven

A shade best described as a warm cognac filled Allison's early

morning eyes as she studied the 6-foot by 8-foot structure in front of

her. Its size dwarfed compared to the small work shed that she

remembered sitting behind her childhood home in Florida, although

there was some resemblance structurally. Both had siding

constructed out of plastic resin wood, giving the small buildings a

prefab-look, only this time it wasn't a shed for her step-father's tools and the family's riding lawnmower. Instead, this time it was a church. Still small in comparison. Still simple. Waiting for purpose.

Mom, if your soul is inside Anastasia, please hang on. Her thoughts drifted to the five-year-old fighting for her life as she concentrated on the crimson shingled roof. Then, she thought of Jeffery as she allowed her line-of-sight to travel up the wooden spire, reminding her of Mount Rainier and everything she found precious in nearby Seattle. Wiping away tears, she focused on the copper-painted aluminum Canterbury-shaped cross at the top of the tower. The end of each arm slightly widened, giving the cross an overall appearance of a circle. When the sun hit it just right, it looked like a giant copper penny. The visual made Allison burst into tears.

"Twenty-four fucking cents, Mom," she screamed at the tiny church; its mandated size purposely limited the congregation to no more than ten occupants at a time, a law enforced after the 2025 coronavirus spread through the religious communities. First, in Nigeria, then Texas, then sporadically attacking church-goers for several months. Large churches quickly became a thing of the past, just like copper pennies, which the US Mint stopped producing in

2022. "That's all I got from you, Mom," Allison sobbed. "What about the fucking quarter you promised?"

Remembering the small box of US pennies tucked in a drawer in her apartment, she thought about how her mother would track down a shiny penny. Pennies corresponded with every year since she had turned one year old. Enola would present it inside a birthday card or memento. Sadly, it was a tradition that served as a reminder of their limited years together. Two months before her mother died, Allison had turned twenty-four years old, and they had laughed about how Allison would have the value of a quarter in just one more year – *you'll have twenty-five cents next year, Allie* – a turning point that Enola May Starks wouldn't live to see.

Reese had attempted to keep up the tradition by giving Allison a penny in 2020, her first birthday after Enola's death, but Allison didn't want it. *No, that's not what I want.* She remembered saying those words to Reese in June 2020. She remembered repeating those exact words a couple of months later. Only the late August rendition was about their relationship, not a penny collection.

Now, she stared at the copper that glistened in the early morning sunlight. The reflection mirrored the mid-August warmth that had gently woken Allison in the back of the Nissan, allowing her to study the small white church from the gravel lot where she had boondocked overnight. It was a familiar corner lot, and one Allison had passed several times before settling in Seattle and before the act of freely driving an automobile had become a thing of the past. She thought about the first time she had driven past the corner of Alder and Burnside, thought about the Evangelist preacher, megaphone in hand, shouting out messages about the rapture and new beginnings. Now, she knew he was right. Parts of the world had died. People and places she would never get back. *Mom, I need you.* Allison's thoughts focused on her mother as she read the sign in front of the tiny church – Portland People's Chapel. *Ironic,* she thought. *Portland People's Chapel existed where the preacher once stood.* Closing her eyes, she thought about 2019. It was the year a tsunami chased her and her fiancé, Reese, from Seaside, Oregon. It was the year her mother died in an Alaskan mudslide. It was the year *her* world collapsed. Change followed.

Automobiles became homes. Recreational vehicles became hair salons, barbers, dental offices, nail salons, massage parlors, chiropractic offices, or other small businesses. Abandoned airplanes became homes, usually located in a desert oasis for wealthy people that didn't want to live near a city. Conversion vans and box trucks became housing for the lower-middle-income working class. Luxury apartments became homes for the white-collar workers that remained in or near a city. The primary source of transportation became monorails. The currency became a person's index finger. Marriage became an outdated custom. Child-rearing was no longer a planned goal, and having a child typically occurred following unexpected circumstances. Churches became tiny places of worship that accommodated up to ten people at a time. Drive-up fast food became walk-in take-out. Health care became accessible to all American citizens. Community colleges were free for all high school graduates. Hemp fuel replaced gasoline. Hotels and motels became small government-run hostels.

There were numerous hostels up and down the coast where Allison could have lodged for free after having her print scanned, a courtesy provided for GFS vacation travelers. Still, for her first night, she preferred to stretch out in the back of the 2035 Nissan Altima, where the rear seats morphed into an eight-inch mattress after a simple voice command. Throughout the night, the surface monitored Allison's movement and temperature. If she was too hot, the bed released cool air. If she was too cold, the therapeutic foam warmed her body with its built-in heat sensors. If she was restless, the cushioned bedding provided extra support.

Now, on a Sunday morning, she watched six or seven people walk into Portland People's Chapel, where a few small pews waited. Allison watched them as she paced the corner lot, where she became comfortable with an older woman's smile and wasn't able to resist asking for prayer, a ritual she never believed in but found herself desiring for Anastasia.

"Do you mind praying for a sick child who is in the hospital?" Allison questioned the friendly face.

"Oh, my darling, of course not." The woman's smile widened, a sign that she welcomed the task of prayer.

"Her name is Anastasia. She's five years old."

"It will be done." The woman's formality matched her attire – a dark navy-blue skirt that hung knee level and a button-down blouse that portrayed several shades of scarlet in its floral pattern – safflower, a flamed flesh tone, vermilion, vivid crimson, and bright red – all of which accented the woman's dark auburn hair in the morning sun and gave her dark green eyes an exaggerated sparkle as she studied the side of Allison's Nissan.

"Thank you." That's all Allison said before turning around to walk back toward Flo. Quickly. Her mind wanted to escape the uncomfortable position she had placed herself in – asking for prayer. Besides, she was curious about what had grabbed the woman's attention, even though it had been ever so slightly, just before the woman excused herself and walked into the small church.

Allison looked around the back of Flo, her cyan-colored friend, spotting Pumpkin, who had just relieved himself like a dog in a nearby patch of grass. The attention-grabber was kicking up dirt with his hind legs as he looked in Allison's direction, letting her know he finished, then jumped back in the open driver's window.

"Pumpkin, are you a dog reincarnated?" Allison asked the question aloud as she backed Flo out of the small church lot, which was no longer used for parking but was more of an outdoor congregation area before and after church services.

Pumpkin just looked at her as she drove through Portland, her old stomping ground and a place of memories from another lifetime, so it seemed. Seventeen years had passed since Allison had been with Reese in Portland. Now it was barely recognizable.

A monorail system ran through Portland's center, from which Automobile Community Zones flowed in every direction. Each ACZ area took center stage around tiny gardens. Monorail riders could view parks with walkers and bicyclists and enjoyed views of refurbished high-rise buildings, some now free public colleges, some functioning as medical offices, and some free housing for the elderly.

Two hundred miles later, Flo broke the silence. "Incoming call, Dr. Starr," The cyan-colored female seemed to have developed a personality.

"Thank you, Flo," Allison spotted a sign as Jeffery's voice took over – Medford 11.

"How's my favorite doctor?" Allison could hear the emptiness when he spoke. It was apparent Jeffery missed her.

"I'm almost to Medford. Next – Ashland. Then, I'll be going over the big-boy mountains and into Hornbrook, California," Allison rattled off her upcoming route. Her voice was full of excitement as she thought about the countless-trips she had made driving that exact route. Years of monotony. Traveling back-and-forth. Sometimes for groceries. Sometimes for laundry. And sometimes just to spend the day away from the dry Northern California soil. Medford's monorail stayed steady with its skyline view and followed their conversation through Ashland and Medford before stopping near an old Arco Gas Station that was now called R-Co-Hemp.

She listened to Jeffery talk about how busy the lab had been all morning as she made her way over the highest elevation on I-5. The August air worked to cool Flo as she quickly climbed the highest point. The slight chill reminded her of the last time she saw Reese – Early Fall, 2020. Briefly, a small pool of water formed in the corner of her dark brown eyes. Emotions she didn't want to address tried to fight their way to the surface.

"I'm glad you're taking your time," he replied. "Let it soak in." Allison had been doing that since Seattle, taking in the new world, remembering the old world, and trying to figure out which one she belonged in. A part of her suspected she belonged in both.

"How's our patient?" There wasn't a point in pretending Anastasia wasn't a priority in the conversation. She was.

"Her condition is about the same. Nausea. Fever. Aches. A slight heart murmur," Jeffery followed with good news. "She's a fighter. Ben feels certain she'll be able to handle surgery by Thursday."

"That's four days away, Jeffery." She was stating the obvious, but her tone clarified that it was too long of a wait.

"He's afraid he'll lose her if he doesn't give her system a chance to get stronger."

"What do you think?"

"I think it's a gamble either way." He knew she would ask his opinion, so he already had an answer prepared. "She needs strength, but kids especially can take a sudden turn for the worse, so I've been staying late, checking her vitals, watching for any sign of decline."

"Anything?" Allison knew Jeffery was going above and beyond. He was a molecular biologist, not a surgeon, and not even a medical doctor; although, Allison would trust him with her own life.

"Nothing," he answered. "In Anastasia's sleep last night, she told Miles to run." Jeffery wondered if that was a detail he should have left out.

"I think Pumpkin used to be a dog," Allison said as she processed Jeffery's statement about Miles.

"You think he used to be Miles?" Jeffery knew Allison's mind was there, as he had learned about Anastasia's reaction to Pumpkin's photo.

"He jumps out the driver's window whenever I stop, does his business in a patch of grass, then jumps back in," Allison laughed. "Twice so far today," she added.

Jeffery smiled, first after visualizing Pumpkin's dog-like behavior, then again after imagining the afternoon glow of the California sky on Allison's milky-white face. "Pumpkin is supposed to be with you." His scientific mind knew it was unlikely that Allison's cat was Enola's dog in a past life, but a part of him wanted to believe it was possible. "He needs you, not as much as I do, but he needs you."

Now, Allison was smiling. "I need you too."

"Send me a photo of some Cali mountains," Jeffery said before reading an incoming lab request – Carol Adams, thirty-two, possible polycystic ovarian syndrome, her doctor requests lab work to determine hormone levels. "I love you."

"I love you too," Allison felt the words leave her quickly.

Dr. Allison Starr didn't continue traveling past the mountains of Hornbrook, California. Not yet. Instead, she took exit 789 and made her way past an abandoned Chevron station. She took an old windy asphalt piece of highway, writhing past two campgrounds near the Klamath River, campgrounds that she knew had once been full of RVs and cars but now appeared to have only a handful of tents in each.

She turned right, making her way over a weathered bridge and up a steep gravel incline. The road narrowed, and unforgiving drop-offs guarded its borders. Pumpkin studied the dusty highway, its guts now covering a once clean car window. Allison saw a large lake out her driver's side window. Pulling between several oddly shaped trees, she maneuvered into a spot overlooking the water below. In the distance, she could see an old dam. *Still functional?* She wondered but didn't ask anything out loud. Tonight, she would survive on a Cup of Soup, a granola bar, and a bottle of unsweet tea. Pumpkin hopped out the open window and jumped onto the hood of the 2035 teal-blue Nissan when he heard the sound of kibble hitting the inside of a bright silver bowl, one Allison was hovering over on the car's front hood, and one he knew meant dinner.

"We need a night without other people around," Allison said to Pumpkin, who was already chowing down. "Look at the sunset, Pumpkin. Its colors match you." She watched the hazy blue August sky fill with apricot and orange. Then, reaching her left arm inside Flo, she pushed a small button near the steering wheel. Flo blinked, making her seem more human. "Send the photo to Dr. Jeffery Linus," Allison leaned into the steering wheel, steadying herself with both hands, as she spoke to Flo's automated command system after taking a photo with the automobile's built-in camera device.

With her granola bar in hand, Allison watched the last bit of the apricot sky blacken. Tonight, she would sleep in total darkness with the sound of a slight purr near her chest.

Twelve

Monday morning Allison Starr wiggled her way down I-5 South, passing several spots of recent wildfires. The toothpick-shaped trees reminded her of the description so vividly described by her mother, Enola Starks. *Charred toothpicks dotted both sides of the Dalton. Black remnants stood like unused spider legs where Alaskan hideaways for birds and wildlife once hid.* It was an entry, unfinished, in a small leather-bound journal, one rescued from the mud-covered 2017 Jeep Cherokee, the vehicle barely two years old, but one her mother had driven for just over forty-thousand miles.

Passing a bright yellow car-carrying transport trailer on I-5, Allison eyed the seven meticulously placed vehicles. Dark-navy, seal-silver, tan, white, khaki, light-gray, and deep mocha. No cherry red. *My mother's car is probably someone's home now,* Allison thought. *She'd like that.* Pumpkin also seemed to eyeball the carefully stacked cars.

"Those are being delivered to ACZ areas, Pumpkin." It was a good feeling knowing homelessness had ended in the United States. However, Allison didn't want to sugarcoat things and knew her world still needed more new ideas and continuous improvement. Even she couldn't ignore the vast strides made. Free college education to those who earned it. Transportation modifications that stopped global warming in its tracks. ACZ communities have restrooms, showers, vegetable gardens, chicken dens, and an immediate sense of belonging. No having to worry about having a safe spot to sleep and having the opportunity to attend a local free college or tech school gave people hope and a fighting chance to make a better life for themselves. A decent career meant having money. Having money meant improved housing and better food. It was a cycle based on positivity.

Allison pulled into the southbound Lakehead-Lakeshore rest area by eleven, less than a hundred miles into her drive since morning. Sure, she could have stopped at a hostel for a shower, meal, and day's rest, but she remembered that all the rest areas up and down I-5 had free showers and vending machines with sandwiches for GFS workers and travelers. She wanted a less popular choice – a cold shower at a rest area, followed by a cold sandwich. Pumpkin seemed to agree. As Allison placed the Nissan in the park position, he jumped out the passenger window and sniffed a nearby almond tree in an adjoining orchard. Allison commanded him to hurry and prompted him to jump back in the window. Before leaving the apricot furball, she watched his body stretch on the dash under the shade provided by a nearby tree that hovered over the front end of the car like a watchful hummingbird. Allison recognized the olive tree's dark green spear-shaped leaves. She reached above her head long enough to finger one, examining its silver-colored belly; she remembered the olive trees near Los Banos, another city holding memories of her past captive.

"They're olive leaves," she informed Pumpkin as she turned around one more time before making her way to the shower, long enough to study the car windows. *Three inches down on both sides.* Satisfied that it was sufficient for a cross breeze, she quickly made her way to the cold water that waited. *Flo will adjust the dash temp if needed.*

Freezing water hit the top of her scalp and made its way down the front of her forty-two-year-old face. Grabbing a bar of soap from her cosmetic bag, she lathered her hair with the thick and creamy suds, allowing the mixture of grapeseed oil and coconut milk to drip down her shoulders and chest. Allison's upper body resembled that of a mid-twenty-year-old who spent a lot of time working out. A perfect trapezius muscle worked its way across Allison's back and showed off every time she moved her shoulders and neck. But, of course, there wasn't a part of Allison Starr that wasn't beautiful.

After rinsing, she could still smell the overpowering scent of coconut, reminding her of her mother. *We're lying in total darkness, and all you can think of is coconut.* She could still remember listening to her mother's words as they watched The Great American

Eclipse from Gervais State Park in Oregon. It was August 2017. The conversation flowed with exchanged giggles, and now, almost twenty years to the date, she could still remember how she responded to her mother's laughter. *Mom, the world is ending.* Allison joked back with her mother. Vaguely, Enola recalled the feeling of doom from a different period in time. Breathing deeply, she focused on the scent of her daughter's hair, letting total darkness surround them. Her lungs struggled for air as Enola took a few extra seconds before responding. The words came with certainty and experience, words that made the hair on Allison's neck stand up, then and now.

No, it's not ending. It's beginning all over again. Allison repeatedly reproduced her mother's words as she made her way back to Flo, the 2035 cyan-colored Nissan that held her mother's reincarnated dog, or at least she suspected. As she reached for her driver's door, she felt the reality of her mother's statement. The world *had* started all over. The unfamiliarity of 2037 was in front of her, but she continued driving. A familiar female voice broke the silence after another two hours. Flo's authoritative announcement warned of an excessive heat wave for all of California and Arizona.

Two of the states that Allison planned on spending a lot of time in during her five-week vacation. *An excessive heat warning remains in effect from two-p.m. PDT Monday until nine-p.m. Wednesday. Please use caution, Dr. Starr.* Allison played back the announcement in her mind. She knew it would be a couple of hot days unless she reacted quickly. Making a break for the coast and working her way south would help. It was time for Allison to quench her thirst by reaching her first planned destination. Allison studied her Nissan's built-in GPS. Pushing the red *trip* button, she listened to the first male voice she had heard since starting her day. *Funny,* Allison thought, *most men don't use directions.* She laughed to herself, but even Pumpkin sensed she was amused. *Dr. Starr, you traveled 174 miles on Saturday, 308 miles on Sunday, and now on Monday, you are currently located in Sacramento. Would you please tell me your destination, Dr. Starr?* Allison knew she had already driven over 250 miles since early morning. Slowly taking her time was part of the pleasure, first stopping to take a cold shower, then accepting a free sandwich from the vending machine. After processing her fingerprint and acknowledging that she was currently a GFS vacation-approved driver, food dispersed.

Surrounded by nearby smoke, she felt the coast summons her closer, a chance to breathe a lighter batch of air. The additional wildfires and excessive heat created an atmosphere that was thick and smothering. She needed the Pacific Coast. In five and a half more hours, she would be sitting on Santa Monica beach, watching the sun melt into the Pacific Ocean. *Hurry.* That was her last thought before she pressed her foot on the accelerator, clicked off cruise control, and watched the odometer's digital number display climb to eighty-seven. There were no rules for Allison Starr. Not today.

Hours of blurred memories passed Allison's driver's window, obscured by smoke and haze, the latter of which Allison might assume was a good dose of pollution, but not in 2037. Air quality had improved over the last five years unless nature was fighting pests and disease on its own. In that case, nature became boss, and GFS firefighters kept the nearby ACZ areas, upscale housing, businesses, and cities safe. Allison noticed several firetrucks yield to an oncoming train out Pumpkin's passenger side as she passed a sign for Tulare, a sign that she knew meant another 170 miles to Santa Monica. The single locomotive pulled at least forty graffitied boxcars, several tanks that she suspected held hemp fuel, and a covered hopper that Allison could tell carried clay, probably for ACZ's gardens. The fast-moving train raced parallel beside miles of almond trees, a pasture of cows, and a withering cornfield. The middle of August showed no mercy. To her driver's left, Allison saw the smoke thicken, fearing that the Sequoia National Forest might be in trouble, even though she knew it was at least sixty minutes east of her, hidden by brittle golden peaks.

Once again, the silence broke. This time, Dr. Jeffery Linus' voice filled the Nissan's interior.

"Business is booming today, but I've never stopped thinking of you. Where's *my* girl?" Allison evaluated his word choice. She was happy they were a couple, but she was hesitant to belong to anyone. Belonging to herself was the only way she knew to be anymore.

"I am fifty minutes away from beautiful," Allison announced, keeping all other details to herself.

"The Pacific Ocean," Jeffery announced. Allison could hear the confidence in his voice. Allison knew he had figured parts of her out, but she also knew there were parts of her he'd never master. Hidden parts.

"Imagine my toes and Pumpkin's paws covered in Santa Monica sand in about twenty more minutes."

"Just in time to see the sunset." Again, he was right.

"I can't wait. It's been too long." Allison kept the memories of the last time she was in Santa Monica with Reese to herself. Then, changing the subject quickly and with purpose, she asked, "How's Anastasia?"

"Her surgery is Thursday morning." Jeffery was disappointed, maybe even angry that Ben Gerhart didn't want to operate sooner. *She needs to be a little bit stronger.* Jeffery's thoughts attempted to agree. Although, his mind could still hear the attitude in Ben's voice. *I want to wait until Thursday.* Too long, in Jeffery's opinion.

"Fucking Gerhart." Allison didn't need to say more. Those two words agreed with Jeffery's thoughts.

"I spent time with her this morning." Showing his empathic side worked with Allison.

"Thanks, Jeffery." It served its purpose. "I love you."

"I love you too." He processed her tone, trying to decipher whether she felt it as much as he did. "Enjoy Santa Monica."

"I will." Silence took over, but not immediately; instead, it occurred minutes later, after Allison pulled into the large parking lot beside the pier. There were only three other cars, all with GFS displayed. Pumpkin jumped out the lowered passenger window, following Allison to a patch of sand that hadn't seen footprints in months.

Settling into Indian position, Allison faced the vibrant orange mixture: a swirling potion of peach marmalade, desert reds, summer squash, and Florida tangerine. As the sun dipped into the Pacific, she imagined Anastasia Elpis' soul dressed in those colors, perfectly matching her most dominant personality traits – happy, courageous, passionate, and determined – just like Allison's mother – Enola May Starks.

Thirteen

Flo's movement mimicked a magician's wand, effortlessly gliding around each mountain curve in California. Oil machines from days gone by sat silenced like dead soldiers. The perfection of hemp fuel had left the oilfields littered with unused rusty steel arms, permanently frozen in a decade that no longer existed. Allison's left and right view offered a look at the historical battlefield as she spent the day exploring the community that stretched north of Santa Monica. Stopping in Agoura Hills, Allison evaluated the living conditions. Renovated planes were situated in the middle of well-kept grounds and shared by a coterie of retired people living a lifestyle that excluded the common man and woman. Most were former airline pilots with their families, choosing to live in isolation and conducting themselves like royalty – the kings and queens of Agoura Hills.

Allison looked on, eyeing rehabbed Boeing 757s, which surrounded an elite country club overlooking the Santa Clara River. A deep hunger sat in as she realized she had been surviving on necessities and as her mind imagined the lavish lunches and formal dining that occurred in the ritzy social club. Confidently, Dr. Allison Starr approached, her facial expressions relaxed and her doctor credentials in hand, as she requested a seat. Several onlookers watched Allison place her index finger on the table's keypad, listened to her order a beer-battered cod sandwich with coleslaw, and whispered as she sipped a large ice tea. Unrattled, Allison slowly enjoyed the well-seasoned cod and creamy slaw while informing the server and nosey listeners that she was in the area doing medical research. *Fuck them,* she thought, knowing she could have talked her way into a guest cottage for the evening if it was something desired.

However, she preferred to conduct her night's sleep in a hidden corner along the Santa Clara River or the Rio Santa Clara, as the waiter referred to it.

Nonetheless, she desired the side of the river as her accommodation site for the evening, opting to leave the life of luxury behind her. *Royalty is not for me,* she thought. *Driving is.* It was a more profound realization that occurred after wandering north the following day. She hadn't put much thought into the direction of her Arizona-bound trip until almost noon. Then, without admitting why, she purposely continued north, allowing her soul to direct her, and ignoring that fact that her attention should be on making her way south – but not yet. A part of her old life existed another two hundred and fifty miles from where Allison now sat. She had hurried past her secrets two days earlier when making her way to Santa Monica, but now she was thinking clearly and quietly, accepting the fact that she had a hidden demon to face in the small town of Redding.

Wednesday's noon had faded when Flo pulled into the lower corner lot of the Mercy Medical Center in Redding, California. She put Flo in the park position while her brown eyes stared at the off-white building that still served as a major hospital. Attached to a mirrored counterpart, it often reflected the nearby mountain sunrays. She didn't remember which of the two buildings she had spent almost two weeks of her life in seventeen years ago. Still, Allison knew she was on the second floor, in the hospital's south ICU wing, and she could even visualize the Our Lady of Grace statue that lurked at the end of the hallway.

"I almost died there," Allison Starr informed Pumpkin, who was wondering why they had stopped. Allison had avoided telling anyone about that part of her life but knew it had been festering long enough inside of her and knew telling Pumpkin was a safe outlet. Remembering the breathing tube, feeding tube, sedation IV, pain-med IV, wrist restraints, ankle restraints, and uncomfortable feeling of catheterization, Dr. Allison Starr allowed herself to become Allie Narducci once again. A hidden part of her life broke through a solid rock dam, releasing pieces of her soul into Flo's interior.

"It was a hot August day which prompted Reese and me to head to the river. Two cars, his with one dog, mine with two, and both with paws that fought to keep balance on bumpy dirt roads as we followed each other and made our way to the Klamath River.

Reese and I spent the day sitting by the river, laughing about the dusty town of Hornbrook and commenting on the secrets that swelled in its belly. We spent a couple of hours that afternoon looking at land for sale. At one point, we fed wild horses a few bruised apples that had rolled around in a cooler in the back of my Yukon," Allie Narducci paused, looking at Pumpkin, who seemed to be listening to the details of her confession. "I don't remember who started the fight. I barely remember getting in my car and speeding away, leaving all three dogs to his care. And, I don't remember hitting guardrails like a round silver ball in a pinball machine, first the right side of the curvy mountain road, then the left." Allie Narducci wiped tears from her face. "The car spun like a Mariner's baseball toward home base. Hard. High. Deliberate. My body tossed like an unrestrained rag-doll out of my driver's window." At that moment, she looked into Pumpkin's eyes. "I remember thinking about my decision to leave my dogs in his care as the car flipped in the air. I remembered thinking that eventually, my anger would dissipate, putting me back with Reese where my furry friends' wagging-tails would be anxiously waiting." She took a deep breath, allowing her mind to recall even the most minor details of the accident and then silently admitting that she still wondered how she had escaped death. She tried to rationalize it out loud. "Maybe you are reincarnated, Pumpkin. Maybe Anastasia Elpis is my mother's soul. And, just maybe, my Aunt Dixie has watched over me throughout the years." Allie wiped away tears that blurred the former Catholic hospital in front of her. "Because I know one thing," she cried, "I felt my dead aunt's hand on my back. I felt her gently place my body in a nearby field of brittle California yellow-eyed grass." She sobbed uncontrollably. "The car burst into flames as soon as it hit the ground. Unrecognizable. Gone. Every trace of my identity burned beyond recognition." She thought about Reese. She knew he had expected her to come back to their camping spot after she had cooled off and after realizing where to live wasn't an argument worth ending a relationship – their relationship.

She wondered how many times he had called the police or the nearby hospital. No trace. No Yukon reported. The police recorded the license plate as illegible. The local hospital didn't have any record of a Narducci. Reese had no way of knowing she had been in an accident. Her body clung to life in another county. Sedated, her breathing assisted by intubation, her life rested in the hands of a hospital three hours away – details Reese had no way of knowing. Her cell phone endlessly rang, its rugged plastic casing engulfed in flames. Reese had no way of knowing she was unable to identify herself to the police or medical staff. Almost two weeks passed before doctors extubated Allison and before she could exercise her vocal cords, just enough to give the team at Redding Hospital a fake name – Alice Norton. Nothing fancy, just something that matched the initials A.N., something she felt she could remember, and something that would serve as her identity until she left Mercy Hospital.

A week after leaving the hospital, Allie Narducci landed a job in a deli. There the owner allowed her to sleep in the back on a cot at night. A month after leaving the hospital, Allie had ordered and received a copy of her birth certificate, was issued a California Driver's License, had purchased a ten-year-old Kia, and made her way north to Hornbrook.

There, she watched Reese leave with his fishing pole as the mid-September sun dipped into its evening position. It was a Sunday ritual. He would be gone a couple of hours. It was enough time for her to locate the camper key in a rusty metal box underneath the front hitch, enough time to write a two-page letter explaining how she had been in a car accident, enough time to grab her clothes and other personal items, enough time to load Shiloh, Yoda, and Serenity, their cat, but one she always considered hers, into the rust-colored Kia, and enough time to decide that leaving Reese and Zeus behind was the right decision. Zeus was *his* dog. Now, she was sitting in front of Mercy Hospital, wishing she could have parts of her old self back.

"I almost died in that hospital, Pumpkin." It was a repeated fact that she announced through muffled tears and lungs that fought for air. Allison ordered the Nissan by voice command to roll down both the front-driver and front-passenger windows. Pumpkin turned his butterscotch eyes away from Allison for the first time since she had started talking and bunny-hopped into a nearby patch of familiar-looking Cali-yellow-eyed grass. Allison exited and then walked toward the hospital, its mirrored entrance facing the Seven-Up Peak Mountain for almost ninety years. She thought of her Aunt Dixie as she walked into the sizeable off-white building and headed to the second floor's ICU. Allison recalled the taller structure, then remembering Pumpkin had gingerly made his escape out Flo's window. She searched the base of her legs planted inside the closed elevator. *At my feet. Inside a building. Silly cat followed me onto an elevator.* Those three silent observations made her think Pumpkin had to be a dog in a former life.

After reaching the second floor, Allison was shocked to see the same Virgin Mary statue. She walked close, stopping to look into the face that starred endless nights at her. Virgin Mary's face appeared in her repetitive dream. Mary, the mother of Jesus, hovered over her, first during her last night at the hospital and at least two dozen times in the ten years following her release. She hadn't had the dream in nearly seven years and hadn't given much thought to the porcelain-colored face – until now.

It would be best if you had a significant change in your life, Allison recalled the professional dream psychic's advice on the other end of the phone. That was in 2030, only two years away from finishing med school. It was a phone call she would never tell others about out of embarrassment, first for spending 150 dollars an hour to seek someone's opinion and second for consulting a phony psychic. *You need to use your abilities.*

But, back then, Allison Starr believed in the possibility of a real psychic. Now, she didn't believe in psychic powers. Allison believed in coincidence. She felt that most people want to improve their quality of life, and she thought her one-time call to a psychic proved how an average phone solicitor could hone their skills to provide helpful advice. Nothing more. Satisfied, she hung up the phone seven years ago, a necessary call that ended her reoccurring dream.

Today, Allison tried to live her life as a realist; however, since Anastasia Elpis had come into her life, she felt herself believing and feeling things she hadn't felt in years. Maybe there were things science couldn't explain.

Rounding the last right-hand turn, Allison spotted ICU South. Pumpkin stayed in step, hiding from any passersby.

"Hi," Allison whispered over the ICU intercom system. "I'm Dr. Starr from Seattle," she knew using her credentials, once again, would be the only way to gain access. "I need to speak with the charge nurse." Direct. To the point. Allison heard a light buzzer seconds before reaching for the door. She stood at the ICU nurses' station, long enough to remember details: *Bed one. Breathing tube.*

Feeding tube. Monitors. Beeping. Suctioning. Coughing. Gaging. By the time the charge nurse worked her way to the monitoring station, Allison had relived two weeks of her life. And after Allison rattled off words like *investigating, quality-care, research, planning,* and *team-building* in *respected* hospitals, followed by *thanks* and *nice meeting you*, Allison Starr made her way to the parking lot, passing the emergency door entrance.

Reese Kabula stood directly in her line of sight.

Fourteen

She would recognize those eyes anywhere. Teasing-blue. They were the same ones she fell in love with when she was in high school, and they were the same ones Allison loved during their seven years together, and they were the same ones she still loved but tried hard not to admit. His youthful body hadn't aged much. If anything, it was a little more defined, highlighting the shoulder and neck muscles she last remembered seventeen years ago. Calculating his age, she said the number out loud.

"Forty-five," she made the announcement louder than she meant to. For a moment, she thought Reese had turned his head toward her voice but was glad he hadn't. Now, she could make her own decision on whether to say hello or not. "No," she answered out loud a second time but in more of a whisper. Her feet directed her to the parking lot where Flo was waiting. Pumpkin followed. "What are the fucking chances of that, Pumpkin?" This time the volume of her voice freely filled the inside of her cyan-colored friend. "Reese Kabula is standing in Redding, California. Seventeen years later. I ask you again, Pumpkin, what are the fucking chances of that?"

Pumpkin looked at Allison. Puzzled. Head tilted like a dog who was trying to understand a human conversation. Then, being able to empathize, he jumped over the console and landed in her lap. Allison looked down at her fingers as they massaged the ball of apricot hair rubbing against her stomach. The furry head faced north, then faced south, unlike Allison's eyes which met the eastern skyline, concentrating on the all too familiar build that had just walked up to a new Dodge Ram 7000. The truck was blue, the same color as his eyes. Allison silently imagined Jeffery Linus' description of the vibrant color – *azure*. A bright yellow GFS sticker was in the upper corner of the driver's right window with a word underneath

that Allison couldn't make out. It wasn't until he backed up to exit

the hospital parking lot that Allison could read the letters. Finally,

her mind deciphered the bold print. FIRE. That's when she examined

the Dodge's truck bed: a water tank, a mechanical reel with a hose,

and several old school pieces of equipment (shovel, t-hook, ax).

He's a rural firefighter. Her mind had determined his

profession, but it didn't stop to evaluate her intentions. She simply

followed him. Slowly and discreetly, she followed him two hours

north, exiting I-5 just before Hornbrook, a town she knew all too

well. She tailed Reese as he veered toward a small area called

Montague. She kept in tandem but not too close, passing cattle

farms, a small ACZ area, and rolling hillsides dotted with renovated

twin-engine planes, now functioning as family dwellings. *What the*

fuck am I doing, Pumpkin? Her voice targeted Flo's driver's side

dash, where Pumpkin had sprawled his cat-body in a resting

position. However, his butterscotch eyes remained in pursuit of the

azure, *maybe cobalt*, Dodge Ram 7000, functioning as a rural

firetruck less than a mile ahead of them. *Why am I following Reese?*

A man who I left a lifetime ago? A man who has seen me at my worse? A man who has seen me at my best? And a man that I still

Allison interrupted herself, leaving her thoughts buried in her heart for Reese Kabula. Instead, she studied the off-beaten route. It felt familiar.

Left on Ager-Beswick Road. Ten minutes and several left and right turns later, she watched a combination of azure and cobalt fade. A cloud of dust separated them. *Still unpaved?* The thought sent chills down Allison's spine. Seventeen years later and little had changed. *He's heading toward the property I wanted to buy. The land I wanted to build a house on together. A cabin. A place the two of us could call ours. A couple of acres that the two of us couldn't agree to build on.* She watched him pull up to a small two-bedroom log cabin. Simplicity. Something she had always wanted. Mountains filled the backdrop. Two large pine trees towered above the small home but didn't attempt to hide the large section of the wrap-around porch. It stretched across the back of the log cabin, a blueprint she had shared with him seventeen years earlier, facing a mountain peak that had always been her favorite. *I don't want to live in the middle of nowhere, Allie.* She could still remember him saying sternly. *I won't be happy here.*

Well, I don't want to live on the coast: too many people, Reese. I like open space. I want to feel free. The irony made her laugh out loud. Rural firefighter Reese Kabula was living the life she had wished for seventeen years ago. Mountains. Open space. Nothing surrounded him. And, Dr. Allison Starr was living the life he had wanted. The smell of the Pacific. City life. Apartments, ACZ areas, and an endless monorail track, all of which bubbled Allison's world.

"That's fucking ironic," Allison spoke to the observing feline in front of her. "It tore us apart, sent me driving off in a rage that resulted in a car accident, one that almost killed me, and then," she paused, "we both opted for the opposite lifestyle." There was a part of her that wanted to put Flo in the park position. She imagined walking up to him. *Was he single?* She searched the immediate area. No swing sets. No tire swing hanging from the giant pine. No birdbath or birdfeeders. No frilly curtains. The absence of the items lessened the odds of a female presence and children. "Do you think he's single, Pumpkin?" No answer. Only a slight purr.

It was the last sound Allison heard before shutting her eyes in the darkness under a sky full of Northern-Cali stars. Undetected, she settled into the back of Flo behind large pines that kept her hidden.

Her body stretched in all directions. So did her heart.

Tonight, she would sleep as close as possible to Reese

Kabula. Then, at first light, she would head southeast.

Fifteen

Dr. Ben Gerhart sat with Karen Elpis early Thursday morning. His eyes were as sterile as his operating room, and his voice rattled off facts with little empathy.

"Your daughter's pre-existing condition has left her with a weak immune system. Her body was a petri-dish for the onset of staphylococcal food poisoning. Unfortunately, the germs have made their way to her heart. She has endocarditis. Someone with a strong immune system and a rigorous course of antibiotics would be able to recover. Today's operation is necessary because she, Anastasia," –

remember to use her name - is not improving with treatment."

"Is she strong enough to operate on?" Karen Elpis searched

Gerhart's face, an emotionless canvas. No sign of comfort

highlighted Gerhart's tone. He was an unempathetic medical

informant. That's all.

"Yes, the fact that she has been stable opens the door for a

successful operation." Ben tried to show some humanity.

Opens the door, Karen processed the words. Her posture

tightened. Not until she saw the doctor with caring blue eyes enter

the small ICU, did she allow herself to breathe and was able to find

her voice again.

"How will the operation help?" She looked over Gerhart's

head, where he had been seated, and into the face of Dr. Jeffery

Linus, who had entered the room, while she waited patiently for

Gerhart's answer.

"The operation is needed to help us determine what damage

bacteria has caused to your daughter's heart values and lining." He

remembered to use the young girl's name again, hoping to avoid any

criticism he was sure Jeffery would make sure came his way later.

"I'm hoping Anastasia will be a good candidate for AHT. The procedure will remove the deadly bacteria from her blood by filtering it through a dialyzer." He forced a warm smile. "First, my team has to look inside."

"Okay, Dr. Gerhart." She tried to smile, but sadness held the corners of her mouth captive.

"She, Anastasia, will be taken by PTP to OR in another hour." Ben smiled a nervous smile at Karen Elpis as he stood and smiled a forced one at Jeffery as he exited the ICU, leaving Dr. Linus to coddle the worried mother, something Ben didn't have the patience or desire to do.

Jeffery's blue eyes (cerulean, a lighter shade of blue) met the worry in Karen's hazel eyes. "I'll keep you posted every step of the way, Ms. Elpis," Dr. Linus took her hand as he spoke. "I'll make sure you are updated regularly." Jeffery smiled before speaking again. "Let's go get some coffee and chat for a few minutes while Anastasia is resting."

Dr. Linus led Karen Elpis down a small hallway to a corner waiting room before excusing himself long enough to grab two Kona Peaberry coffees from the doctor's gourmet coffee machine. He sat, sipping his coffee, listening to Karen tell a story about Anastasia's first trick-or-treating experience, one that occurred ten months earlier, when the five-year-old insisted on making her costume.

"Of course, that just meant picking out the material," Karen laughed. "I was the one who stayed up all night, stitching it together under the Seattle moonlight, while Anastasia slept like a baby in the back of our Nissan Versa." She took a long sip of the creamy Kona Peaberry. "She had the cutest outfit in the ACZ on Halloween night. I even made shoes out of the same material. My thumbs were sore from poking a sewing needle through suede half of the night," Karen reflected proudly on her injuries as she flipped over the work ID hanging on a silver lanyard around her neck. The front of the ID displayed where she worked as a hairstylist, Wind Blown. The back showed a slightly faded photo of Anastasia dressed in a nut-meal-colored suede native Indian princess dress and matching hand-stitched moccasins. Her long brown hair was a mixture of out-of-control curls and displayed two chicken feathers, which dangled from the longest strand. "Anastasia had just turned five years old on September ninth that year." Tears formed in Karen's eyes. "Now, I don't know if she'll see six years old."

Jeffery had just taken the last sip of his Kona Peaberry coffee, thinking of Allison, knowing it was her favorite, and hoping his answer to the overstressed mother would be something she'd find comforting. "Anastasia will be a part of your life forever, Ms. Elpis," he whispered. "You'll never lose her."

Making their way back down the corridor, they arrived in the ICU just in time to watch Anastasia's eyes open. "Mommy, I'm tired."

"I know, baby," Karen spoke softly but with strength. "You'll be able to sleep more in a few minutes."

"Dr. Starr will make me count again." The five-year-old's announcement met a look of regret on Karen's face, so Jeffery tried to ease the tension once again.

"Dr. Starr wanted me to tell you that she misses you and loves you and that you're in good hands with her friend, Dr. Paz." Jeffery watched Anastasia crack a smile.

"That's a funny name," she replied.

"Yes, it is," Jeffery smiled back before escorting Karen Elpis alongside the PTP, who had already begun rolling the bed toward the scheduled operating room. "You tell him I said he better take good care of you."

"I will," the small child looked over at Jeffery Linus, who was signaling Karen Elpis that they had reached the last area that family members were allowed to enter. He stood near, watching Karen plant numerous kisses on her young daughter's face, before finally releasing her daughter's hand, reclaiming the fingers that had once stayed up all night hand-sewing the small girl's Indian dress and matching moccasins.

Dr. Linus sighed, letting the empathy that consumed him settle, long enough to reassure Karen Elpis that Anastasia was in good hands and long enough to make it down the hallway and to a hidden corner in the doctors' lounge. First, *I have to call Allison.* That was his only thought as he settled into a corner chair near the smell of gourmet coffee.

"Dr. Paz will take good care of her." It was his third sentence, following a meaningful *I love you*, and after announcing that Anastasia had just entered surgery. "Hopefully, Gerhart will be able to rule out damage to her heart values and lining and will be able to use AHT to filter her contaminated blood."

"Thanks, Jeffery." He wished she had said *I love you* first, just as he had, but Jeffery knew there was a part of Allison Starr that he hadn't won over, not yet. "Please keep me posted." And then, "I love you."

Allison watched the mountains of Northern California roll past each side of Flo. The teal-blue Nissan sparkled underneath the early morning sun as it handled each twist and turn. Finally, she steered away from Hornbrook, California, gently. While she watched Interstate-5 carve through mountains ahead of her, Pumpkin looked at the ass-end of Flo, directing Allison's attention to the rearview mirror. *We can't go back. Now's not the time*, Allison thought. Pumpkin seemed to understand Allison's silent thoughts. His fur was still moist from Allison's tears, emotions that poured out after she decided not to approach Reese Kabula. She knew where he was if she changed her mind. But, for now, she was southbound, passing trees and mountains that she had seen three days earlier when she had traveled that same stretch of road – making her way south on I-5.

It was a long haul, first on 5-South, then deciding to mix things up, she took the 505 to 80-West. Allison was driving on roads she hadn't been on in almost twenty years, but she still seemed to know her way. Effortlessly. Seeing a sign for Vallejo, she knew she was close to San Francisco. Driving was the medication that helped settle her nerves. Unfortunately, Allison could do nothing to help the five-year-old consuming her thoughts, so she decided to fill her own body and mind with beauty so that the positivity would saturate the universe.

Making her way over the Golden Gate Bridge, Allison picked up coastal highway one, letting Flo move her hips from side to side around each curve. Jeffery had called four times by two in the afternoon. Each time Flo patched the call through with an announcement – you have received an incoming call from Dr. Linus. Each time Allison pushed an automated reject button on the steering wheel gripped by her right hand. The reject button prompted a preprogrammed message: You have reached Dr. Allison Starr. Unfortunately, I am unable to take your call at this time. I will call you back as soon as possible.

Allison Starr knew. She could feel it in her bones. If it was her mother's soul, it was in trouble. The Santa Ana winds had carried the message down I-5. The lights on the San Francisco Bay

Bridge shined an eerie orange, making it appear in mourning. A large harbor seal had raised his head above the Pacific Ocean's deep-blue surface and pointed it in Allison's direction as she walked the shoreline of Bean Hollow Beach. *Did the seal know too?* Allison wondered.

Now, sitting with her only company, Flo and Pumpkin, she made a return call while parked near the Bean Hollow's Rocky coastline. Jeffery Linus picked up right away.

"Hey Allison, I tried to call you," the voice answered.

"I know," then, "sorry."

"Are you okay?" Jeffery Linus knew she was worried.

"Maybe." It was the one word that explained Allison's behavior – the unanswered phone calls, the emotional disconnect he heard in her voice, and the silence that grew between them after Jeffery spilled the details about Anastasia's morning surgery.

Allison listened to and absorbed Jeffery Linus' words as she watched The Pacific Ocean whip plankton and algae into a meringue foam. The bubbly sea reminded her of Jeffery. Then it reminded her of something more profound. A wakeless feeling made her heart crumble as she observed the turbulent ocean. She could see Reese

Kabula's soul in every unsettled wave.

Sixteen

Friday night, the wind howled in a ghostly rhythm outside Flo. Allison could feel the heat sensors kick on inside the Nissan in an attempt to fight the damp chills that came down in the form of a shower from the late August Pacific. The sound of large male elephant seals cried in battle on the shoreline. Allison knew some of the males weighed close to 5000 pounds. For a few minutes, she tried to imagine the giant mammal's daily diet but then remembered her own, a ration of peanut butter and wheat thins, both of which she had picked up at the hemp fuel station, fifty miles back on Coastal Highway 1. In the dark, she listened to the sound of whipping wind and crashing waves. The sound of nature continuing despite the world's many changes came to a halt when Flo patched Jeffery Linus' call through. It was 9-p.m.

"Are you still at the Elephant Seal Vista Point in San Simeon?" He had listened to her talk about how the male elephant seals were sparring partners and how their battles resulted in bloody whiskers and wounded pride earlier in the evening. Jeffery was attentive. An obvious observation made clear when he called her, updating Allison after knowing what stage of sepsis Anastasia was fighting.

"Yes, the left side and right side of Coastal 1 are in a boxing match now," she replied, trying to regain her sense of humor. "The left side of the highway is still smoldering from recent fires, and the right side is mocking the job of a firefighter, spraying sea mist and foam into the smoky air," she added. "It sure limits visibility, making it impossible to drive."

"I can imagine," Jeffery followed up with a slight chuckle. "I'll cut to the chase, Allison." He knew she wanted details about

Anastasia. "She's in stage one." He could have stopped there. Details weren't necessary for someone with her medical background, but he wanted to hear himself be positive out loud. "Systemic Inflammatory Response Syndrome," he rattled off. "SIRS is spiking her fever. 101 right now. Her nurse has ice packs and Tylenol keeping it down."

"What other symptoms is she having right now, Jeffery?" She wished he was with her after hearing his name roll off her tongue. Having him hold her in a world where the sea and land had collided (a replica of her feelings) would be comforting.

"Her blood leucocyte count came back high," he sighed.

"How bad?"

"10,500."

Allison knew a white blood cell count that high in a child her age meant she was trying to fight infection. "She's a fighter."

"Yes, she is," Jeffery said. "So are you."

"I got it from someone." It was a follow-up statement that she didn't consider fully before announcing. It reminded her that another soul could be involved – her mother's.

"I love you," Jeffery said.

"I love you too. Goodnight." Allison blew a kiss into the air and heard one in return.

August twenty-second brought blue skies, the high sixties, and a clear winner in the fight between land and water. Sea fog had beaten smoke in the middle of the night and had celebrated by bathing Flo in a light mist. For a Saturday, it was beautiful. Allison stood admiring five or six large elephant seals below the fence line. Like Pumpkin, they looked relaxed and comfortable, an obvious comparison made after Allison noticed Pumpkin asleep on the driver's dash, his new favorite spot.

"We've been gone one week, Pumpkin," she announced loudly, making sure his eyes opened in response. "Four more weeks left." Allison thought about staying on Coastal Highway 1 until she hit San Diego but imagined sparse hemp stations scattered in occasional small towns. "Let's make our way to Highway 101. I need real food, a shower, and a faster pace."

By two, Allison was watching her jeans and t-shirts fluff in a Santa Maria laundromat. She felt grounded in the middle of a small ACZ area, listening to local Spaniards complain how one load of laundry took seven dollars to wash and three dollars to dry.

"Diez dólares," the Spanish woman rolled both her tongue and eyes. "No print. No wash." She held up her right index finger. "Mucho dineros." She looked directly at Allison, seeking agreeance.

"Si, mucho dineros. Muy caro." Allison responded, sympathizing with the friendly woman. However, Dr. Starr's Spanish had its limits, something Allison knew was her fault, a direct repercussion after cheating in her undergrad Spanish class. After staying up the night before to write in microscopic letters on one permitted 8x10 index card and using her college textbook, Allison followed the example set by others in the college classroom. Like the other students, she took advantage of any assistance after the professor would leave the room, which he did routinely following an exam administration. Quickly, she looked for clues in the textbook, matching them with an example she took note of in class on her organized notecard. The method was always the same: skim the book, compare the models meticulously written on the notecard, and respond to test answers after identifying a simple sentence structure and a matching correlation. It was the only class Allison made a B in, which she always assumed meant BARELY getting by. Now, ten years later, Allison attempted to engage with

Spanish locals, her brain still recalling tidbits from the Spanish class taken long ago. *Maybe the professor left the room on purpose. Perhaps he knew referring to the textbook and taking notes would help us retain basic concepts.* Still, Allison wished she knew more Spanish. She wanted to converse with the forgotten people, the souls who didn't ride the monorail, the people who earned their pay selling fresh vegetables, making fresh bread, working on nearby hemp farms, or taking care of other people's children. They knew the meaning of hard work. Allison studied the woman's index fingers, both of which she waved in the air. She knew those fingers belonged to hands that had kneaded bread, carried baskets of laundry to the ACZ area nearly a mile away, had canned vegetables, had planted gardens, and had wiped the mouths of white-collar workers' children. The woman had a valuable place in the rapidly changing world. Maybe that's why she wanted to give the woman a ride to the ACZ area, especially after watching her struggle to carry a large basket of clean clothing. Flo wouldn't mind. "Conducir hacia el sur," Allison spoke the words slowly, after recalling how to say *drive south*. "Necesitas montar?" Allison questioned again in English, "Need Ride?"

"Si." The woman smiled. "I no ride in car since child." Brown eyes, similar to Allison's, glowed, matching the woman's wrinkled smile as she revealed pieces of her cultural immersion – she too had learned tidbits, keeping English words handy.

By three, Allison left the woman's home, a 2025 dark blue Chevy Tahoe 3500, with a glass jar of freshly canned green beans, two homemade corn fritters, and a generous slice of ham from the monthly slaughtered community pig farm. *Good still prevails in the world*, Allison thought as she waved and shouted "adiós" toward Bianca Salvador, who was smiling ear-to-ear.

Saturday night Allison took a quick shower at the Gaviota State Park Rest Area off Highway 101 before filling her belly with ham, green beans, and the best-tasting corn fritters she had ever tasted, their insides sweet and buttery. Pumpkin quickly ate his dried food after having a taste of each thoroughly mixed in his bowl.

Jeffery called just as Allison had finished a list of places and locations that she wanted to see in the next four weeks: Antelope Canyon, Grand Canyon, Bryce Canyon, Zion National Park, and Canyon de Chelly. She was still stretched out on Flo's cooling sensors when the call was patched through and didn't realize she was talking out loud to her co-pilot.

"We might as well add San Diego, Pumpkin. We're not too far, and I've never been there."

"Make sure you go on a whale watching tour if they still offer those," Jeffery added to the conversation, making it a three-way. Allison giggled after realizing his voice was floating in front of her.

"Funny, I can't see you, but you're here," Allison stated.

"I'm always with you." Jeffery's reply sent a slight tingle down the back of her neck and across her shoulders. That was something Allison's mother would always say. Then, sensing the delay in conversation, Jeffery added, "Sorry, too much?"

"No," Allison said, but then added honestly, "it just made me think of my mother."

"She's always with you too." Jeffery almost let it go but wanted to acknowledge her feelings before continuing. "Anastasia was asking about you when I made my last stop to see her this evening. She was propped up with several pillows, attempting to eat hospital Jell-O and downing ice chips like candy."

"Orange or lime?" It was a question meant to lighten the mood, but one Allison hoped he'd answer with orange.

"Orange," he announced. He had seen the lime Jell-O heading in her direction and had switched it with the patient's tray next door. Quickly and without remorse.

What child eats lime Jell-O? Allison and Jeffery's brain waves synchronized like trained swimmers, but that was just the tip of the iceberg. There was a connection between them that neither one of them knew existed.

Jeffery jumped – right into her arms.

Seventeen

Protruding above the horizon, where the Pacific Ocean and sky seemed to meet, a 70,000-pound slate-gray whale covered in white barnacles peeked his head above the water. His hunger was satisfied after sucking up a mixture of larvae and ocean crustaceans. Like most humans, he had traveled long distances during his lifetime and had been in numerous relationships. Allison didn't notice him until he careened out of the water, exposing his pectoral fins, which disappeared quickly below the surface, and became substituted promptly with two large flukes, which spread like angel wings in a pool of bubbles the color of snow. The sight made Allison feel at home.

"Holy crap, Pumpkin," Allison choked on her words. "Did you see that California Gray?" Pumpkin wasn't entertained and found the sand beneath his cat paws more interesting. Still, Allison continued to carry on her conversation. "Did you know whales have lots of partners during their lifetimes?" Allison thought about her Marine Science class in college, an elective class she chose to complete during the same term as Spanish I. Marine Science first captured her attention in high school. Her soul felt drawn to the sea, then, now, and even long before she presently remembered. Allison continued her conversation with Pumpkin, "But somehow, they manage to find the right mates, have the right calves, and create their pod." She wished Pumpkin would participate in the topic she found so fascinating but settled for Jeffery's input as it escaped the inside of the open car window and flowed into the misty air where Allison stood, her body leaning against Flo.

"Whale pod?" He had come in on the last word.

"I'm glad someone's interested in my rambling," Allison giggled. "Pumpkin is targeting a mound of seaweed right now."

"I'll have you know Marine Science was one of my favorite classes in my Maryland high school." *Another thing in common*, Allison thought without interrupting Jeffery. Instead, she let him continue, taking the conversation to a much deeper level. "The Chinese believe invisible thin red threads connect people to anyone they are supposed to meet, even if it's only briefly. I believe those invisible threads first connected mammals."

"Thin red threads?" She asked, interested in hearing more.

"Whales bond together biologically or through friendship," Jeffery informed her. "They have a wide range of clicks and whistles that together sound like a finely tuned orchestra underwater, the vibrations bounce off rocks and other sea life, creating a red thread that helps them locate other whales," Jeffery said. "People do that too." Jeffery anxiously explained, happy to have a person in his life that seemed interested in the world both above and below sea level. "The ancient Chinese believe that we are all predestined with these invisible red threads, so we will eventually find our way to the people we're supposed to meet or be with."

"What if the thread snaps?" Allison asked.

"They can't. If anything, connections grow stronger as we age, bringing us to others that we have a lesson to learn from."

"Are you and I connected with an invisible red thread?"

"Absolutely." Jeffery pictured Allison at the end of a red thread, connected to his soul, a crimson bond, before his earliest memory, in a matrix of infinite tiny lines. "We would have met somewhere, if not Swedish Medical, then somewhere else."

"Do threads end?" Allison stared at the Pacific. It was a body of water that seemed endless but became something else as she studied its surface. It was the bible for her soul.

"The belief is that they don't. The lines that connect us can loosen, fade, and even drift into the unknown, but eventually, they become closer and tighter."

"So, we end up where we're supposed to?" Her question waited for an informative answer. She hoped for insight that would make her feel better about Reese Kabula. Her mind needed comfort and peace when she thought about Anastasia Elpis. Her soul wanted answers that would explain her mind's scientific dilemma with Enola

Starks' existence. And, her heart slowed its beat waiting for a reply that would make her feel less indecisive about Jeffery Linus.

"Yes, the universe puts everything in place." Jeffery's tone was authoritative. Biochemistry and Molecular Biology had made Allison's world spin slower, without so much uncertainty.

"I love you." She said it because she felt it in the core of her existence.

"I love you too." Jeffery was willing to live in as many moments as he could with Allison Starr.

After spending two full days and most of a third in San Diego, Allison turned Flo east. It was nearly nine p.m. when Allison pulled over at the Laguna Mountain Summit. Topping just over 4000 feet above sea level, she imagined the mountain top would be an excellent place to try the ROSAT 36-Mini. Remembering exactly how to use the handheld version, Allison pointed it at the south cluster of stars. Nothing. The tiny ROSAT did not detect any dark matter invisible to the naked eye, but it directed Allison's attention to the Milky Way. Next, she studied the northern sky. A large circle of color, primarily purple, flashed on the read-out screen. *Is that dark matter?* Allison questioned a second time before recording a live photo of the read-out screen and transmitting it to Jeffery's lab.

Allison was exhausted when she finished her shower at the Sunbeam Rest Area off Interstate 8 in El Centro. She scanned her index finger for a tuna sandwich and coke out of a freshly stocked vending machine and rationed out Pumpkin's Meow Mix with two spoons of tuna shared from her sandwich. Then, Jeffery called – his nighttime routine. Allison could hear the excitement in his voice as Flo patched him through.

"Did you notice the spherically shaped purple? It looks like a halo around the center of the Milky Way." He sounded like a five-year-old opening his first present on Christmas morning. "Allie, it even has a slight globular shaped carrot-orange and drop of banana-yellow in the very center."

She wanted to tell him not to call her Allie. No one had called her Allie since her mother's death, but she missed hearing it; besides, it was hard to correct a man who made the word *globular* sound attractive and created vibrant colors using produce in their namesakes.

"You have such an eye for detail." She looked at the saved screenshot once more. "I see it now. It's beautiful."

"Allie, it's dark matter," he followed up with clarity, "It's what human souls encompass."

"Are you saying that dead people are dancing around the Milky Way?" She almost laughed at how ridiculous her question sounded.

"A lot of progressive scientists, myself included, believe it's part of the one percent Gerhart failed to inform the professionals in his seminar about." He spoke slow and deliberate. "It is the collection of spirits waiting to be reborn."

"Are souls always that color?" Allison's words caught in her throat as her emotions fought to believe in the human spirit.

"No, it's like mixing a cake batter," Jeffery answered. "A person's spirit or soul is somehow uniquely color-coded to that individual, so there are endless variations."

Allison wondered what color her soul was. *What color is Anastasia's? What color is my mother's?* They were questions she kept private but questions that stayed with her throughout the night.

"I love you, Jeffery." The words left her twice in one day.

"I love you too, Allie." It was the third time Jeffery used the name her mother had always called her. And, it was the third time Allison didn't mind.

Eighteen

On the twenty-sixth of August, Allison parked Flo underneath Interstate 8 that stretched over Gateway Park. It was an attempt to hide from the 104-degree temperature that ate away at Yuma, Arizona's soul. She could easily spend a couple of hours. First walking by the edge of the Colorado River, which flowed through Yuma, she made herself a chicken-salad tortilla with chicken, mayonnaise, celery seed (something her mother always added), and fresh flour tortillas.

Jeffery called just as she had finished her last bite of creamy

chicken salad, minus what she had shared with Pumpkin, following a

long walk by the river, one where Pumpkin stuck all four paws in the

water like a small dog.

"Your fairy castle cactus misses you," then he added, "so do

I."

"I see your fingerprint that I downloaded successfully gained

you entrance into my apartment, Dr. Linus."

"Yes – I'm in there like swimwear." *Jeffery is an old soul.*

No one says that anymore, Allison thought before releasing a slight

chuckle and before responding.

"I knew I could count on you." Allison wanted an update on

Anastasia, but it was nice to small talk first. Jeffery must have felt

the same way, studying the small photo at the opposite end of the

window sill in Allison's bedroom. The photograph was old and

faded, a snapshot in time memorializing sixty-nine years ago.

"So, who's the young girl in the Cherokee Indian costume?"

He knew it was probably Cherokee, as he could read a faded sign in

the far background – Qualla Indian Reservation. He was well-versed

in Indian culture, another subject he found fascinating – Native

American History. He recalled learning how the white man broke treaties and ran most Cherokee Indians off to Oklahoma, except for a few, who settled in Qualla Valley.

"That's my mother, Enola Starks. She was seven years old at the time."

"She's beautiful." Jeffery avoided saying what he wanted to say. *She looks identical to Anastasia Elpis's in the photo, the one Karen Elpis proudly wore on the back of her work ID badge.* So instead, he hinted indirectly. "She reminds me of someone I know."

"People always said we looked alike," Allison replied, assuming he meant her, "but I don't see it."

"You do look a lot alike." Jeffery didn't want to make her feel uncomfortable, so he settled for the best reply but was able to throw one more subtle hint out there by using the young girl's name. "Anastasia seems to be getting stronger."

"Seems?" She didn't like the uncertainty. It reminded her of the small towns she had traveled through getting to Yuma. Like the drifting sand they were built on, they recreated each day, sometimes each hour. Not knowing the future and losing most of their population to more significant areas with monorails and government housing, they survived day-to-day on the purchases made by the few passersby that stopped at the small diners. Travelers made purchases at their mom-and-pop hemp stations, and the town budgets received monthly credits from the government for their wind turbine machines. Still, even that drifted like the sand, depending on the kilowatt capacity each device produced.

"Her fever is maintaining under 100 on its own, and her heart rate is steady." Jeffery gave it to her the way he always did – straight, an honest realization that prompted him to add on the following, "I think she looks a lot like your mother's childhood photo."

Allison processed Jeffery's input. She did have light blue eyes that reminded her of Enola's but had never considered their other common features. Then, remembering the photo of seven-year-old Enola, Allison saw similar cheekbone structures and smiles. Both high-boned, and both dimpled in the cheeks when smiling. "I think they share a lot of the same heritage," she confessed.

"I think the four of us do," Jeffery announced, referring to himself, Allison, Enola, and Anastasia, and knowing Cherokee

Indian ran in his bloodline too. "My mother was Cherokee and Scots-Irish."

"Wow, Jeffery, we could have lived on the frontier in our past lives together," Allison joked. Still, her thoughts were of theories she had once never dreamed possible – *reincarnation, past lives, and even the existence of red threads connecting people who are supposed to meet.*

"Red threads," Jeffery announced in sync with her private thoughts.

"I love you," Allison said once again because it was there, deep inside of her.

"I love you too, Allie." He had permanently changed her name.

That night she stopped at the Love's Truck Stop in Yuma, where showers were free for all GFS drivers, grabbed an ice-cold drink, bag of ice, small thermal ice chest, and topped Flo off with hemp fuel. *I'll take care of you, and you take care of me.* Allison's thought cemented her friendship with her intended recipient, Flo, and left Allison satisfied, knowing that her cyan-colored friend would keep her body temperature comfortable in the late-night

August heat. Even Pumpkin had stopped jumping out as fast at each pit stop, enjoying the fact that Flo kept the dash from getting too hot or too cold. It was always just right.

Thursday's morning temp soared. By noon it was 100, and by the time Pumpkin slowly trailed Allison's shadow at the Painted Rock Petroglyph Site in Dateland, Arizona, it was 105 degrees out. Hot. Sweat poured down Allison's face as she studied the prehistoric etchings on each rock. A bulgy-eyed alien with eight legs, a three-legged human-looking specimen with four arms, a creature with the eye of a hurricane for its face, and a prehistoric-looking dragonfly was standing next to a five-legged dog, maybe a cat. It wasn't just the heat that made Allison question some of the large rock carvings' authenticity. There were also sole imprints in the desert clay leading off-trail and near some of the boulders. *Graffiti?* Allison wondered but then began to look at the bigger picture as she made her way on foot back to Flo. Pumpkin followed.

"Humans started evolving on earth almost 300,000 years ago," Allison spoke to Pumpkin, who had just moved in front of her. "We have evolved anatomically at a dramatic level," Allison's tone was instructive, a characteristic she often had when analyzing something she cared about, "but we've kept some basic characteristics, such as limbs, fingers, torsos, heads," then, she finally added after further consideration, "and souls."

Allison's furry student had lost interest in her historical update and had already jumped back inside Flo's open passenger window, comforted by the cooling sensors that were fighting the unforgivable Arizona heat. Allison was disappointed in Pumpkin's dismissal but continued processing silently. *Souls. Recycle. Evolve. Repetitive characteristics.* Suddenly, it made sense to her. *If Anastasia contains my mother's soul, there would be change, but there would also be some traits that would withstand the test of time.*

That night, Allison pulled over in Buckeye, Arizona, within the Maricopa Monorail System's visual distance. She watched people board, scan, sit, wait, and on the incoming monorail, she watched them stand, pause, and disembark. Humans were predictable, survivors, routine mammals, and resilient.

Mom, I know you're out there. Allison closed her eyes in a dark corner of Buckeye.

Within, Allie felt a mixture of the deepest sea and the highest mountain top hug her soul. It was as if hundreds of years floated inside of her.

Nineteen

The last Friday in August, Allison fought her way through the Coconino National Forest as she made her way to Flagstaff, and Anastasia fought to take each breath after taking a sudden turn for the worse during the night.

Jeffery had called Allison several times that morning, but Flo was parked alone at the top of a deep ravine. At the same time, Allison and Pumpkin made their way on the unmarked Blue Wash Trailhead below, maneuvering deep into a canyon in Cave Creek,

Arizona. Pumpkin kept pace, even in the heat, until Allison reached

the spot of the waterfall. Dry. Barren. Allison should have known

but had forgotten that an August Arizona is not like an August

Seattle. At one point, Pumpkin stopped walking. Exhaustion had set

in. Allison reached down, bringing the furball to her chest, before

finding the nearest shade of several large boulders, and sharing a

water bottle with Pumpkin. First, Allison took a large swig, then she

cupped her right hand and poured water into it with her left, holding

it in front of Pumpkin, who lapped the water before it had a chance

to disappear between the cracks in Allison's fingers.

"Does that feel better, Pumpkin?" Allison watched as he

lifted his tongue in a rapid motion, finishing the puddle that pooled

in the bottom of her palm. He looked grateful but had reached his

limit in the early afternoon heat, so Allison strapped her backpack on

her chest and placed Pumpkin inside the largest compartment, like a

newborn baby. Then, sticking his head above the zipper line, he

watched Allison make her way up the steep embankments, around

jagged rocks, and on loose gravel that waited for one wrong step.

"Don't worry. I won't let us fall," she assured him and herself.

By the time Allison made it back to Flo, she felt like a considerate friend was waiting. Air conditioning, cooled seats, and an ice-cold bottle of water from the restocked beverage center (something routinely done by a station attendant each time Allison stopped for hemp fuel), followed by three messages from Jeffery, waited for Allison.

Message one: *Call me as soon as you can, Allie.*

Message two: *Anastasia has had a setback.*

Message three: *Just call me.*

By the time Jeffery had explained Anastasia's symptoms – muscle pain, chest pain, shortness of breath, a fever that had returned, low blood pressure, and a rash on her stomach, Allison knew.

"She's developed MRSA."

"She's not doing well," Jeffery pointed out the obvious. "The staphylococcus bacterium is not reacting to any antibiotics."

"What are her chances of recovery, Jeffery?" Allison wanted his opinion. One she was sure would be honest.

"Given her age and symptoms, I'd say she has a fifty-percent chance of survival." He had always been straightforward with Allison, so he let his mind evaluate the possibilities before continuing. "Organ failure is her biggest threat," he took a deep breath, "so far, she's not showing any signs of organ failure."

By the time Allison had stopped talking to Jeffery, Flo was in the middle of Coconino National Forest, somewhere on 17 North, and was determined to make Flagstaff by nightfall. It had been over twenty-five years since Allison had been there, the last time with her mother. *I was sixteen*, she remembered. It had been a late August trip, just the two of them, a plane first to Phoenix, then a puddle-jumper connection to Flagstaff. After renting a 2011 Honda Accord, Enola drove Allison to the Grand Canyon South Rim via the Historic Route 66, stopping to take hundreds of photos. Allison could still recall her favorite – a picture of the two of them, out on a ledge that stretched 7,000 feet above the canyon floor, their faces glowing like the painted desert. A mixture of sandy-brown, desert-gold, earthy-green, and rich-red warmed their shoulders in a world where jagged rock stood tall, the most oversized slabs darkened by shadows that bounced from red cliffs and the snaky ravines far below.

"Mom, I don't know what to do," Allison spoke out loud as she pulled into Flagstaff. "Do I continue my route or head back to Seattle?" She knew she couldn't do anything to help Anastasia, at least not medically, but a part of her wanted to sit by the young child. However, according to Jeffery, Karen Elpis was usually at her daughter's side, and most of the time, Anastasia was sleeping.

Pumpkin stirred after hearing Allison's unanswered conversation. Again, it seemed the furball knew Flo was maneuvering to a parking spot. This time in the back of The American Hemp Travel Stop in Flagstaff, carhop waiters or waitresses would approach each GFS vehicle to take orders for grub, everything from salads to burgers. Pumpkin spotted the young waitress first. Her hair bounced as she walked in old-fashioned black-and-white penny loafers and her light-blue satin skirt kept rhythm with each strand of hair that glided down the back of her solid black blouse. She couldn't be more than seventeen and had a smile that captured Allison's attention. She stepped to the driver's window, greeting Allison as ma'am, which made the hair on Allison's neck stand at attention. *I guess I am officially old,* Allison thought while listening to the carhop waitress rattle off the Friday night specials.

"Fish sandwich. Junior cheeseburger. Blackened chicken salad," and after moving her hair from her nametag and tucking it behind her left shoulder, "oh, and tacos."

"I'd love a blackened chicken salad and coke," Allison replied, accepting the fact that it was a combination of healthy and evil. "Thank you …" Allison's polite conversation came to a dead halt as her hungry eyes read the name on the young girl's employee badge. "Nola."

Pumpkin watched Allison's private reaction, which occurred after the carhop waitress bounced away. First tears. Then laughter. Finally, more conversation that Pumpkin couldn't understand but sensed made Allison happy.

"Okay, Mom, I'm going forward." She looked at the darkened sky, thinking of her mother. She knew very few people called her mother Nola, but she also knew it was her preferred choice. "I'm taking the waitress's name as a sign, Mom." Pumpkin hopped back on the dash, where he waited for his share of chicken from the chicken salad and where he watched Allison's face glow in the Flagstaff moonlight. The rare coincident had settled the decision. Tomorrow, Flo would head further east. But, first, Allison would try to sleep.

It wasn't easy. Morning came after a long night of tossing and turning. Flo tried everything possible to give Allison some peace, altering the temperature and pressure for Allison's unsettled body weight. Nonetheless, Dr. Starr started the day determined and used every moment to explore lonely stretches of highways, deep canyons, and majestical valleys.

By nightfall, Flo pulled into a near-empty rest area in Monticello, Utah. Flo's headlights stared up at the large white arrow pointing to a large hole in the canyon wall, almost life-like. *Good eye*, Allison thought after noticing the painted arrow that centered above Flo's headlights. Allison studied the arrow's intention, *a large hole.* It was a lonely space in the center of such a massive boulder, one that would otherwise appear indestructible. Allison empathized,

feeling she, too, had an empty spot within. *Refuel. Keep going.* She

took the hole as another sign, exiting Flo. Heading into the women's

restroom and lounge, she focused, first by standing under a cold

shower, then grabbing a fresh sandwich on the way out. She was

happy to see the machine had Comb Ridge Burgers, famous gourmet

burgers that started in Bluff, Utah, now stocked in Utah's vending

machines at GFS truck-stops, the monorail stops, and a delighted

surprise – rest-stops. After scanning her index finger, Allison pushed

a button for the double-patty burger with cheese, lettuce, tomato, and

pickle. The following words appeared eye-level across the front of

the vending machine: Thank you for choosing Comb Ridge. We are

preparing your burger. Inside the large metal machine, Allison could

hear robotic movement and imagined arms like Dr. Chrome

working. Open bun. Hamburger patty. Cheese. Hamburger patty.

Cheese. Lettuce. Tomato slice. Pickle. In less than three minutes, a

small door opened. Allison reached in, retrieving a foil-wrapped

burger, which felt hot to the touch.

Pumpkin woke when he heard the car door open, and Allison could tell the scent of cooked ground beef had also been a factor, proven after he devoured his dried kibble mixed with one of the patties. Tonight, they both ate well, their reward for a day filled with driving near the edge of scary ravines and unforgiving drops. As Allison slowly ate her burger, she thought about each step of her day. After leaving Flagstaff, she made her way to Canyon de Chelly in Chinle, Arizona, where she stood at the edge of an open canyon with Pumpkin, one that plunged into the earth's belly. Her favorite view in the canyon was Spider Rock Overlook, the last ravine within the park. Its green shrubbery covered the canyon floor like the red carpet at the Emmys, welcoming its distinguished visitors. The two sandstone spires stood over 800 feet tall. Allison inhaled deeply at their beauty and exhaled much more profound from a spot within her soul as she watched the sun bake the steepled spires. *The desert oasis is my church;* she had thought then and still agreed with now, as she devoured the last bit of ground beef from her left hand.

Sipping an ice tea she had pulled from Flo's refrigerated storage, she thought about how Flo mastered the Oljato-Monument

Valley right at sunset. Allison had felt like a parishioner, seated before majestic sandstone buttes, painted in the blood of Gods, a natural red-sand, a place where even an atheist felt holy.

Refreshed, and after the day's review, her mind felt content. Maybe tonight, she would find better sleep in the back of Flo. Stretching out, Pumpkin lightly purred beside her. The mesmerizing sound soothed Allison, nudging her into a deep sleep. Unfortunately, she couldn't hear Pumpkin's purr increase with intensity as her dream enveloped them both.

But she could see the large white wings that swooped down, grabbing both her and Pumpkin. First, she eyed Canyon de Chelly that towered toward her stomach. Then she strained to tilt her head upward, glancing at the feathered creature.

For a brief moment, she felt her Aunt Dixie's presence, a loss before her mother's and one that hit them both hard.

Twenty

Utah was an accident. Like the birth of Anastasia Elpis, it just happened, and once Allison sunk her teeth into the unplanned state, there was no going back.

National parks were fee-free for GPS drivers and their passengers. Allison knew it might be another five years before she had a steering wheel in her hands, so making a hard left on 313 West with Canyonlands National Park as her morning destination seemed like the logical thing to do. Grand View Point Road flirted with Flo's tires, begging for traction every curve, which the cyan-colored automobile handled perfectly. Pulling into a teardrop-shaped circle, Allison looked at Pumpkin, who had been watching a peep-show through the front window: massive boulders, solid rock walls, giant slabs of earth, circular domes, towering rock toothpicks, and deep crevices that looked like they could swallow Seattle whole.

"Let's check out the Grand View Point." She thought about leaving the driver's door open for Pumpkin's exit, but he had already jumped out the passenger window and was making his way to the overlook's waist-high rock wall. "Careful, Pumpkin," Allison said after watching him jump on top of the wall, the only thing separating him from sudden death. *What am I thinking?* Allison thought *Cats have nine lives.* Allison found her thoughts funny and laughed out loud.

Dr. Allison Starr took a moment, wondering how many lives humans had. *Was my mother on her second life?* Then, *or has she had many?* And then a bigger question, *have I?* Starring at Grand View Point's canyon floor, Allison studied the shape – a sizeable three-fingered handprint branded into the earth's crust. It reminded her of a mummified three-fingered hand from in the Peruvian desert, found twenty years earlier, one she had read about in her Human Evolution class in undergrad. *Is human life recycled?* She wished Jeffery were with her. He'd have opinions, maybe even answers.

"Are you there?" Jeffery Linus' voice echoed over the canyon floor, granting Allison's wish to talk to him. *Timing is everything,* she thought. After hearing Jeffery's voice transmitting from her awaiting vehicle, she made her way back to Flo. Like a well-trained dog, Pumpkin followed.

"I was just thinking of you," Allison said without fear of putting her emotions out there.

"That's the best news I could ever hear," he replied. "Do tell," he followed up with a slight laugh.

Allison and Jeffery spent hours talking about human evolution, about documented cases of déjà vu, about reincarnation, and finally about Allison's dream where she saw an angel. However, she avoided telling Jeffery that the white-winged creature felt familiar or that she imagined the aura of her deceased Aunt Dixie. Instead, she focused on Anastasia's current condition.

"No change?" Allison wanted confirmation.

"All her vitals are still the same," Jeffery followed up. "Still no sign of organ damage."

"That's good," she wanted to think positive.

"Yes," he stated about Anastasia, and then changing the subject, "You remind me of an angel, Allie." His out-of-place comment formed quickly, a combination of the guilt he felt for not revealing his unshared dream and the familiarity he felt with Dr. Allison Starr. Jeffery thought about his dream, one he first remembered having when he was eight years old. He had also seen an angel. It wasn't until he turned eighteen, making his way into adulthood, that he finally convinced himself that it isn't an angel's job to save a brave Indian buffalo hunter and that dreams are only dreams. After all, modesty would never allow him to reveal himself as the honorable hunter. Still, the vivid scene played in his mind. He ran toward the edge of a cliff. His body served as a decoy, dressed in dried buffalo hides. Giant bison followed him over the life-taking cliff to their deaths. The brave Indian's actions supplied thousands of pounds of buffalo meat to his tribe. The fact that the hunter survived, somehow leaping in midair to a ledge twenty feet ahead, dubbed him a spiritual leader. Members of the Indian tribe bowed in his clever defeat, claiming he must have walked on the backs of plunging buffalo. He knew differently. He could see the eyes of the angelic figure, and he could still feel the angel's talons as they wrapped tightly around both of his forearms, carrying his body to safety above the dust created by the South Dakota stampede. *I was a hero—a warrior.* Jeffery Linus kept his thoughts private, except for the small comparison he made every time he thought about Allison Starr's eyes. "You remind me of an angel," he said again. "You are heavenly and gracious," Jeffery announced, his voice matter-of-fact. "You are a soul that I feel like I've known for hundreds of years."

"You think too highly of me, Doctor." She didn't believe the two attributes were part of her characteristic makeup. Being heavenly and gracious were not parts of how she saw herself. Jeffery saw a side to her that she didn't. He saw a beauty deep within Allison Starr. He had witnessed her compassion and humanitarianism at Swedish Medical first-hand, and he had never met a woman so capable of surviving on her own. Perhaps it was those hidden qualities that had drawn him to Allison Starr. Whatever it was, he was hopelessly in love with a woman who sat almost one-thousand miles away, one he wished would fully verbalize their connection.

"I feel like we crossed paths before," he stated the obvious again, hoping this time she'd feel obligated to respond at a deeper level.

She did. Allison's response struck Jeffery like a lightning bolt, sending a spiderweb of 300 kilovolts racing through his soul.

"I was the angel that carried you," Allison said.

Twenty-one

A bright yellow Aspen leaf landed on the dash beside Pumpkin. Flo had sat, windows open, in a continuous breeze next to the Piute Reservoir for nearly four hours, and Allison had no intention of moving her metal friend until Thursday morning, an intentionally late start. The Piute State Park was empty of other travelers, leaving Allison private time to wade into the reservoir, deep enough to bathe. She leaned back, floating on the surface, letting her toes come just above the water's surface, allowing the second day of

September's sixty-degree temperature to blow across her naked chest and stomach. Allison's long brown hair, which had darkened throughout the years, floated like jellyfish tentacles in the water around her head. Inside her head, she replayed the informative declaration she revealed to Jeffery a few days earlier before carrying on a brief five-minute conversation riddled with inquisitiveness banter. *I was the angel that carried you.* She didn't have an explanation even though he had repeatedly asked for one. Honestly, she didn't even know why she said it or what it meant. Baffled, she effortlessly floated offshore. Pumpkin watched from the shoreline, where signs of an early fall surrounded him. The implementation of new environmental policies had addressed global warming. Summers were shorter, falls were longer, winters were kinder, and spring disappeared slowly.

During the last two days, Allison had noticed the Utah temperatures were exceptionally comfortable. She made her way on 191 North toward Green River, a small town hidden off 70 West, and then by Tuesday, after changing direction once again, she plunged south to Capitol Reef National Park.

Sitting under Cassidy's Arch in Capitol Reef, Allison realized how her mother must have felt during the last fifteen to twenty years of her life. Allison equated growing older to the feeling of having a clogged artery, one that she had witnessed so many times in those small sterile operating rooms at Swedish Medical. Her mother must have felt the walls of life closing in around her.

Allison was still young at forty-two, but she was old enough now to appreciate every detail that seemed unimportant just a decade earlier. Leaves were no longer just leaves. Allison noticed whether they were smooth, wavy, indented, or toothed along the outer edge. Her attention to detail had intensified. She estimated that the Piute Reservoir's water temperature was in the mid-sixties, just by the air surrounding her. She knew the surface was smooth, knew by its color that its depth was taller than a three-story building, and knew her body's outline entertained the large rainbow trout and smallmouth bass that weaved with her shadow. But age had given her more than keener attention to detail. It had given her the desire to fill every moment with happiness.

That night, Allison realized she had a solid two weeks before she would need to return to her Seattle apartment. *Two weeks is not a lot of time*, she thought, as she stared at the infinite number of stars in the night sky. Almost ready to doze off, Flo patched through a call from Jeffery Linus, the first one in two days, since she had remarked about being an angel that saved him. When? She didn't know. Where? She didn't know. And, even though he had pleaded for her words meaning, she wasn't able to give him more. She didn't know about his childhood dream. Allison Starr was utterly unaware that he still carried the vivid details of being plucked from a herd of stampeding bison with him as an adult. She didn't know about the dream that still felt real to him.

"Hey, Allie." He wanted to address her using the less formal salutation. She desired it too. They both still felt tender from the last phone conversation.

"Hi, Jeffery." She was going to say Jeff, but it didn't fit him.

"I got the photo you sent of Piute Reservoir," he paused. "Beautiful." There was no point in bringing up unanswered questions. Allison's comment, matching the actions of an angel that once saved him from sudden death, was coincidental – nothing more.

"It is. There are so many stars here. I tried using the Rosat36, but it wasn't picking up anything." She worked to keep the conversation flowing. It worked. Jeffery didn't dwell on her revelation. Instead, he recognized his sensitivity to the slightest hint that an angel saved him. Allison had no way of knowing about his dream. *Coincidence*, Jeffery reminded himself.

"That's not unusual. Sometimes a sky full of stars takes center stage," Jeffery laughed. "Maybe you'll have some luck tomorrow evening from Bryce Canyon. That's a pretty high elevation at the top." He had never been there but had always wanted to. *Someday, I'll go with Allie*, he privately imagined.

"I forgot I gave you my route, Doctor," she said, then recalling how she had sent a text message with the photo of Piute Reservoir – my prelude to Bryce Canyon. "I'm not sure if I'll spend the night inside. It hit me today that I only have a couple of weeks left. There's so much I want to see before I come back."

"You're doing great. Just relax and go with the flow," Jeffery suggested. "Doctor's orders."

She needed his humor. It was the perfect cure for the uncomfortable feeling she was fighting, and it was an opportune mood-setter for what she wanted to ask.

"How's Anastasia?"

"I'm baffled. Anastasia is not improving, but she's not declining either," he answered. "She's a strong little girl." *It's almost like she's purposely waiting*, but Jeffery didn't say it where Allison could hear it.

"Just keep me posted," Allison instructed. "And, don't forget to water my fairy castle cactus."

"It's on my schedule," he replied, remembering that Friday (*or was it Saturday*) was watering day – only a few drops.

"I love you," she said first.

"I love you too," he smiled after replying. "Enjoy Bryce Canyon tomorrow morning."

She did. By noon, Allison had Flo parked over 8,000 feet above sea level. Allison studied the Natural Bridge Viewpoint. Its solid rock arch accommodated the height of a small RV in the days when RVs were operational. Like the two tunnels she had driven through earlier that morning to enter the park, yet more refined, its outer arch displayed rocky spikes that looked like lace from a distance. She imagined the amount of erosion and change that had taken place to create such a masterpiece, where sixty million years earlier, there had been a river flowing through the canyon. Now, a medieval world of carved castles, fortress walls, and mysterious dungeons teased her to the very top of Bryce National Park, where she took deep gulps of air in an elevation over 9,000 feet.

She felt so small facing the enormous canyon below her, a realization that reminded her she was just a speck in the world.

"Pumpkin, we're almost unnoticeable," she announced, wondering who would notice if she were gone.

It was a harsh realization that occurred that night in her dream. This time, when Allison's angel appeared, any doubt that it was her Aunt Dixie disappeared. A maze of color blurred her vision of the mysterious creature, so she concentrated on the blend of vibrant colors: Carolina red clay, freckled tangerine, mountain green, cornbread yellow, and cast-iron black. The combination created a flashback of her five-year-old self. She was sitting in her Aunt Donna's Asheville, North Carolina kitchen. Butter dripped down her small arm as her mouth devoured large bites of freshly baked cornbread. She licked each finger. Slowly, and one at a time.

The flashback prompted Allison to study her grown-up hands. They gripped the rusty metal chains securely bolted into the rock wall that climbed alongside her. She was almost 1,400 feet up the rock altar. Allison's pulse quickened each step of the hike,

leaving her struggling for breath. It wasn't until her blue eyes

realized the large metal bolt's fate. She watched it dislodge from the

sandstone cliff at the same time her mind processed the fact that it

was too late to save herself. Falling backward, she was comforted by

the underbelly of her large angel. Allison's eyes remained fixated on

the winged creature, while her peripheral vision saw earthy greens

and desert reds quickly flow by her. The colors coated massive rock

slabs like paint. There was no chance for survival. Gone.

Allison Starr woke up screaming at 3-a.m. Friday morning. It

was only a dream, but the feeling stayed with her as she guided Flo

along Zion Canyon's Scenic Drive. Stopping at The Grotto by 9-

a.m., in a parking lot that was once for shuttle transportation, she

parked Flo and made her way across the small foot-bridge. Pumpkin

kept pace even when the terrain turned into a series of wiggling

switchbacks. It wasn't until the climb became steep and narrow that

Pumpkin started to slow. Finally, Allison reached to scoop him,

placing him inside a make-shift sling she had tied from an oversized

scarf, one her mother had passed down to her on her twenty-first

birthday, and one that she had felt the need to pack when leaving

Seattle. Now, she *wanted* that closeness. No, Allison *needed* the familiarity of a two-decade-old scarf never worn, and one never washed. Even though time weakened the scent of her mother on the floral linen, she swore she could still smell her mother's coconut shampoo. It was the comfort her mind needed. She continued the hike, convincing herself that rusty bolts and falling to her death were parts of the bad dream.

Still, scarf or no scarf, Allison felt her life slipping away from her as she reached Hogsback. The steep and narrow walkway, one she had never seen before, looked all too familiar. It was identical to what she had seen in her dream. *Stop it,* Allison demanded. *Keep going.* But, after glancing at her right hand, she suddenly felt extra precautions were needed. Her fingertips, each frozen by the abominable chilled temperature, were stained a dark reddish-orange. It wasn't a result of Utah's September cold. *Rust,* her mind deciphered.

Reaching in the sling, one she had created from her mother's hand-me-down scarf, Allison gave a slight pat to Pumpkin's head. That's when she noticed – even her furry friend shied away from the iron corrosion. Allison took it as a warning. "Okay, Pumpkin, let's call it a day."

Maybe some dreams aren't dreams.

Twenty-two

It was only logical that Allison Starr should have been driving north.
After all, she was down to eleven more days on the road after today
– September sixth. But, instead of heading north, and making a
beeline to Seattle, Washington, Allison acted like a typical Sunday
driver, at least modeling the ones she remembered before the
POTUS implemented driving restrictions. Allison's actions were
slow, meandering, and without direction. The only reason she wasn't
wholly lost was that she had been on 89 South forever. It wasn't

until she saw a sign for the North Rim of The Grand Canyon that she purposely continued south. *It's only 45 more miles*, she thought, after slowly making her way through Jacob Lake, a small wooded town that had the best frybread she had ever eaten. Picking up 67 South, she broke off a small piece of frybread, which Pumpkin batted from one side of the dash to the other, a game that lasted at least ten minutes and one where he was more excited playing with the new texture than nibbling on it.

Jeffery called to say he had sprinkled a few waterdrops on the fairy castle cactus late Saturday after checking in on Anastasia one last time before leaving Swedish Medical for the day. "It's doing great," he commented. "I think it loves the higher window-sill." He didn't mention how he stood in her apartment for over an hour, eyeing Allison's décor. He had observed her decorating taste, noticing how she delicately folded a sizeable quilted bedspread over a wicker corner chair in the bedroom. Curious, he held it up to examine the layout – old patches of childhood clothing carefully bound together in the shape of a giant star. He could tell the swatches had come from baby clothing. Some belonged to her:

swatches of pink with flowers, velvet red, white lace, and faded

letters on what looked like a newborn gown – University

Community Hospital. There were also swatches that he guessed had

belonged to her brother: a royal-blue patch, a portion of a football

jersey, and a FUBU patch that he knew belonged to popular boys'

jeans when he was a young teen. He made sure he folded it back,

neatly hiding pieces of her life held together by strands of nylon

thread. They were pieces of her life that she would never see again.

The analyst side of Jeffery studied the small bedroom vanity on the

opposite wall. No hairbrush, just a detangler comb, and one that he

couldn't help but touch just to feel her presence. No perfume. No

make-up. Allison Starr smelled like nature, a mixture of

honeysuckle, fallen leaves, and crisp spring water. Make-up couldn't

improve her natural beauty. Allison was already perfect.

Everything seemed simple about Allison Starr, but nothing

was. The kitchenware was heavy-duty enamel, matching black, and

the dishes boasted a floral pattern with bright matching solids. A

Wall-T.V., a simple couch that was more for comfort than show, and

a magazine with a cover boasting about national parks lie within reach, so it didn't come as a surprise when their current phone conversation focused on an announced new route. At the same time, he pictured her sitting on her simple gray couch and flipping through a travel magazine. Jeffery knew Allison Starr was a planner, even though she tried to hide that fact.

"I might as well see the Grand Canyon," she announced after rattling off the road she was on and after chatting about frybread. "Eleven days will be enough for me to do that and still make it back on time. I think."

"Just be careful," Jeffery followed up, knowing perfectly well that asking her to come back early wouldn't be good for their relationship. She needed every hour she could get behind the wheel of a car. "Try out the Rosat36 again if you have time."

"Definitely. I tried it out last night," she announced, "nothing." She thought about where she had pulled over for the evening – Page, Arizona. "I think the lights around the dam and bridge in Page made it too bright."

"Probably," Jeffery said, although he wasn't familiar with Page. He only knew it was in Arizona. His mind pictured a large dam holding back the Colorado River. He knew the river flowed through Southern Arizona. His mind imagined the vast number of electrical units and floodlights that bordered both sides of the bridge. *Way too bright*, Jeffery concluded. He knew a well-lit bridge wasn't the best place to spot dark matter. "No worries," Jeffery tamed his silent thoughts; *it's not always visible even in the most optimum conditions.* He didn't damper the issue with extra details, keeping his last thought private – *seeing dead people's souls isn't an everyday occurrence.*

"I'll find a couple of dark spots around the Northern Rim of The Grand Canyon," she followed up. "And, I know, Doctor. You want pictures."

Jeffery Linus laughed out loud before saying what he felt. "I want you," he didn't slow. "I love you."

"I love you too."

Just before nightfall, she found a GFS service center at the end of 67 South. They offered hot showers. She had taken way too many cold showers so far on her trip. It was time to heat things up. Then she would locate an entrée to accommodate the frybread she had already devoured. It was a simple plan, one that started with Allison parking Flo near Bright Angel Trailhead. There were no other visitors at the North Rim, so it was a perfect night to try the ROSAT36 after her welcomed shower and eating something nutritious.

Allison was surprised that the Grand Canyon Lodge had hot water. It was the first time she had felt steam on her face since leaving her apartment in Seattle. Slowly lathering and savoring every minute in the shower, she thought about the angel in her dreams, almost prompting her to make a phone call to another professional dream psychic. *Is it just a coincidence that I'm parked next to a trailhead called Bright Angel Point?* It was a question she asked herself as she applied a second glob of shampoo, hoping her hair would revitalize after air drying.

Pumpkin waited for her to return to the car. Like a well-trained dog, he did not jump out the open window that Allison had inadvertently left down. Instead, he waited until Allison tossed her shower bag in the back of Flo. Then her teal-blue Nissan friend took a turn at waiting while Pumpkin followed Allison up a steep trail. The well-trained furball stopped whenever Allison slowed, her eyes searching for an unobstructed view of the Grand Canyon. She waited patiently with the ROSAT36 in hand until the sky had completely darkened. At an elevation of almost 9000 feet, Allison felt close enough to touch the stars. Using the ROSAT36, she mastered several shots: the southern sky, the eastern, and the northern. Unfortunately, the western sky was not accessible from where Allison was standing, blocked by tall pines reaching the nearest star batch. Even with her back to the prominent soldiers, she could smell the scent of pine-sap filling the air around her. Pumpkin stayed close, fearing what might come out of the thick dark forest – deer, mule, bison, or even a bear, worse yet a mountain lion, one that might mistake him for a sacrificial cub.

It was nearly 10-p.m. when Allison returned to Flo and patched through to Jeffery's cell. "I just sent you three photos that I took on the ROSAT," Allison announced after hearing Jeffery's hello. She could tell he was still in the lab, working later than usual, but she knew he would want to look at them and give his opinion on the presence of dark matter.

"I'm looking at the southern shot now from Bright Angel Point," he excitedly announced. "I see some orange and yellow. Faint, but it's there." He hurried on to the second photo, but before he could comment on that one, Allison interrupted his thoughts.

"What do you mean southern and Bright Angel?" Baffled, she wondered how the hell he knew where she was and, even more precisely, what direction she took the picture.

"I guess I didn't explain that part," he answered in a curious tone. "The ROSAT36 prints off four identifying pieces of information near the bottom of each photo: the location coordinates of the dark matter, the location coordinates of the photographer (unless it is the same or nearly the same as the first set of coordinates), the ROSAT's aimed cardinal direction, and an official date/timestamp." Jeffery didn't see any dark matter in the eastern sky and had already moved on to the northern shot when Allison piped in.

"So really, I should be watching you, Doctor," she chuckled, thinking about how easy it was to load his print into her apartment security system. "I need to remember that."

"I do have a few cards up my sleeve," he revealed, before adding, "nothing on the second shot, but the third shows some purple, which is beautiful." Allison looked at the photos, which rotated in slideshow mode on the handheld device. Honestly, she couldn't see much. Maybe on the first. Nothing on the second. And, okay, a hint of purple on the third.

"I see a little purple," she confessed. "So that's dark matter?"

"Yes." His voice skipped a beat.

"Souls?" Allison was still trying to wrap her head around the fact that spirits were floating among the stars.

"Absolutely." He sounded ready to defend a thesis. "It could be thousands of souls, and together it just happens to create such a perfect faded hummingbird-magenta-purple."

Allison smiled. That was a mouthful. It was also why she migrated toward Jeffery Linus, the world's most renowned color enthusiast. "I love you."

"I love you too." He smiled into the vocal transmitter on his lab desk that communicated directly with his cell phone.

"How's our patient?" She didn't need to use her name. He knew.

"Okay," his smile faded. "I'm looking at Anastasia's most recent stats, taken just before you transmitted the photos."

She could hear the concern in his voice and now understood why Jeffery was at the lab so late. "What is it?"

"Her blood pressure is way too low." Jeffery sighed. "She's in trouble."

Twenty-three

Anastasia Elpis had a slow but consistent drop in blood pressure since Sunday evening. Dr. Ben Gerhart tried everything humanly possible to halt the decline, but his patient's five-year-old body was not responding to fluid replacement as he had hoped. Instead, his patent was constantly babbling, which only Karen Elpis seemed to comprehend. Rattling off nearly inaudible numbers, Karen listened. *Three. Seven. One. One.* Out of order, Karen thought, then acknowledging that her daughter was receiving a lot of sedation, she encouraged her daughter to start over.

"Start over, baby," the mother urged. "Count backward like Dr. Starr taught you – three, two, one."

"Three. Seven," then taking a last unassisted breath, "One," Jeffery could hear gurgling coming from the child's throat. Anastasia's mother clenched her daughter's hand.

"Try again, baby girl," Karen whispered between sobs into her daughter's ear. "They have to put a breathing tube inside your throat," Karen cried. "Like this, baby girl – three, two, one…."

"Three. Seven. One. One. Seven," the child's lips parted for the breathing tube, her tiny body sedated by Dr. Paz, who had been at the child's head. It was a haunting decision but one that Gerhart felt wasn't optional. Not until he could figure out a way to eliminate her symptoms – low blood pressure, difficulty breathing, confusion, and if he didn't get a handle on her condition – further complications.

It was a Tuesday morning when the young child lay intubated. Jeffery had kept Allison posted every step of the way.

"She has almost half of the symptoms for septic shock," he stated sadly. "I heard her trying to count, but she couldn't master it. Instead, she kept scrambling up the order."

"What is Gerhart going to do to treat it?" Allison wasn't trying to blame Ben but couldn't help but wonder if Dr. Ben Gerhart could do more.

"I know he put in a request for Norepinephrine, a vasopressor medication, which will constrict her blood vessels and increase her blood pressure," Jeffery stated. "And, I saw Ben consulting with your team MCE, who programmed Dr. Chrome to maneuver several possible scenarios successfully," Jeffery informed her, "which I'm sure means he's even thinking of another possible surgery." Then for reassurance, "I think he's doing everything he can."

Allison shook her head, trying to believe Anastasia was going to be okay. "Stay on top of it," she replied with a lump in her throat.

"You know I will," Jeffery answered quickly. "I'll see you in nine days." Jeffery was already counting them down. He knew Allison was planning on returning to Seattle by the seventeenth, a Thursday, plenty of time to get her life in order before her Saturday shift at Swedish.

"Yes, you will," she answered, smiling slightly. Then, changing the subject completely, she asked a question that had been weighing heavily on her mind. "When souls exit the earth, how do they do it?" The wording wasn't exactly the way she wanted it to be, but she hoped he'd catch on to what she was asking.

"Are you asking how they get from the body to the galaxy?"

"Yes, that is what I'm asking." She couldn't imagine spirits or souls just haphazardly leaving the earth. *There has to be some sort of system.* Both the logical and organized facets of Allison Starr were taking over again.

"In 2030, NASA dedicated an entire task force to study EMP – Earth Magnetic Portals. It's been seven years, and I know some scientists are still shaking their heads no, but the task force is continuously uncovering supportive evidence that proves these portals exist." Jeffery settled in for more questions. It was a topic he could talk about all night.

"What evidence do they have, Jeffery?" She knew he subscribed to and read every document released by NASA and just about every scientific world branch. It was yet another thing she loved about him. He was a wealth of information.

"They've tested the pull of dark matter with large magnets that they sent up into space." He continued to explain. "By sending magnets the size of a semi-truck into space, they were able to watch the magnets pull the dark matter in whatever direction the magnets floated," he announced, hurrying to the good part. "Do you want to know how they watched that?" He asked but didn't wait for an answer. "ROSAT," he took a breath, "Allie, it's amazing."

"So dark matter is attracted to magnetic fields," she summed up, as she pictured souls leaving the earth and headed for a magnetic field in the galaxy, "but do they exit earth from a certain point?"

"Yes," Jeffery answered, finding her inquisitiveness sexy as hell. "Dark matter leaves earth through an EMP and travels into the galaxy where the magnetic field is at least a hundred thousand times stronger."

"Where are the exit EMP locations on earth?" Allison's mind placed science right in the middle of the Holy Book, so much so that she could scientifically explain almost anything.

"Believe me, the EMP task force is going crazy trying to figure that out," he smirked. "It's like an ongoing Indiana Jones movie, but never being able to locate the Holy Grail." He shrugged his shoulders, wishing he could have a stab at finding a magnetic portal on earth. "Every time they think they've located one, it disappears before they can get a team to the site, leaving the task force with no proof."

"Are you saying the magnetic field changes location?"

"Yes," he took another deep breath, soaking up the intelligent conversation. "The magnetic field breaks down into energy particles and moves to another location, possibly on the other side of the world."

"How many Earth Magnetic Portals does NASA think exist in the world?" Allison Starr was utterly buying into it; suddenly, the existence of a human soul made sense.

"NASA has no idea," Jeffery answered, "Although, given the infinite number of energy particles that flow between Earth and the galaxy, I would say the EMP are somewhere near a million, give or take."

Allison breathed the Littlefield, Arizona air. It was warm, ending the second Tuesday in September. "Have I told you that I love you?" She looked up at the Littlefield sky, still light, but her heart could feel the multitude of souls dancing above her, forming a painter's pallet that only the ROSAT could see.

"I hear it in your voice," he answered, hoping he didn't sound too cocky. "I love you too, Allie." He blew a kiss into the air. It hoovered quietly in Swedish Medical's laboratory, like a soul in transit – waiting for its host.

Twenty-four

Anastasia Elpis turned six years old on the ninth of September. It was a breezy seventy-three outside when Karen Elpis caught a monorail to Swedish to be at her daughter's side. The mother worked that morning at Wind Blown, first cutting and styling a regular's hair, then washing a load of white towels in the far end of the rehabbed RV. Earning a little extra money delayed her early morning arrival to Swedish, pushing it to noon. Still, she arrived with the newest interactive FurReal toy – a long-necked yellow giraffe with black spots, one that wiggles its tail and ears. The giraffe

answers almost two hundred basic questions. A college graduate
with a crisp button-down shirt had programmed the mammal's
internal computer to participate fully, customizing it to use
Anastasia's name in almost every response. Karen didn't stop to
think about the nearly two-hundred-dollar price tag. She only
thought about the smile that it would bring to Anastasia's face after
her daughter was extubated and weaned from sedation.

"Wednesday will be the day," said Dr. Ben Gerhart just
twenty-four hours earlier.

It wasn't until Karen rounded the corner and caught the look
on Dr. Jeffery Linus's face that she realized it wasn't going to
happen today, not tomorrow either. She clinched the bright yellow
giraffe as her body reacted – her physique melancholy – as she
sauntered to the eyes that interpreted hers – worried.

"Let's go to the waiting room and talk," Jeffery caught her by
the arm.

"No," Karen almost shouted, "I want to see Anastasia." She
was trying not to sob, trying not to think the worse, and trying to
keep herself together.

"She needs to remain intubated, Karen," Jeffery said right away, fearing she might think Anastasia had passed. "But there are some complications that we need to discuss."

They were the same complications that Jeffery had spent the morning discussing with Allison as she stood on the horseshoe-shaped glass skywalk that stretched over the west rim of the Grand Canyon, her eyes focused on the canyon floor 4,000 feet below. She had spent Wednesday morning driving through the Joshua Tree Forest in Arizona, stopping to take photos of large Joshua trees that bent in every direction, mangled and twisted into one-of-a-kind art. Bright yellow desert flowers scattered at their twisted trunks, creating a world that looked both dead and alive. Then, just before the sun had reached the afternoon sky, Allison had paid the fee to enter Hualapai Tribal land so that she could walk along the edge of golden-brown cliffs. The escarpments were unforgiving; one misplaced foot, and she'd need *her* angel, one she recently admitted had watched over her many times in her life. One that Allison knew must be getting tired from saving her. One she imagined was her deceased Aunt Dixie.

After Allison answered Jeffery's call, her feet froze in place on the sheet of glass. Below, a river twisted in the canyon. Pumpkin matched her stance and carefully remained at her ankles, uncertain that the glass would hold.

There's nothing you can do for her, Allie. She replayed Jeffery's words from their phone conversation that had ended thirty minutes earlier. *Just breathe and think positively.* Following his advice, she used every ounce of effort hiking to Guano Point. Pumpkin had opted to be carried and was leery when Allison made her way too quickly on the hard-red clay surface. He knew, just like Allison, that a mistake would be fatal. Still, a part of Allison needed to stand as close to the edge as possible. A portion of her hoped her soothing angel would appear, so she could beg it to save Anastasia.

Meanwhile, Dr. Linus was trying to save Karen Elpis from falling apart.

"Anastasia has developed small blood clots," Jeffery was holding Karen Elpis' hand, sitting in the small family lounge, his eyes level with hers, and his bedside manner a mixture of empathy and straight-forwardness. "That's why she can't have the breathing tube removed," he added. "Her blood flow and oxygen level are both compromised; she wouldn't be able to breathe on her own fully." He pulled a monogrammed handkerchief from his lab coat. He carried it with him for emergencies. Jeffery placed the small square-cut fabric, a cotton and synthetic blend, in his lab coat pocket every day because it was his father's and because it reminded him of his father's boy-scout personality. *Better safe than sorry,* his father used to say at least five or six times each month. The initials D.S.L were once embroidered in bright red but had now faded to dark pink. David Styles Linus would be proud of his son for letting a grieving mother use his handkerchief and even more proud that Jeffery chose to carry it around. *Better safe than sorry.*

"How many blood clots?" Karen Elpis wiped the tears rolling down her face with the hand that had been holding the bright yellow giraffe before returning the damp hanky to Dr. Linus and stroking the plush toy that lay in her lap. "Can the clots be destroyed?"

"Dr. Gerhart is working on that now," Jeffery answered, still holding and then squeezing her left hand with his right, then answering her first question. "The problem is that there are well over a hundred clots." That was a lie by omission. Yes, there were well over a hundred, but Jeffery played it down, knowing that Anastasia's morning blood work results showed that there were well over a thousand. He also knew at least 900 reasons why Karen Elpis didn't need that specific detail. The first reason being hope. She needed *hope.*

"Can I sit with her?" Karen asked before adding, "It's her birthday."

"I think you should spend as much time as you can with her," Jeffery answered quickly, "and she would love to have the giraffe placed beside her in bed."

The mother smiled, although slightly, before standing to hug Dr. Jeffery Linus and excusing herself to make her way to Anastasia. It wasn't the birthday celebration she was hoping for with her daughter, but just being near her right now would have to be enough.

Karen Elpis slept sitting up as nightfall filled the small room. Occasionally, she'd open her eyes to watch the machine help her daughter breathe and to make sure the yellow giraffe was still placed under Anastasia's left hand where she had put it. There wasn't any sign that her heavily sedated daughter could hear her voice, but just after 11-p.m., Karen Elpis spoke to the now six-year-old.

"Happy birthday, baby girl. I love you with all my heart. Please get better for me. Don't leave me. I need you way too much. You're my greatest joy. I can't lose you." Wiping tears, she made a promise. "I'm taking you to the Woodland Park Zoo as soon as you're out of the hospital."

Karen couldn't afford things like that. Splurging on the interactive toy giraffe had set her back, but this wasn't a matter of money. She wanted her six-year-old to see the African Savanna display at the zoo. The young mother wished to see her daughter's blue eyes open wide as she stood near the wild grasslands, wanted her child-sized ears to catch the corners of her smile as she listened to the roar of the African Lion, and wanted the interactive FurReal giraffe tucked underneath the edge of the hospital linen to manifest in real-time.

"I promise." It was a promise that Karen hoped she could keep.

Twenty-five

Desert mountains surrounded Flo as Allison and Pumpkin bounced along 95 North from Vegas. At first, the highway stretched two lanes in each direction, and then it dwindled to only one. The Nevada wind hissed into the three-inch opening on Allison's driver's side, where she had purposely left the window lowered. Pumpkin kept watching from the dash, sitting up straight as he noticed a coyote the color of red rock scurry across the potholed highway. Very few GFS automobiles traveled up and down 95 North; miles and miles of empty land hugged both sides and appeared lifeless but were home to rattlesnakes, scorpions, black-tailed jackrabbits, and bighorn sheep – to name a few.

Allison noticed Vegas was a different animal. It was a bustling desert city, filled with crowded monorails, busy to-go restaurants, and brightly lit casinos. It was the third city where she had stopped to do a load of laundry and the first where the print, play, and pick-up (PPP) method was not only preferred but encouraged. Print scanned—Play at a nearby casino is authorized—Pick-up time for clean laundry assigned.

The slot machines bustled inside The Mirage, a short walk from PPP Laundry, where Allison decided to try her luck after regaining her composure. Minutes earlier, she had almost lost her footing when a loud BOOM exploded on her right. The iconic Mirage Volcano had survived a changing world, a fact verified as it shot flames into the darkened sky and sent a massive amount of hot air in Allison's direction. At that moment, she was glad she had left Pumpkin in Flo's care, windows up, where he lounged inside, and where the inside temperature was a controlled sixty-eight. Pumpkin would have been scared to death. *He'd be down another life,* she thought, as she held her index finger on the Triple Red Hot 7's start button. Red Hot. Bonus. 7. Nothing. Bonus. Red Hot. 7. Nothing again. Bonus. Bonus. Bonus. She watched the WIN display move quickly. 121. 242. 343. 721. In just a matter of moments, she had won seven-hundred and twenty-one dollars. An acknowledgment flashed across the screen – Congratulations, Dr. Starr, 721 dollars is currently depositing. Your bank balance will be updated soon.

Leaving at that time would have been a good idea. But, unfortunately, even though the casino's financial network had transferred the money to Allison's bank account by the time she had stood, her self-control lacked the discipline to head back to Pumpkin. Not yet. Two index prints later, after ten minutes in front of Wheel of Fortune and another fifteen minutes in front of Megabucks, Allison knew she had lost all but one-hundred and thirty of it back to the casino. Still, it was a lucky night. One-hundred and thirty dollars and a basket of clean laundry put a pep in her step as she made her way back to Flo, leaving behind sin-city, a world where index fingers, debits, and credits were all part of a nightly ritual. *At least people can't overdraw themselves anymore, like in the old days,* Allison processed. No more advances. No more bookies. People could only spend what their printed finger acknowledged as available.

Now morning, Vegas was seventy-four miles behind her. Making her way back to the desolation of 95 North, she didn't take a break until Amargosa Valley, first stopping at Area 51, an alien hideaway, for gas, a coke, and a picture of a six-three bright green alien that stood lifeless next to the snack aisle. She sent a copy to Jeffery, waiting for some sort of smart-ass comment, but continued driving when he didn't answer. *Busy*, she thought.

By afternoon, Allison had made her way through Beatty, Nevada, and was standing in a small ghost town called Rhyolite, directly in front of a replica of The Last Supper. A talented artist named Albert Szukalski had delicately portrayed the menacing white-draped figures, which eyed Allison from a wooden platform. *Thirteen,* Allison quickly inventoried. *Jesus in the middle, and six disciples on each side.* The hollowed-ghosts made from plaster-soaked fabric didn't need eyes to stare through her. She could feel the recreation of Leonardo Da Vinci's Last Supper penetrating her, sizing up her beliefs, as each faceless ghoul was wondering why she hadn't accepted the blood and body of Christ. For a moment, Allison allowed herself to stand in the path of judgment, envious of the human characteristics the man in the middle had during his earthly life, unselfishly sharing his final moments with friends. The analysis made her think of her mother's last moments. *Did she think of me? Did she feel lonely?* Then, she thought of Anastasia. *If my mother's soul is inside the young child, is she disappointed that I am not there – again?*

She didn't have the answers, not until a giant darner landed on Jesus' ghostly shoulder, its vibrant blue spots calming her concerns, its nearly six-inch wingspan signaling her to keep going. *Forward,* she remembered what her Aunt Dixie would constantly say to her mother, and somehow, she imagined it was being said to her too. *Forward.*

Maybe that's why she decided to steal more time on the road before booking it home to Seattle. *I have plenty of time to get myself by to my apartment by the seventeenth,* she rationalized as she guided Flo into Death Valley National Park. Multi-colored canyons, miles of desert sand, and a mountain peak replicating a giant corkscrew greeted her. She had never been to Death Valley, and it made logical sense that she should at least peek in from the Nevada side, especially since she was so close.

It wasn't for another two hours, nearly six-p.m. when Jeffery called.

"You didn't like the alien photo I sent?" A slight giggle followed Allison's question, one that filled the desert silence surrounding her, in the corner of Death Valley, on a nameless dirt road that wiggled its way between Grapevine Peak and Rhyolite, somewhere northwest of Pioneer Road.

"I do…it's just that I've been slammed in the lab all day," he added cautiously.

"It's more than that, isn't it?" She could tell by the tone in his voice.

"Yes," he answered, knowing time wasn't on his side, "She's gone into organ failure." He didn't have to say more. Allison knew Anastasia's time was nearing, just like Jesus knew at The Last Supper. "She doesn't have long," he added, knowing the best approach with Allison was honesty. He knew her medical experience answered most of the questions she probably had on her mind but added, "It's not only her heart now," he choked back tears. "The lack of blood flow has also affected her brain."

Allison took a few minutes, letting it all sink in, before speaking. "She'll be gone by morning." It came out as a statement, but she hoped Jeffery would correct her, adding on more time, anything.

"Yes," it was the coldest word Allison had digested in a long time, but it's all Jeffery could give her. He could hear the love of his life whimpering on the other end of the communication device. "She's not suffering." He found some comfort in knowing the six-year-old wasn't feeling any pain and was hoping Allison would too, but he also felt anguish knowing Anastasia wasn't able to hear Karen Elpis' last *I love you* or share a final kiss. The child would be gone by morning. There was no way to save her.

"Life's not fair, Jeffery," Allison said.

"I know, Allie." Then he tried hard to make sense of Anastasia's time on earth. "She was here for a short time, but for a huge reason," he said. "Maybe your mom's soul is part of her existence, and maybe it was Anastasia's job to show you that." Jeffery didn't know if he was making sense, but he believed reincarnation was possible. He had listened to Allison discuss the unusual connections and had witnessed some on his own – the dog paw birthmark, the continued chitchat about her imaginary dog named Miles, and Anastasia's memory of having mud in her throat. Jeffery had witnessed Anastasia screaming for Miles on several occasions. Something that made the hair on the back of his neck curl was the odd connection Anastasia encompassed with the Indian heritage, something he knew the child hadn't been introduced to in Seattle or even learned about, for that matter. Jeffery knew it had been part of Enola's family tree, and more daunting, he knew it had been part of his own. *Did I know Allison's mother in a previous life? Did I love her daughter then too? Was the angel who saved me in my childhood dream, Allison? Are we all just recreated vessels carrying repeated souls? Red threads?* Jeffery had a million unanswered questions and some answers he felt confident having. "She was supposed to be here for you, Allie."

The darkened desert sky had settled around Flo, who was waiting patiently in a patch of yellow tarweed and small cacti. Allison struggled to speak. "Hug her for me, Jeffery." She couldn't address Jeffery's theory about Anastasia's purpose. Not now. "I'm going to stay put for tonight." She looked around, realizing she couldn't find her way back to the main road even if she tried. The eleven-p.m. sky was black onyx, darkening everything around Allison Starr. Fate had left her with no choice but to stay put. "I love you."

"I love you too, Allie."

Jeffery wandered to the doctor's lounge before midnight, where he saw Ben Gerhart's face hanging in defeat. He looked different, almost human. If Jeffery didn't know better, he'd swear Gerhart felt something more than anger or superiority – his usual MO.

Karen hadn't left her daughter's side since arriving by noon on Wednesday, her daughter's birthday. Haircuts would wait. A shower wasn't in the cards, and sleeping was something Karen Elpis hadn't done in nearly two days. As a matter of fact, Karen Elpis had spent the last thirty-six hours by her daughter's side, taking less than a handful of bathroom breaks. The worried mother refused to join Jeffery in another heart-to-heart conversation in the family room, afraid she might miss Anastasia's last few moments, even though Jeffery assured her it wouldn't happen that way. Removing the breathing tube would be a decision Karen Elpis would have to make, but only after Dr. Gerhart convinced her it was time.

By two-a.m., Gerhart finally approached Karen Elpis, not as a doctor but as a father of two grown children. He took off his authoritative doctor hat and put on his empathic dad-face, one he never wore at the hospital.

"I'm sorry, Ms. Elpis, Karen, but Anastasia won't be able to recover from the organ damage," he reached for her hand, a gesture he had kept off-limits since working at Swedish. "She'll never be able to breathe again on her own." He looked her in the eyes. "I'm a father. If Anastasia were my daughter, I'd let her go in peace, without pain, without suffering. She wouldn't want to be on a breathing tube forever." He stopped talking, long enough to look across the ICU room and into the face of Jeffery Linus, who had given up on trying to talk Karen into another coffee break and instead was sitting in support with Karen. "It's time," Ben said.

Karen Elpis sobbed uncontrollably. She knew Anastasia wasn't going to recover, a slow realization that grew from the quiet conversation between Jeffery and Karen over the last two hours.

Karen knew Dr. Linus wouldn't mislead her, and then hearing it come from Dr. Gerhart solidified her decision.

"I just need an hour to say goodbye."

Both doctors respectfully left the small ICU room, leaving Karen alone with her daughter.

Twenty-six

The wind shook Flo unforgivingly. Allison had tried to sleep in the back of Flo, hoping the pitch-black sky would mask her emotions. Finally, just after 3-a.m., she surrendered. Nature won. Reaching for the ROSAT36-Mini, she occupied her time by trying her luck. Pumpkin attempted to follow in the windy darkness but quickly retreated after the desert sand embedded around his whiskers. He jumped back inside Flo before Allison shut the driver's door.

"Okay, ROSAT, let's see what's hidden in the Nevada sky." Then, remembering she had traveled on the small unnamed dirt road over cattle bars and past a sign which read: ENTERING Death Valley National Park, she corrected herself. "California sky." She was ten minutes into California. Aiming the ROSAT into the galaxy above her, she thought about all the backroads she and Reese used to explore in California. Never this one, not near California's Death Valley. Now, she stood alone in its darkness aiming the ROSAT into the sky. First one direction, then another, and after rotating her stance, a third, and finally the northwest direction. Nothing transmitted across the screen. Disappointed but forgetting to click the ROSAT into off position, she brought it straight down, level with her line of vision. Suddenly, she realized that the ROSAT was flagging a mass of color directly in front of her, probably less than five hundred feet. Record. Transmit. Record. Transmit. Record Transmit. She took her eye away from the ROSAT, looking in the same direction. A coal-black sky stared back at her. No color. Quickly returning the ROSAT to the northwest direction, she searched for what she had briefly seen. Now, nothing.

Maybe I was wrong. Allison tried to convince herself she was mistaken, then remembering the vibrant colors, "What the hell was that?" She questioned herself as her mind recalled the colors and shapes that she felt sure she had witnessed. Allison was confident she had seen a peach color replicating Florida's underwater sea coral. Her dark brown eyes had seen a dark crimson red, its richness matching the swirling belly of Arizona's Marble Canyon, and its shape mimicking a woman whose skin matched the color of clay. Allison could still visualize the dandelion yellow matching what she believed to be her mother's favorite wildflower. Allison's thoughts continued, replaying a crisp sherbet orange, its shape morphing into a younger woman. *What the hell did I see?* Then asking herself more scientifically, *was that dark matter leaving a portal on earth?* She shook her head no, hurrying back inside Flo, one hand holding the ROSAT and the other wiping tiny desert sand crystals from the corner of each eye. *That's it;* she announced to herself, *The Kaleidoscope-Effect.* Her scientific mind had already given the phenomenon a name, as she processed the only logical scientific explanation. *The ROSAT didn't record color or shape. My eyes were playing tricks on me.* Puzzle solved, at least in Allison Starr's opinion.

Sitting in a small corner of California, somewhere above Pioneer Road, an untraveled area hidden between Grapevine Peak in

Death Valley, California, and Rhyolite, Nevada, Allison grabbed the ROSAT one last time, hitting the playback button. In a few minutes, she imagined she would see total darkness. Nothing.

That's what happened precisely, after a tiny red lithium dot, no bigger than a pin-head, lit then quickly faded. *Out of battery*, she thought, *are you kidding me?* The lithium 3000, which powered the playback capability of the ROSAT, needed to be charged. She searched the inside of the foam-lined case in the dark of night. Nothing. No cord. No extra battery. Her world had gone dark.

For Anastasia Elpis, the world had also blackened. The young child lost all brain activity at the precise moment when Gerhart and Linus walked in together. Above the head of her ICU bed, the Nicolet Monitor showed that all brain activity had stopped at 3:12 a.m.

Karen Elpis was still holding her daughter's hand when both doctors looked first at the monitor and then at each other. Gerhart conceded to the fact that something or someone was watching over six-year-old Anastasia Elpis. Now, disconnecting Anastasia from the breathing apparatus would occur without the possibility of discomfort for the young patient. Doing so while the child's brain still showed any sign of activity would have prompted her tiny body to struggle for breath, a scientific reaction that her mother did not need to witness, and one that Gerhart didn't want to be the mother's last memory. The universe had given Karen Elpis the gentler option.

"Ms. Elpis, would you like to remove Anastasia's breathing tube?" Gerhart thoughtfully questioned the mother. "You have that right." Offering the dreaded task was the correct thing to do; although, he couldn't imagine her wanting the responsibility.

"No, Dr. Gerhart," Karen answered. "I can't." Then, after squeezing her child's hand tighter and longer, "I trust you."

"Your daughter's brain activity ceased minutes ago. All medications have stopped. Extubating will only take a few minutes." He thought about Karen Elpis' personal beliefs. "Did the hospital chaplain already visit with you and Anastasia?"

"Yes," Karen smiled. "She has been blessed by the hand of God."

"Very well." Dr. Ben Gerhart moved slowly, explaining each step. "I am going to shut off the ventilator. Anastasia's body will not react. This step is necessary to extubate." Gerhart was a kinder version of himself.

Karen shook her head yes, and reached for Jeffery Linus' hand, who was standing right next to her.

No reaction. The patient looks like a tiny angel. Those were the thoughts Ben processed privately before continuing, first by deflating the tube cuff, then by gently removing the tube. The hospital did not need Dr. Chrome to remove life support, although, right now, Ben Gerhart wished it was the job of a bionic arm, not his own.

Once again, Jeffery removed his father's monogrammed handkerchief from his lab coat pocket, holding it within the grieving mother's reach. Karen smiled through tears before accepting it and wiping her tears on the faded letters D.S.L.

David Styles Linus smiled too.

Gerhart glanced at the time on the monitor above the child's head once again before speaking, "Time of death – 3:12 a.m." Gerhart choked back tears. Watching a child die was the most challenging moment of his medical career. "Take all the time you need with Anastasia," Gerhart said to Karen. "I'll make sure the PTP doesn't arrive too soon."

Karen handed the tear-drenched hanky back to Dr. Linus, who was in the process of turning to exit with Gerhart.

"Could you stay?" Karen asked.

"I will stay as long as you need me to," he quickly answered. It was five-a.m. before Karen let go of Anastasia's tiny hand. Watching the PTP cover her child, she turned away from her life with a bright yellow giraffe in hand.

Jeffery Linus rode the monorail to Karen Elpis' ACZ community, ensuring she was safely in her 2019 Ram Pro-Master Conversion Van, where he knew things would never feel the same ever again.

By six-a.m. he was home, mourning the loss of the youngest angel he had ever known.

Twenty-seven

By the time Jeffery Linus got home, it was well into Monday

morning. Exhausted, he called Swedish. Good. There was always a

biochemistry intern jumping at the chance to run basic lab requests,

one that was willing to tend to stat scripts and wanted to get his feet

wet in a major hospital's Molecular Biology Department. Phil

Hoffmann, an intern at the local university, volunteered

immediately. Done.

Jeffery needed to catch up on missed sleep, so he quickly dozed off after trying to reach Allison a second time with no success. It was somewhere between lunch and dinner when he opened his eyes in his small Seattle apartment. Thinking of Allison, he reached for his cell. One missed call. Sitting up, he dialed. He had to give her the information she knew was coming.

"I didn't want to keep calling," Allison announced after Flo patched Jeffery through. "I knew you were probably at Swedish late." It had been almost midnight when she last spoke with him, and he was still at the hospital, running circles between Dr. Ben Gerhart and Anastasia Elpis' ICU room. "I also wasn't ready to hear the news." Allison had spent the better part of the morning, well into the afternoon, walking through the California desert with Pumpkin, stopping beside towering rocks for shade, sharing bottled water with her furry companion, and accepting the fact that Anastasia Elpis was probably gone from this world. Even more gut-wrenching was the feeling that her mother's reincarnated soul went with her.

"I made sure Karen Elpis got home okay this morning." It was an informative statement that confirmed Allison's thoughts.

"I'm sorry, Allie. Anastasia is gone." Two short sentences alleviated any doubt.

"I know. Something inside me felt differently," Allison announced, then changed the subject to avoid details. "I sent three pictures to the lab that I transmitted from the ROSAT, all duds, sorry." Her stomach fluttered, stopping her from sharing *what I think I saw* details. "I forgot to turn it off, aimed it too low across the valley in front of me, and…" she cut to the chase, "I think the playback needs charging."

"No worries," Jeffery soothed her. "It's been a long night for both of us," he said. "I'll check the photos tomorrow." He placed his feet on the marble flooring, cold to the touch, but he liked the way it shined after the natural light peeked through the opening in his bedroom curtains. "I'm hanging out at home all day today," then following up, "I need it."

"I hear you." She knew what he meant. Mental exhaustion had taken its toll. Stretching the limits of science had restlessly tied Allison's stomach in knots. She didn't know for sure if her mother's soul had existed inside Anastasia, but a part of her believed it had. Still, there were too many unanswered questions. *Did Anastasia have a separate soul? Were they the same? Was her mother in the cosmos now, waiting to be reborn?* They were all legit questions, and they were all unanswered questions. "We both need our rest," she continued. "Enjoy your day, Jeffery."

"You too, Allie." Then remembering Allison's goal of being back to Seattle on the seventeenth, or Friday the eighteenth at the latest, he questioned her progress. "Are you still sitting a thousand miles from me?"

"One-thousand, seventy-eight," she rattled off, a route she had programmed into Flo's hard-drive. First, it would take her up through Reno, Nevada. Next, through Lassen National Forest, and would eventually spit her out just under Mt. Shasta, California, where she'd grab Interstate 5 and take it home. "I'm under six hours to Reno, so I'll make that by tonight."

"Be careful traveling," Jeffery added. "There's a lot of long lonely highway in that stretch."

"I will," Allison replied, then, "I love you."

"I love you too," Jeffery said but needed to say one more thing before disconnecting. "You were supposed to meet Anastasia Elpis for a reason, Allie," he reminded her again. "Red threads."

"I know," she said, then after final goodbyes, Allison directed Flo to 95 North. She needed to be on a road that felt the same way she did – alone.

Just before Reno, Allison went through Virginia City off Nevada's 341. It wasn't what she expected, having once heard about the many eateries, quaint shops, the town's psychic palm-reader, small pubs, a homemade fudge store, and a few colorful candy shops that caught the eye of every kid passing by. Now, it was a ghost town—empty of patrons. The only things that stood in Virginia City were churches, each with broken steeples and weathered shells. Now, each structure stood infiltrated by wild horses and tiny field mice.

Without stopping, Flo slowly made her way through the deserted Virginia City. The emptiness prompted Allison to think about everything she had seen since leaving her corner of the California desert. She had seen numerous mining towns littered with rusted equipment over one hundred years old and had driven through sparse farming communities. Allison had made her way across several Indian reservations. And, recently she stopped at two state parks where a few other GFS travelers were walking. No monorails.

No big cities. Towns survived using increased farming productivity, operating hemp fuel stations, and earning income from struggling mom-and-pop diners – except for places like Virginia City, the sacrificial lambs of America's new world. Those places had folded and now stood as ghost towns representing the old America.

Reno was different. Even in the dark, Allison could see the bustling monorail system that ran from one end of Reno to the other, numerous casinos, crowded restaurants, beauty salons, gyms, hospitals, schools, medical offices, and several extensive daycare facilities. Reno had done a three-sixty, eliminating its homeless and drug population, creating jobs for the masses, and treating the addicted. Most of Reno's working people flourished in the hospitality, medical, food, or entertainment industry. As a result, Reno was economically sound, a feeling that even a passerby like Allison felt.

It was a feeling that she also felt when talking to Jeffery. He called right after she had finished a shower and laundry at a GFS rest area outside Reno and had made it to Tahoe National Forest's west side. The September air was cold at the high altitude, and Flo worked to warm Allison as she stretched into a comfortable position in the back of the Nissan, where Pumpkin had already found his place beside her.

"The stars are amazing in – Gold Run," she struggled to remember the name of the small mountain town as she settled into a conversation. "I'd try for another shot at seeing dark matter, but the lights are too bright in the rest area, and the ROSAT needs charging."

"The fact that you were able to pick up some dark matter at the Laguna Mountain Summit in Southeast Cali makes me so happy that you took the ROSAT with you," he babbled like a child. "I'm sorry I forgot the charging cord," he said, realizing it was in the lab's wall safe. "Just enjoy the California stars," he said, then added, "California must be a hotspot for views of the cosmos."

"There are so many mountains and summits," Allison agreed. "It's amazing." Even though unsaid, there was a secret part of her that wished she had never left California, especially Northern California, where she had left behind huge mountains, jutting plateaus, valleys that twisted like garden snakes, and a large piece of her heart. "I can see Orion." She looked at the three bright stars that formed a straight line in the hunter's belt, then shifted her eyes to the brightest shining star directly above his belt, tracing his armpit with her eyes and following along his arm to the bow he was holding.

"Allie, that's amazing," Jeffery's voice smiled. "I wish I was there to see it with you." Then he thought of the constellation that he knew would be located above the mighty hunter, Orion. "Do you see The Bull, Taurus?"

"I don't know what to look for?"

"Look above Orion," Jeffery directed. "Try to find the red star."

"I see a red star," she informed him.

"Good," he said. "The red star is usually located in the middle of the bull's horns."

"Oh my God," Allison's voice heightened. "I see the bull!" Now, she sounded like a bit of a kid in a candy store.

"It's amazing," Jeffery said. "The cosmos is magical."

"Jeffery, do you think Anastasia is out there?"

"I do," he answered, "and so is your mother."

"Thanks," she said, needing him to ease her pain.

"I guess now it is as good of a time as any to let you know that I got a message from Karen Elpis when I woke up late this afternoon," he continued, "Anastasia's funeral is Monday afternoon."

Allison searched her mind, trying to remember what day it was. "Tomorrow is Saturday, right?"

"Yes." Jeffery knew that being on the road makes days run together.

"I can make Interstate 5 tomorrow morning." She thought about how Sacramento was only another hour or so from her. "Then I'm only 750 miles away from Seattle." She calculated the math in her head, factoring in the seventy-five miles she had to knock off in the morning just to get to I-5. "I'll be home Sunday evening," she announced.

"Really?" Jeffery tried not to sound too excited, as he didn't want a funeral to be why she came home early. "You think you can make it?"

"Definitely," Allison answered. "I need to go," she added. Without clarifying, Jeffery knew she was talking about the funeral.

"Then, I'll see you Sunday evening when you get home," Jeffery announced. "Be hungry," he added, thinking about a romantic dinner together. It would be their first in nearly five weeks.

"I'm starving," she said, "but not for food."

Jeffery wondered if she could see his cheeks flush a powdery red.

"I love you," he said firmly, but his thoughts read his body language. *I'm hungry too.*

"I love you," Allison said back. Although, he wasn't the only one with a hidden thought. *I feel like my heart is stretching in two different directions.*

Twenty-eight

Allison made Sacramento by eight-a.m. Pulling into a strip plaza near a busy monorail station, she eyed a Chick-fil-A. Then, happy that some things hadn't changed, she made her way inside, stepped up to the counter, and ordered a large unsweet tea and number one – a chicken sandwich with waffle fries. Her eyes focused on the storage area that used to be a drive-up window. No more. Patrons were walk-ins only and weren't allowed to sit within the grab-n-go styled restaurant, reminding her that even the things that seemed the same were different.

For the next 270 miles, she convinced herself that different doesn't mean less. *People, places, and traditions change,* Allison reminded herself as she eyed the Hornbrook exit. *Sometimes people and the environment around them become more robust, better, wiser, and take less for granted.* Her deep analysis nearly caused her to exit the interstate, but the sound of Jeffery Linus' voice over the automated phone system brought her back to the here-and-now. Her foot grew heavy on the accelerator as she listened to the euphoric voice that filled the empty spots inside her.

"Allie, do you know what you've done?" Jeffery's tone was celebratory, which immediately made Allison search her recent actions, trying to locate something she had done worth celebrating.

"By the sound of your voice, I deserve some sort of award," she announced, still not knowing what news was so spectacular.

"I've been staring at the ROSAT photos you transmitted all morning," he announced quickly. "You recorded dark matter on the earth's surface, Allie!" Scientists had proven that dark matter exists in the cosmos. Yes. But, directly on the earth's surface? No.

"What do you mean?" She remembered the theory she had founded as she stood in the darkness of the California desert – The Kaleidoscope-Effect – a rare phenomenon occurring when tiny desert sand crystals aggravate the cornea, causing an explosion of color and shapes. *Had my scientific mind overcompensated once again?* Allison questioned herself, remembering the colors and odd shapes she had seen in the small corner of her darkened desert oasis.

"You recorded ground-level dark matter," he took a deep breath. "This is huge!"

"You're talking about the photos I inadvertently shot near Rhyolite, Nevada? So, they weren't black?" And then, "I did see dark matter?"

"You knew?"

"I imagined it. I guess briefly, but I figured there was no way dark matter could be that low. So, I convinced myself that it was a crazy reaction my eyes were having to sand crystals," she confessed. "It was windy on the California-Nevada border that night."

"The coordinates show you were definitely over the Nevada line. The ROSAT picked up the dark matter less than 500-feet away from you, in the corner of Death Valley, just inside California," he rattled off, after verifying the sole set of GPS coordinates printed on the bottom of each photo. Only one set of coordinates was published on the picture, confirming that the dark matter was directly from an EMP. Otherwise, *there would be two sets of coordinates printed on the image.* He reminded himself. Furthermore, it was in "Death Valley, an area known for its magnetic fields." His hands trembled as he thought about what the scientific world could learn about the human soul and afterlife because of Allie's discovery.

"I remember you were telling me about the EMP task force created by NASA," she said, trying to recall the acronym's meaning. "Earth Magnetic Portals?"

"Yes, exactly," he announced. "You found a portal on earth, Allie." The nerd in him wanted to shed happy tears. The man in him fought to keep his scientific explanations sound and organized. "You witnessed souls being pulled to a portal on earth directly after death." He shook his head, trying to keep his composure. "That area pulled the dark matter together, from hundreds of people that had passed and was getting it ready to transmit to a more substantial portal in the galaxy, one with a magnetic field that is –

"at least a hundred thousand times stronger." She finished his statement while remembering the glow in his sea-blue eyes. "Sorry for interrupting, but now you have me excited." Her mind was busy wrapping its self around the fact that she had witnessed people leaving earth. "Should I go back there? Can you meet me there? We could get more documentation." Allison Starr was almost as excited as Jeffery Linus, a reaction that made him love her that much more.

"Believe me, Allie, if I thought there was any way the portal was still there, I'd get a NASA EMP task force to meet us there first thing tomorrow, but –

"It breaks down into energy particles and moves to another location." Then realizing she had finished his sentence once again, "Sorry."

"Yes," he confirmed, and then repeating something he had once told her, "Possibly on the other side of the world."

"I get it." She was absorbing everything like a sponge. He held her interest even a thousand miles away, which now had dwindled to about half of that. *Five hundred miles away,* she thought, passing a sign that welcomed her to Oregon. "What should we do with the information we have?"

"I need to call a buddy of mine that works for NASA," he responded. "I'll let you know what he says." And Allie, "I love you."

"I love you too." She followed his smile to Roseburg, Oregon, where she stopped for the night. Tomorrow she would see his smile in person, only 350 miles from where she was settling into the back of Flo for the evening.

Even though late, Jeffery called his buddy on Florida's east coast, just as Allison's brown eyes grew heavy. She quickly fell into REM sleep. Her pupils fixated on the satin wing bars that floated above her, attached to off-white feathers that gently brushed her hair as she slept. Allison could feel the gentle motion on her face as her angel glided above her. It maintained a nonthreatening, and somewhat hypnotic rhythm, even when the feet-less angel's talon swooped low, giving Allison an up-close inspection of the creature. This angel looked different. Her gut told her it wasn't her Aunt Dixie. Not this time. For a moment, she imagined it was a large white bird, but the middle of the heavenly creature had a naked human torso. Allison's scientific brain studied it, watching for movement, noticing how the abdominopelvic muscles pushed it forward and controlled each breath taken by the mysterious creature.

Moving her eyes, she searched the top of the gender-neutral torso for a face. Milky white skin stared back at her, holding Allison's attention captive, giving her x-ray vision. Allison's eyes focused on the creature's inner anatomy. Exterior details were unimportant, as Allison's inquisitive nature soaked in the forgiving and trusting vibes, both of which sent her into a deep sleep. The creature stayed, watching over her.

Stirring after several hours, Allison opened her eyes, almost expecting her angel to be inside the back of Flo. Instead, searching the outline of her own body for its existence, she only found Pumpkin.

He purred gently, seemingly calmed by the middle-of-the-night visitor. Allison wiped brown locks from her eyes, sitting upright, her mind focused. She concluded that it was only another dream, although she felt her mother's presence had watched over her. Opening the back-passenger door, she took in a massive gulp of Roseburg, Oregon air – a mixture of wine vineyards and trickling mountain waterfalls.

She didn't notice the fuzzy white feather that floated out of the cyan-colored Nissan and into the six-a.m. sunrise when she opened the car door. The owner's purposely plucked feather hurled through the Oregon sky, motored by invisible gusts of wind before it came to a resting spot near a pinot noir grapevine.

The tattered plumage, new growth from a recently passed soul, had been a sign that Allison missed. One from the reincarnated soul she knew best as Enola May Starks – her mother.

Twenty-nine

The middle of September brought non-stop rain to Oregon, masking the crunch sound between Allison's back molars as she downed a bag of unsalted almonds that she had picked up two hundred miles back. The downpour had delayed her morning start, not that she wasn't fully capable of driving in the rain. Still, she found it mesmerizing and stared at the mountain pass in front of her for hours.

Jeffery's day had started precisely the opposite. The Seattle sky was bright and sunny, and there was nothing about him relaxed. Instead, his hand trembled as he worked through one lab request after another. Jeffery had spent over an hour on the phone, approaching almost 3-a.m. Florida time, with his buddy at NASA, Dr. Steven Olympus, someone he knew through high school in Maryland and someone that excelled in New York State's graduate program. Steven earned a degree in Nuclear Chemistry and Astronomy, a combination Jeffery always found confusing. However, NASA saw the unique degree as a gold star, quickly putting Dr. Olympus in charge of several cutting-edge programs, one being the EMP task force.

The old friends followed up with a second conference call around 9-a.m., pacific time, which left Jeffery's head spinning, but not from exhaustion. No, it was from total elation. It was one thing to be recognized by NASA and given a ROSAT36-Mini for running one of the country's best molecular biology hospital labs. But it was utterly different from being offered a leading position working with the EMP task force.

"You're exactly right, Jeff. The portal terminated in Death Valley by now. But the fact remains that you uncovered an Earth Magnetic Portal. Hell, you even documented its magnetic pull of dark matter. NASA needs people like you. I would like you to sign a contract with NASA to be a GFS remote EMP investigator, taking a team from location to location, sometimes on the other side of the world, monitoring magnetic fields for dark matter. It's too big of a discovery to relinquish to the team I have in place. I need you to establish a second team with fresh eyes."

Jeffery remembered the conversation almost word for word. There wasn't a question in there anywhere; instead, it was more direct. *I need you to,* Jeffery thought, *monitoring magnetic fields.* The chance to travel non-stop in a world where time often stood still was terrific, but the opportunity to scour the globe for dark matter and use equipment that cost trillions of dollars was something he never imagined he'd do. Jeffery Linus was forty-five years old, and he knew this offer would never come again. Jeffery also knew that the recent intern who had filled in for him at Swedish would jump at the chance to run the lab. He didn't even have to pick up the phone to call Phil Hoffmann. He imagined his young heart would skip a beat when offered the opportunity, just as Jeffery's heart was malfunctioning at the moment. The muscular organ operated at a faster pace than it usually did.

Gathering his composure, he made it clear that he wanted Dr. Allison Starr on his team. She was the real hero. Without her, the EMP would have gone unnoticed, and its documentation of dark matter would have never made it to NASA's file of evidence. It was an example of being in the right place at the right time. *Allison's destiny* Jeffery imagined.

"Yes, her degree is in cardiovascular anesthesiology, but she would be an indispensable member of the team. After all, it was Dr. Starr's discovery," he corrected Steven a third time. It was a fact that grabbed Dr. Olympus' attention. Steven Olympus extended an offer to Allison in her absence.

"Done," Steven Olympus spoke firmly. "I'll electronically send you a contract within the hour with your name on it and an offer for Dr. Starr."

During a quiet 10-a.m., Jeffery Linus signed the contract and electronically scanned it, sending it to NASA. *Done,* he thought. Allison didn't have to sign her offer. She just had to be on a GFS flight to the east coast of Florida on Thursday morning, the day before Allison had initially planned to be back in Seattle.

The following two hours were a blur. Dr. Linus sat with the hospital administrator, recommending intern Phil Hoffmann. Jeffery explained how the chance to run an EMP task force at NASA would be good publicity for the hospital, ensuring that everything would be in place by Thursday, his departure. No, their departure.

It wasn't his place to announce Allison's resignation. He knew she'd do it her way. Instead, what he wanted to do for Allison was make her arrival in Seattle as comfortable as possible.

Leaving Swedish Medical's Cherry Hill Campus around two in the afternoon, he picked up a bundle of fresh purple asparagus with one hand. With the other, he gathered two celebratory cuts of porterhouse steak, followed by a bottle of the small store's best vintage red wine and two long stem candles with crystal holders. He carefully balanced everything in the trench of both elbows before reaching for a reusable cloth grocery bag. He felt organized, reborn. Exiting the store, he heard the computerized cashier speak to him – enjoy your meal, Dr. Linus. Your debit amount is 183 dollars – then he made his way to Allison's apartment via monorail. While in transit, he thought of the new life they'd have together. It would be one of travel and adventure. Jeffery and Allison would celebrate each discovered Earth Magnetic Portal by sitting together in areas rarely explored, testing the atmosphere and ground for magnetic activity, and using sophisticated mechanisms to look at the cosmos. Their hearts would quickly beat when they witnessed dark matter dancing like the Northern Lights – ghostly and without restriction. Even after reaching Allison's apartment, he thought about what they could give the world together. First, there would be a unification of spiritual and scientific followers. Second, Jeffery and Allison would unite believers and non-believers by proving that life and death are part of a continuous cycle. Millions of people will bathe in solace. The world will be filled with people who know that death is temporary. It is not the end. Loved ones are not gone; their souls are recycled. Tiny churches will no longer feel the need to assemble in mourning, but instead, they will gather in the celebration of rebirth. Like young children on Christmas morning, family members would speculate how their deceased loved one's soul would reinvent itself.

Jeffery's eyes traveled up Allison's eastern bedroom wall, stopping at the fairy castle cactus, bouncing from one spire to another, and smiling at the beautiful display created as a whole – the traverse heights offered coexistence, yet each spire stood independently. He smiled. His right hand worked to mist the magical array, adding tiny droplets of water. Finally, heading into Allison's kitchen, he accessed a copper fry pan and a small amount of coconut oil before searing the two cuts of porterhouse, setting them aside. He would perfect the massive reductions of short loin minutes after Allison's arrival. Now, he ran water over long stems of purple asparagus as he imagined the endless shades created when human souls unite, forming an explosion of color.

For Jeffery, NASA stood for his most sacred belief – the goal of discovery and uncovering the truth. So, as he heard the fingerprint identification pad greet Dr. Allison Starr just outside her apartment, he felt confident that the woman he had grown to love would feel the same way.

"I planned a nice dinner for you," he announced as he watched her walk in the foyer, carrying a cosmetic bag over one shoulder, a duffel bag of clothing over the other, the ROSAT36-mini in her left hand, and Pumpkin in her right. "Let me help you," he smiled, then reached for both Pumpkin and the ROSAT, but not before planting a quick but passionate kiss front and center.

"I smell the garlic, onion, fresh asparagus, and some seriously tended-to beef," she smiled. Her eyes devoured the doctor as he demonstrated his ability to cap off and present the well-planned meal. The display made her hungry; although, her body had a hunger that trumped the pains she felt in her stomach from not eating since late yesterday evening. Simply put, it was raw lust. She had been too excited to get home and too anxious to stop for food, which seemed like the right call, after feeling the intense warmth of Jeffery's kiss, and after seeing the flames flicker above crystal holders on her small dining room table, where Allison sat both her cosmetic and duffel bags before adding to her conversation. "You're a true romantic," she said. "I give you a ten for ambiance, Dr. Linus."

He smiled. Job well done, and to think he was unfinished. *NASA wants us.* He silently played it over and over in his head as he motioned her to have a seat. The short and to the point approach had always worked with Allison. Why stop now? However, Jeffery knew that timing was everything. Let her enjoy some food first. But the announcement should be made before love-making. He didn't want a once-in-a-lifetime career opportunity to be tangled with passion. However, the thought of sitting under a night sky filled with stars, recording dark matter, and changing the view of death for millions, was the most intense orgasmic action he imagined existed.

"Why, thank you, Allie," he said, smiling. "I hope you're hungry."

"Starved," she said but went in for a longer kiss as Jeffery pulled out her chair, an act that let him know it wasn't just food she wanted.

"Me too," he added, his lower groin ached for her, but he kept the conversation light. "Is it okay if we eat now, or do you need time to get settled in before dinner?" His question showed that his finesse was spot-on, careful not to imply that she might want a shower. On the contrary, he had noticed her hair smelled of Oregon pine and hoped she would leave it that way so he could smother himself in her scent throughout the evening.

"No, I want to dive in now." She breathed deeply. Taking in the smells around her – a hint of parmesan and butter swelled from each strand of purple asparagus, two servings of slightly pink porterhouse lightly sizzled in porcelain-tinted coconut oil, diced cloves of crème colored garlic, and yellow onion. The mixture of enticing odors and warm colors relaxed her as she watched him pour a glass of dark red wine into the goblet in front of her.

Somewhere in the middle of dinner, after laughs flowed easily, Jeffery and Allison discussed the where and when for Anastasia's funeral, then Jeffery delicately approached the subject he could no longer contain.

"My buddy at NASA wants me to assemble and oversee a second EMP task force team," he announced, studying her immediate reaction, then quickly added, after watching her face grow concerned. "You're my first pick for my team." Then correcting himself, "Our team."

"You're kidding?" She still looked shocked; although, it was no longer the – I can't believe *you're* leaving – look he had seen seconds ago. Now it was much happier. A – I can't believe *we're* going – look flashed across Allison's face. At least he hoped he was reading her correctly. "We would be dark matter explorers? Together?" Her tone and questions confirmed he was right.

"Yes," he answered. "Three-a.m. stars, milky ways, staring at the cosmos, sailors uncovering the secrets of dark matter –

"We could change the world," she exclaimed.

He didn't wait for a yes. Instead, he saw it across the small table, accented by candlelight that made the darkest part of Allison's brown eyes explode in a half-dozen shades of brown. He could see the colors of her soul – a perfectly baked apple pie, a fallen maple leaf, a bail of fresh stable-hay, a top-secret FBI folder, a carpenter's leather work-belt, and a large glass-jar of sun-tea.

Working as a team, they quickly moved dishes to the kitchen island, their feet sternly planted around the sturdy oak table, and relocated the long stem candles to a nearby look-out point. Each crystal holder carefully displayed the flickering towers. It was a process that only took a few unspoken moments, and it was one they agreed on. Their actions met one goal – clearing the small dining table.

What happened next demonstrated their superior ability to work as a team. The consenting doctors tossed pieces of clothing around the small table. The discarded garb resembled tattered nautical pennants. Their sailor bodies melted into each other on the oval-shaped surface. Allison's body served as a keel, offering

stability for their lovemaking. Dr. Jeffery Linus plunged forward, his

tiller invading the deepest part of Allison.

They sailed into the unknown.

Thirty

The Seattle sky looked like four different seasons, one in each cardinal direction. West, there was a thick wall of sea mist blocking the view of the Pacific. North, Allison could see snow clouds heading for Mount Snoqualmie. Due south, her eyes traced the last of fall, indicating that winter was already claiming mid-September. Finally, east, the sun rose into the ten-a.m. position, fighting its way through smoky clouds.

Rarely did winter come this early, and rarely did fire season last this late. Northern Oregon had made it through the worst of the fire season until things took a drastic change. Even from Seattle, Allison could see the southern sky fighting the smoky demon.

"Eliminating global warming has its price. It has sent the seasons into a whirlpool of confusion," Jeffery said, taking Allison's arm as she stepped into the tiny Seattle church. Then changing the subject, "Someday, days like this will be a little easier." Allison knew he was referring to Anastasia's funeral, not global warming. Death was a straightforward concept, in Jeffery's opinion. He felt certain death was just the end of one life and the beginning of another. He wanted nothing more than to prove it to the world. Death was a painful transition, but by studying EMPs, he could prove that the painful topic should not include the imaginary subtopic of Heaven or Hell. He would spend the rest of his days proving to the world that death was part of a master plan, that it was part of the cycle, nothing lost, a new life started. Earth Magnetic Portals would become a layman's term at the celebration of a loved one's passing.

"She's out there," Allison whispered, keeping her emotions intact. "I know she is."

Jeffery wasn't sure if she was referring to Anastasia Elpis or her mother, Enola May Starks, but he hoped his answer would suffice for either one.

"Yes, and she knows you know that." The problem was, Allison still had doubts. Maybe researching the mysterious dark matter for NASA would help make a believer out of her, but she used the fake-it-until-you-make-it method for now. Even after everything that had occurred, Allison still considered the possibility of coincidence.

Allison's mother hadn't copyrighted the name Miles. Birthmarks look like whatever you imagine. Mud is not an Alaskan trademark; it's in every rainy Seattle corner. Vivid dreams about angels are common. Anastasia's remark about Allison's forehead having the shape of a moon on it could have resulted from anesthesia or the hospital's fluorescent lighting. *Coincidence*, Allison thought, as she took a seat between Karen Elpis and Jeffery. The three of them filled the only available pew on the right-hand side. In the left-hand pew sat Miss Lindsey, Anastasia's daycare teacher, James Retford, Karen Elpis' neighbor in the ACZ area, and his five-year-old daughter, Isabell. The Retford's lived in a 2017 Ford Conversion

Van, across from Karen, in the ACZ community, where Isabell would sometimes wave at Anastasia. Six attendees mournfully looked on as the hospital reverend stood looking out at the two pews.

The non-denominational hospital reverend, Al Kingston, stood with a simple button-down dress shirt, plaid, and his trousers a cross between tan and olive green. He could easily be confused for someone who worked in a phone store, possibly even a tiny diner. His tone was matter-of-fact and lacked any theatrical performance.

"Let us remember Anastasia Elpis. Losing a child of such a young age takes courage. Courage to believe. Courage to remember. Courage to let go."

Allison offered comfort by reaching for Karen's hand, even though she noticed the young mother held herself together and slightly smiled when Reverend Kingston cracked a joke.

"Anastasia is today's movie star. Please close your eyes and imagine her in *All Dogs Go to Heaven VII*, the 2032 3-D remake, where small children live in a magical land with their dogs. Built from candy, rows of box trucks exist in heaven's ACZ community. The dogs run freely. Children stay young forever. And, parents can only visit," Reverend Kingston smiled back at Karen before gently lifting the small golden urn in front of him. "Ashes to ashes. Amen."

Karen mumbled a soft *amen,* followed by a series of numbers – *Three. Seven. One. One. Seven.* – "I love you, baby girl."

Jeffery processed Karen's selection of numbers, his mind recollecting that he had seen the easy but random series before. *Where?* It wasn't until the funeral ended, an event referred to as a *brief dedication to the child's life* by Reverend Kingston, that Jeffery felt comfortable enough to ask Karen about the numbers he had heard her quietly recite.

"Are the numbers something you and Anastasia used to say at bedtime?"

"Something like that," Karen giggled slightly. "It was how she counted when she was under anesthesia," she announced. "She'd mess up the pattern every single time," Karen informed him. "She was confused and often counted out of sequence when sedated." A smile stretched across Karen's face as she thought about the endless hours that they would read books together or practice counting numbers. Still, Anastasia would always count out of sequence after sedation and sometimes before drifting off to sleep in their tiny metal home and always in the same pattern – Three. Seven. One. One. Seven.

"Hold on to your memories," Jeffery leaned in for a farewell hug. "You take care, Ms. Elpis." He turned, walking away, still trying to place where he had seen the number pattern. He'd think of it, but now he wanted to give Allison a few minutes alone with the childless mother.

"I'm sorry you lost her," Allison said, still holding Karen's left hand. "She was a beam of light in a world that needed her."

"She always will be Dr. Starr," Karen's passion showed through, as she took time to comfort her daughter's favorite doctor, one who had done nothing but try to help her child. "I believe the reverend was right," Karen said. "I know my baby girl, and I know she's playing with her imaginary dog in a magical candy-land."

"I believe you're right," Allison said, although she had no idea. Maybe her NASA fieldwork would prove Candyland existed. Perhaps she'd believe in magic. Right now, she felt empty. Lost. "Best always, Karen," she said, then squeezed the mother's hand before catching up with Jeffery.

"Did you ever pay attention to Anastasia's counting pattern when she went under anesthesia?" Jeffery didn't ask the question until they were settled on the Monday evening monorail ride after an afternoon lunch out at Sal's Surfside Restaurant in Seattle. The lunch topic focused on the exciting possibilities they'd uncover working for NASA. They exchanged tender looks and delicate touches across a similarly-sized table matching the one they had made love on twelve hours earlier in Allison's apartment. At that same table, Allison agreed she'd drop by Swedish Tuesday morning to give her resignation. The fact that it was four days before her next scheduled shift was in her favor. Allison knew donating a few extra days of work to Swedish would be appreciated. Besides, she planned on dropping by Swedish tomorrow to see the photos she had transmitted to Jeffery's lab from Death Valley. Curiosity nibbled at her since Jeffery announced that the images contained far more than black-sky lurking in the desert wilderness.

"I always do," she answered Jeffery's question, trying not to sound offended. Paying attention to the babble coming from her patients, young or old, was something she instinctively did. "Anastasia wasn't able to count down successfully after sedation, always counting out of sequence," Allison informed him. "Rattling off a combination of numbers, all under ten." Allison could even remember the numbers. "Three. Seven. One. One. Seven," Allison recalled, although she had guessed the last number based on the shape of the child's lips as sedation took hold of her minor patient.

"I wasn't trying to imply anything," he said, picking up on the fact that he probably sounded like he was questioning her thoroughness. "I just wanted to know if the numbers Karen Elpis heard recited from Anastasia in the hospital were the same."

"Were they?" Allison knew children that age commonly stuck to patterns and sequences to comfort themselves during stressful times.

"Yes," he said. "It's nothing," he added. "I just feel like I've seen that number pattern in print." He shook his head. "Somewhere."

"You work in a lab, Jeffery," she reminded him. "I'm sure you see number patterns all day."

"You're right," he scrambled to move on to a different conversation as they neared Allison's apartment. "Will you stop by the lab in the morning to see me?" Jeffery asked, not thinking about how anxious Allison might be to see the photos she had captured proving the existence of an EMP. Instead, he wanted to assist her with any bargaining-lingo she might need before heading up to the top floor to talk to administration, an essential step in making sure they both boarded a plane in three more days. "I'll buy you a cup of your favorite coffee."

"Deal." Allison stood, giving Jeffery a quick kiss before exiting the monorail. Of course, she wanted to see him in the morning, but the fact that he didn't think about how excited she was to see the photos bothered her. Suddenly, she felt small. A part of her wondered if Jeffery was the type of man who would always be show-cased in their relationship.

"I love you," he shouted to the closing doors.

Allison didn't answer back. She couldn't – she felt like a cannonball hit her dead center.

Thirty-one

Darkness brought the molting angel; its appearance soothed the gnawing pain in the center of Dr. Starr's gut. Allison could see the bright yellow talons with claws that glistened in natural light like razors. She had a clear view as the creature's grip tightened, lifting her body above Seattle. Allison was at the angel's mercy as it securely but gently held her in place underneath its feathered undercarriage. Her eyes looked up, slightly angled forward, to study the human torso she had noticed in her last dream. Angled down, she could see it was carrying her over the highest mountain pass on I-5, the one that separated Southern Oregon and Northern California, a distance that would typically take at least eight hours from Seattle but had only taken minutes. The world was dark below, still sleeping, except for Allison. It was vividly clear. The mid-day appearance felt warm and comforting, sun rays bouncing off her face as the angelic creature circled lower. A log cabin she recognized was directly below her, where she hovered in suspended flight. *Reese's house,* she knew from following him there. Starring down, through what appeared to be an invisible roof, she watched him sleeping. Alone.

The alarm clock woke her at five-thirty a.m. She felt for her bed's closest edge. *A weird dream*, she thought, as she swung both legs to the floor. It was the day she would give notice at Swedish, a significant turning point in her life. Allison wouldn't report to her first scheduled surgical procedure on Saturday; instead, she would be leaving in forty-eight hours on a plane to Florida with Dr. Jeffery Linus. Convincing the hospital administrator that Dr. Paz should assume her position full-time would require little finesse. Allison knew he'd be a gracious shoo-in for the job, as he had happily covered for her during her vacation. He would just continue. Perfect timing.

Riding the monorail felt surreal as Allison thought about how much her life was getting ready to change. Her new life would be one where she would constantly be behind the wheel of a NASA-GFS work van, a driver's position she had already called dibs on during her last conversation with Jeffery. If she weren't driving, she would ride as the passenger in a NASA-GFS plane, through clouds and endless sky to other countries. Thoughts of the future consumed Allison as the Seattle sunrise glowed on her right cheek. The vibrant rays passed through the large monorail window, and its glare permeated the community stretched on the left side, waking up the small ACZ area. It was another day for most people, but for Allison, it felt like she was playing a part in a movie – one that started with a dream. Undoubtedly, she knew that if the day were indeed a movie, it would be fast-paced. It would be a day where analyzing her recent dreams would be too time-consuming. She wished Jeffery was on the monorail ride. His presence would have offered her a safe place to chat about angels and reveal her middle-of-the-night captivity. The much-needed conversation would have cleared her mind.

Unfortunately, Allison knew Jeffery had left earlier than expected and was already at the lab. Jeffery wanted to make sure the intern, Phil Hoffmann, was fully briefed on all standard procedures. After gladly accepting the Swedish Molecular Biology Department's open position, it was a long day of shadowing that Phil did at his own expense. Jeffery had even made sure the anxious intern would receive the department head title following the consummation of his graduate degree. It was a ceremony that would occur in only ten more days. Again, perfect timing.

Allison stopped at the lab before making her way to the top floor as promised. She was anxious to see Jeffery but even more anxious to see the photos she had transmitted from Death Valley. *Exquisite colors*, Allison remembered Jeffery saying on a previous phone chat. Now, she would see for herself. She approached quietly, allowing Jeffery to finish explaining how to prioritize several stat lab requests simultaneously. He stopped, pulling his attention away from Phil, long enough to smile in Allison's direction, then after realizing the young molecular biologist was consistently spot-on, he turned his full attention to Allison.

"Nervous?" He was referring to Allison's top-floor assignment, the one where she'd change her life after fifteen minutes of conversation with the big-wig.

"No," she answered, knowing that's what he meant. "It's my calling." She had no problem making a significant change when she felt it was the right thing to do. "But I am nervous to look at the photos."

Wow, Jeffery thought to himself, *why am I waiting?* He had been so busy working side-by-side with Phil all morning. It was a stress that had caused Jeffery to set-side the mind-blowing discovery, actually, two mind-blowing discoveries, the last of which he made at the crack of dawn just before his replacement arrived. Reaching for a manila folder that he had placed near the ROSAT printer, he stood by Allison, where he pulled out the set of three.

Allison's hands trembled when she flipped from the first transmitted photo, then to the second, and finally to the third, her mind processing the unlikely odds that all three images recorded by the ROSAT-mini had lighting glitches. Almost zero. *It's fucking dark matter,* she conceded privately, and then where Jeffery could hear it. "I can't believe it," she said. "It's gorgeous." Her eyes sparkled as she studied the colors. First, there was a vibrant peach-coral that she recalled seeing during a childhood snorkeling trip with her mother to Key West, one where they floated for hours over coral beds off the most southern tip of Florida. Then there was a rich-red, the same color as the mud that Allison had stopped to pressure-wash off Flo's tires, following a day and night of off-roading in Death Valley. But, the intensity of the bright yellow prompted Allison to close her eyes, just long enough to remember an old photo she had tucked in an apartment drawer.

Faded by time, she had held the image many hours, staring at her mother's ten year old arms as they delicately cradled the summer squash she had grown for a middle-school 4-H competition. Enola May had proudly placed second. Also, on display – a hypnotizing orange that matched Pumpkin's coat perfectly and the shade of her mother's dog's fur – Miles. Next, her eyes studied the shapes. *Human? An older woman? Indian descent? A second shape? That of a young girl? Hair in a bun? Like Karen styled Anastasia's hair?* Knowing her mind saw what she wished for, she kept the imaginary shapes to herself but felt an intense familiarity that triggered a slight tremor from her heart to the tips of her fingers as she struggled to steady the photos.

After handing Allison a promised cup of Peaberry coffee, Jeffery could see her hands were trembling and imagined by the look in her solid brown eyes that the pace of her heartbeat was quickening. Still, he had to tell her about the numbers, the numbers that kept him tossing and turning throughout the night, a number pattern that he had remembered seeing in his lab but couldn't remember on what document. It wasn't until he had gotten to the lab first thing this morning that he had figured it out, less than two hours ago, a discovery that left his heart racing.

"There's more," Jeffery said, his voice getting ready to unwrap the best Christmas present of all time. "Remember when I asked you about Anastasia's pattern of counting numbers after she began anesthesia?" Of course, Allison remembered. It was the only time she had ever felt insulted by Jeffery Linus after she wrongfully assumed he was reviewing her professional capabilities. Of course, she had recorded the numbers recited by her young patient. *Three. Seven. One. One.* And the last number, formed by the young child's lips – *Seven.*

"I remember," Allison said, still slightly annoyed, "Why?"

"Look," Jeffery pointed to the bottom of the photo, which Allison had shuffled to the top of three after taking a third sip of coffee and sitting it on the lab counter. "There's only one set of coordinates signifying that the dark matter was recorded and discovered in the same approximate location." He rattled on, "it's the same on all three photos."

Allison looked, then slowly felt for Jeffery's lab stool behind her. Its structure supported her nearly collapsed body. Weakness had taken over after studying the sole set of coordinates printed at the bottom of the photo. Her hands quickly reshuffled. She checked the other two images and verified the coordinates were the same on all three – 37.00'00.0" N, -117.00'00.0" W. "Allie, Anastasia knew the coordinate numbers where her soul would leave earth," he said, watching her brows come together.

"Are you saying a six-year-old knew the coordinates for an Earth Magnetic Portal?" She was shaking her head in disbelief. *It has to be another fucking coincidence*, she told herself.

"Yes," he answered, "that's what I'm saying precisely. "And, look at the time-stamp."

"2037/09/11 03:12 A.M.," she read it out loud but made no connection.

"That's the precise date, and time Anastasia Elpis was pronounced clinically brain-dead." Jeffery fought to keep his words in control and emotionless, something he felt was necessary.

"Get the fuck out of here," Allison said as her feet attempted to hold her steady, her body anxious to stand, as her knees buckled in disbelief. "Are you saying that I accidentally aimed the ROSAT low? Accidentally took three consecutive photos of an EMP? And, somehow, snapped each photo within sixty seconds matching the exact minute Anastasia died?" Allison didn't attempt to control her voice. It fluctuated like an out-of-control roller coaster. It matched every hair that stood up on the back of her neck.

"Yes, Allie," he looked at her face, her forehead still wrinkled and her mind still searching for a scientific explanation. There was only one. Dr. Allison Starr had been drawn to the precise location at the very moment in time to watch the reincarnated soul of her mother pass from an Earth Magnetic Portal. There was no other explanation. "It was no coincidence." Then, going where he probably shouldn't have, "Your mother wanted you there."

The last statement left Allison speechless. She felt her skin lighten, the color in her face matching the milky-white angelic creature she had seen in her previous two dreams. *Was that my mother?* She didn't dare ask the question out loud, not yet. She physically wasn't able to anyhow. Breathing deeply, she found the strength to stand without holding the nearby counter. Her eyes searched Jeffery's. He gleamed, knowing there was a spiritual world that needed exploration. The look on Allison's face was different – one her mother had described to her after years of teaching high school, a look that only a teacher understands when face-to-face with a student who finally gets it.

The Lightbulb-Effect, Allison thought as she searched for a scientific name to describe how she felt. It was the exact moment that Allison let her heart unwrap. Suddenly, she accepted the fact that science can't explain everything. Dr. Starr was embracing the existence of rebirth. She felt her Aunt Dixie watching over her throughout the years, always suspected her aunt had saved her from a fiery car crash, and was confident that her Aunt Dixie's angelic spirit had visited her before Anastasia's passing. If spiritual connections and happenstance had ended there, she'd jump at the chance to track down EMPs. It hadn't. Since Anastasia's death, she knew a new angel had taken over – the soul of her mother. And, even though it was hard to explain, she felt her new angel was directing her fate. The magnificent creature had earned her trust. She couldn't go.

Instead, Allison reached for the lukewarm cup of Peaberry coffee, finishing it off. The liquid raced down her throat, soothing the damage that had occurred from keeping her mouth open in astonishment. Finding her voice, she looked at Jeffery.

"I can't leave Swedish Medical," she said clearly. "My place is here."

Thirty-two

On Wednesday, Jeffery purposely caught an early morning monorail ride to Swedish. *The early riser gets the NASA contract but not the girl*, he sadly accepted. His promptness would serve two purposes. First, he would be able to box the last of his items from the lab, where he had spent endless hours working over the last dozen years. Second, he would be able to avoid Allison, the love of his life, that had done everything but break up with him during their middle-of-the-night phone conversation, the one where she had attempted to explain why she didn't want to accept the NASA position. He listened, shaking his head at each excuse. *Destiny. Angels.* He recalled her most repeated words. It made no sense to him. NASA was *their chance* to help the world understand the scientific dimensions of an afterlife. *His opportunity*, he corrected his private thoughts. It was an opportunity he couldn't refuse, even if it meant leaving Allie behind.

It wasn't until he exited the elevator at Swedish Medical that his right arm struggled to balance a cardboard box filled with a half-dead philodendron and twelve years of personal ah-ha moments recorded in journal format. And, his left arm attached to the hand that clutched the black case which held the ROSAT36-Mini and charging cable, the latter of which he had double-checked for, that he came face-to-face with Dr. Allison Starr. *Why does she have to look so beautiful?* He questioned himself. Her figure took center stage in the sunlight that poured in the hospital's East Wing, its glow accenting her high cheekbones and long brown hair, which she had pulled back into a ponytail, making her look a lot younger than forty-two years old. He had no choice but to stop as she neared, which immediately filled him with an awkwardness that he had never felt around her, one where his hidden palms each secretively held a pool of sweat, causing him to nearly drop the cardboard box if it weren't for Allison's quick reaction.

"I'll take it. You readjust." He imagined she wasn't just talking about the box. Her word choice fit her so well. *Readjust.* That was something Dr. Allison Starr had mastered. If she was bothered by the fact that he was catching an evening flight to Orlando, Florida, it didn't show on her face. Jeffery would ride a shuttle to Kennedy Space Center on Merritt Island, where he would be briefed, introduced, and inodiated with immediate tasks at hand. Allison would stay behind. She looked well-rested, which honestly pissed the fuck out of Jeffery. There was no point in waiting until tomorrow morning to catch a GFS flight. Jeffery Linus would be leaving Washington state with no scheduled return date in just a few more hours. He would take his exit early.

"Just hand me the stack of journals," he directed. "You keep the plant." It was half-dead like their relationship. "You're much better at taking care of plants than I am." That was Jeffery's only attempt at humor. It was the best he had.

Allison handed him a ten-to-twelve-inch stack of journal notes from the box. Then, she went in for an unreciprocated hug, partially because both of his hands were full and somewhat because he didn't have the stomach to be so fucking cheerful over ending a relationship that he thought was amazing.

"I'm glad you were able to get an evening flight," she said. "I guess NASA has some pull." She referred to the fact that only one or two flights left major cities each week, used chiefly for job-related travel, and all on a newly designed GFS Boeing 9000.

"No reason to stick around," he said. Allison knew he was pissed, but she also knew he'd have to get over it. She wasn't about to be bullied into a significant lifestyle change, especially since she couldn't shake the feeling that she needed to be in Seattle right now. He'd have to understand.

"I told you I need time," she reminded him. "A couple of months to figure out if it's the right decision for me." It wasn't something she was willing to bend on. If he wanted her on his team, he'd find her three months from now, and even more importantly, if the good doctor loved her, he'd love her three months from now. "You follow your dream, Jeffery. It's the right thing for you." Her gracefulness made him feel even more awkward. He sat down the black case, then pulled her close with his left arm, giving in to emotions he wanted to keep hidden.

"I love you, Allie," he whispered to her sun-kissed forehead. "Call me when you're ready." No kisses exchanged—only a one-armed hug.

"Take care, Jeffery," she said as he bent down to fetch the ROSAT. "You will change the world." It was a five-word declarative sentence, but one that had weighed heavily in her decision not to accept the NASA position. She didn't want to play second fiddle. Not ever. She knew she would always be in Dr. Jeffery Linus' shadow – the van driver, the unknown assistant. It wasn't her style.

Dr. Allison Starr watched Dr. Jeffery Linus walk away. She didn't cry. Not a single tear flowed. Instead, she stood silently, letting the morning sun warm her shoulders. For the first time in a long time, she felt at ease. There wasn't a second thought about NASA; instead, she was confident that staying in Seattle was the right thing to do.

By the time Dr. Jeffery Linus boarded his flight at Sea-Tac (Seattle-Tacoma International Airport), Allison had instructed an unscheduled emergency surgery patient to count down using the exact reverse pattern she had taught Anastasia. This time, the countdown would be a success; although, Allison suspected Anatasia's countdowns were too. *You were giving me the coordinates, Mom* Allison admitted, letting her mind believe and accept that it was a sign, one that added to a long list of why she needed to be at Swedish, at least for now.

"Three. Two." The thirty-one-year-old patient never made it to *One*, succumbing to the anesthesia. Allison watched his eyelids hide his dark-brown eyes.

"Good job, Mr. Farren," Allison reassured her patient, although she suspected he could no longer hear her. Still, she stood guard over her patient, wondering how someone so young and overwise healthy can have a heart attack.

"Hal Farren has a slight blockage in the left anterior artery, ultimately discovered after he suffered from smoke inhalation." Ben Gerhart looked at Allison as he spoke, then around Dr. Chrome to his MCE, who had programmed Dr. Chrome to conduct the robotic-assisted coronary artery bypass surgery. Allison had never heard

Gerhart speak during surgery, much less astute enough to recognize

the puzzled look on her face. However, since the unfortunate death

of six-year-old Anastasia, Gerhart's bedside manner had changed for

the better.

"Thank you, Dr. Gerhart," Allison replied to the new and

improved Chief of Surgery at Swedish Medical.

"Dr. Starr. Nice to have you back early." He spoke with

sincerity to Allison, leaving her speechless, before directing his

attention to his MCE, "Good job, Dr. Holm." Gerhart's compliment

was for Steven Holm, his Motions Computer Expect. Holm had

spent years routinely programming Dr. Chrome for scheduled

surgical procedures, the latest of which had just concluded. The

compliment left Dr. Holm questioning the whereabouts of Dr.

Gerhart's evil twin, a proto-type for Ebenezer Scrooge. "Now, the

Oregon firefighter is as good as new," Gerhart followed up before

smiling at both human doctors on his team and exiting. The gesture

left Allison star-struck, especially after watching him stroke Dr.

Chrome gently, his silent bionic arm partner, one he spent hours

hating, as he turned to leave the small surgical room.

"What the hell just happened?" Allison questioned Steven Holm, whom she had known for years. Nevertheless, she felt comfortable having a confidential chat within the private room.

"Anastasia Elpis' death hit him hard," Steven replied. "He's been like this for days now." A slight chuckle followed. "Even being an overloaded go-to hospital for Oregon state's weak and weary firefighters hasn't swayed his positivity."

"The fires are scorching the Cascade Mountain range," Allison said, after reflecting on the five-minute blurb she had watched on her Wall-T.V. before heading to Swedish this morning. "Oregon looked like a war zone," she said.

"Right now, it's devouring over 4,000,000 acres, stretching north as far as Eugene and south as far as Medford," Steven shook his head. "Only twenty percent contained as of this morning. My brother is an Oregon firefighter, so it worries me."

"I didn't know," Allison spoke empathically. "I hope he's okay."

"I heard from him late last night," Steven said. "Exhausted, otherwise okay." Then, "he's happy that Northern California sent up every Northern California firefighter they could get their hands on."

Allison's eyes widened, "Guys from the big cities?"

"Mostly rural firefighters," he answered, remembering what his brother had said.

Reese, Allison thought, then feeling the color drain from her face, "Keep me posted." It was the only polite way she could excuse herself.

Her heart ached. She felt another cannonball hit her—dead center.

Thirty-three

The sky over North Oregon bleeds a dark rust-orange as smoke billows above the highest flames, exceeding the tree-tops of one-hundred-year-old pines. The ground below remains saturated with golden embers. The raging fire's thick appearance mimics the inferno depicted in Virgil's divine comedy – Dante's Inferno – only there wasn't one person laughing. Nearby, the Columbia River Gorge is no longer recognizable. Its embankments discolored a charcoaled-black, another victim of Oregon's spreading wildfires.

Daylight hours did not make the massacre any less heartbreaking. Thick towers of white smoke tilted and weaved into the afternoon sky, revealing black and ash-gray underbellies. Firefighters worked endlessly, trying to contain the raging demon. By Thursday, every hospital within a 300-mile radius was fighting the mighty dragon's damage.

A young girl, age seven, sat in the emergency room of Swedish Medical, her eyes matching her red shirt and her hands blackened with soot. She looked more in shock than anything else when Allison Starr hurried past her after stopping just long enough to whisper words of comfort to the child who sat surrounded by strangers.

"Stay here," Allison squeezed the child's hand. "I'm going to take good care of your father and come right back for you." Then, signaling a volunteer to keep an eye on the child, she forced herself to hurry past. It wasn't the quality care Allison typically gave her patients, but if she wanted to make sure the child's father lived, then she had no choice but to hurry to the make-shift OR.

"This man is a hero," Ben Gerhart announced when his team filled the cramped OR. "He saved his family's life. Now, let's save his." Allison knew Ben was referring to the patient's wife of eleven years, already recovering upstairs on the fifth floor, in a restricted burn wing of the ICU, and his seven-year-old daughter Monique, who waited patiently and parentless one floor below. The child's small blackened hands were now stroking the family's kitten, which had just been placed in her lap by the guarding hospital volunteer. The middle-aged volunteer was a mother herself. She was not afraid to break the hospital's no-pet policy when she accepted the feline from an incoming firefighter. He was the same one that had pulled the young girl's father from the collapsed pool of bright red flames, a blazing red-eyed monster that destroyed the family's home.

Other firefighters backed off, listening to an order they received. Fortunately for the weary father, the solo firefighter hadn't been given such an order and overlooked the obvious danger that he was walking into a landmine. Combustible household products and a living room furnace exploded around him. Still, he couldn't stop, not after lifting the seven-year-old through a broken window and not after watching the face of the child's mother twist in anguish after her husband pushed her to safety, sacrificing himself.

Looking across the emergency intake room, he smiled through blackened cheeks as he watched the young girl coddle the rescued kitten. The firefighter hoped his efforts to save the child's father paid off too. But unfortunately, he was unsure what damage the man's body had endured following the last explosion, one caused by a small gas leak and one that knocked both of them off their feet. Still, somehow, he managed to rescue the girl's father despite being wrestled to the ground by a heavy support beam, one that had hit him directly across his shoulders. Hard. The fire suit had saved him from severe burns, but a sharp pain across his chest prevented him from continuing in the day's fight. So now, he sat discreetly, feeling pressure in his chest but unwilling to demand special attention in a room full of chaos.

"Sir, please sit in the wheelchair for transport." It was the same woman who had accepted the cat from him for the young girl and the same woman who recognized the man as a lone firefighter needing medical care. "I have an OR available now," she announced, her motherly tone revealed that *no* was not an option. "Don't get nervous," she said to the broad shoulders that faced her as she wheeled him into the elevator. "It's normally an exam room, one that is doubling as a small OR today," she assured him. "Hopefully, you don't need surgery, just an exam."

"What about the child?" It should be his last concern, but he had noticed her chair empty just as the elevator began to close, a direct view from his seated posture.

"A transport just took the kitten and the child. They are both at her father's side in a recovery room," the woman's voice smiled. "Thanks to you," she added. "The father had significant burn injury to his upper airway, but nothing Dr. Gerhart's team couldn't repair in a matter of minutes," the volunteer all-knowingly announced. "It was a small reconstructive surgery from top-notch doctors."

"That's great news," the firefighter beamed, still feeling pain shoot from one shoulder to another. "Sounds like you know a lot about what goes on around here."

"During emergencies, we all wear a lot of different hats," the middle-aged volunteer proudly announced. "Now it's your turn to meet the team of doctors that saved him." The information came just as the automated doors opened to a small room that had been converted back to an exam room, at least for the time being.

"Thank you." The words slipped out between teeth that looked exceptionally white against the firefighter's charred face. His pain caused him to squint his eyes upon entrance, where Gerhart's team stood combat-ready. Steven, the MCE, helped the firefighter lie face down on the exam table. Then Allison, who routinely wore a different hat, stepped up. She was willing to function in whatever role was necessary to help her patient. She carefully cut through the back of the man's flame-resistant jacket, exposing another layer consisting of a plaid shirt and a third layer that was a simple white t-shirt. Using medical-grade shears, Dr. Starr studied the firefighter's bare skin. Even Ben, a once sanctimonious surgeon, now found pleasure performing tasks well below his paygrade – this time, the well-known surgeon performed a basic but thorough exam of the patient lying in front of him.

"No burns," he announced after making an initial inspection. "No irritation from chemicals," he continued. "Possible carbon monoxide poisoning," he surmised, after noticing the bright red skin near the shoulder blades and lower neck, a discoloration that his grandfather might have referred to as a farmer's tan, had it been higher around the neck. Finally, Gerhart turned his head long enough to study the results of the patient's chest x-ray, displayed on the wall directly in front of him. The x-ray was a safely and routinely performed procedure and furnished immediate results.

The patient stayed in position, face-down on the medical exam table while Gerhart studied the findings – NO LUNG DAMAGE. Simultaneously, a small blood tube was collected from the patient's left arm and transported via a pneumatic tube to the lab. Phil Hoffmann, the new head of the Molecular Biology Department, was already processing the firefighter's metabolic panel. ORGAN FUNCTION – ABOVE AVERAGE and PLATELET COUNT 270,000 per microliter. Both results were on the same wall facing Gerhart. *Just as I suspected,* he thought—a *clear case of carbon monoxide poisoning.* Then confidently, "See to it our brave firefighter receives a ten-minute treatment in the hospital's hyperbaric oxygen chamber," Gerhart's demand was for Dr. Steven Holm. The computer expert spent less than three minutes programming the exam room's hard-drive. It immediately opened a hidden panel at the patient's feet. A pulley system slowly slid the exam table into the hyperbaric chamber as directed by the computer. The patient did not need a mask in the 2037 HOC, only the cooperation to lie still during the session. Allison watched the glass capsule enclose her patient and felt the need to comfort him.

"Everything will be okay, Mr.-," she stopped herself after realizing she didn't know her patient's name. Her eyes searched the wall facing Gerhart. *His name will be on the lab report,* she thought. Then after finding and locating it, her heart skipped a beat.

Reese Kabula. And then, knowing it was the same day that she and Jeffery originally were scheduled to catch an early GFS flight to Florida, *perfect timing, Mom. Now, I understand why you kept me here.*

Thirty-four

A mysterious gray cloud hung low in the October sky above Eleuthera Island, making the locals feel more secluded. It had been hours since Jeffery could see the newly planted pineapple field, one he knew was directly behind him. Darkness had set in, directing his feet to stay buried in the damp soil. The location was his team's fourth assignment since arriving in Florida three weeks early, and his actions were always the same. Waiting.

Jeffery's EMP task force consisted of five scientists, including himself, and under his direction had been thoughtfully assigned to monitor their section of the thin island. Jeffery knew from his research that Eleuthera Island in the Bahamas had a strong magnetic pull, and a part of him wondered if the founding Greek's had not named the island after witnessing the movement of colorful spirits as they were drifting to the cosmos. *Freedom*, he thought about the meaning of the Greek word Eleuthera. *That would be an appropriate name.* It was just a hunch, but one Jeffery's gut felt was worth investigating. Unfortunately, he knew the small Caribbean hiding spot had a history of interfering with compasses, causing them to malfunction even more in the last ten years. Still, he also found himself swept up in the local folklore, which boasted stories about colorful circles of transparent smoke dancing and weaving above the beds of magnetic rock around the pineapple fields before being released like giant glow-in-the-dark balloons of helium into the sky.

It was almost five a.m. before the EMP scientist stationed closest to him radioed, breaking Dr. Jeffery Linus' comfortable stance that he had been maintaining.

"Do you read me, Dr. Linus?"

"Yes, loud and clear, Dr. Comings," he answered, wondering why his team insisted on using such formalities when all five of them had a doctorate in one thing or another. *First names*, he remembered telling his team when they met three weeks ago in Cape Canaveral. Their attempts were short-lived, which Jeffery accredited to their desire to hear and use their recently earned credentials. Each team member under Dr. Linus had received their qualifications within the last year, and each still liked how the formal salutation rolled off someone else's tongue. "Do you see anything, Kate? I mean Dr. Comings," he corrected quickly.

"Yes, Dr. Linus, my G37 is registering off the charts," Kate Comings quickly announced, but not before everyone in the EMP task force, a total of ten eyes became fixated on the aurora type show that lit up the sky less than a mile due west. Jeffery allowed his mind to process and record the facts as he began to record using a more sophisticated version of the ROSAT36-Mini: *The Gaussmeter's scalar scale exceeds 500 SI units. The vector scale shows an alert in the westward direction. The cosmos' magnetic field is much stronger than NASA imagined, proven by its ability to lure dark matter from such an intense EMP.* He steadied his thoughts and hands as he continued to aim the ROSAT37-Plus at the western sky. *Keep recording.* He reminded himself. *Absorb everything.* He did. *Golden honey. Pumpkin spice. Warm hibiscus. Barn red. Emerald. Christmas light white. Bride's ivory. Baby blue.* It wasn't until he regained his composure and was able to control the excitement in his voice that he pinched a small button sewn into his NASA shirt, connecting him with his team.

"Dr. Silk, were you able to record dark matter using the B-field Ring Apparatus?"

"Yes, Dr. Linus," Rubin Silk answered. "I've got at least five minutes of transmission."

"Dr. Hubbard, any digital images using the DMC?" Jeffery hoped his answer was yes, having learned that the Dark Matter Camera 900 was a megapixel playground.

"I'll be able to knock your socks off, Dr. Linus" Jeffery could hear the tone in Peter's voice, a result of his MIT degree. The college graduate seemed to be smirking over the clear and very secure communication transmission airway.

"Dr. Petra, any good news to report from the HULA?" Jeffery breathed deeply, waiting and hoping the Hubble Laser could measure the atoms' vibrations in the field.

"I'm looking at the numbers now, Dr. Linus," Sarah Petra's attractive voice slid easily into Jeffery's eardrum. "You're going to be impressed."

Then, thinking about the doctor that had announced the all-eyes-alert over the communication transmission airway, he spoke with gratitude. "Dr. Comings, I can't tell you how much I appreciate your decision to sound the horn," he said, wanting to make sure that Kate Comings knew her importance. "You were on the ball with the Gaussmeter37 tonight," he exhaled. "The higher-ups are going to shit themselves when they find out the G37 exceeded 500 SI units."

Laughter broke from each EMP member as they zipped up padded cases and slowly made their way to the center of the largest pineapple field in the twilight sky.

"Thanks, Jeffery," he smiled when Kate Comings spoke over the team's communication system, partially because of the data they had gathered and partly because one of his team members finally used his first name.

"Good job, Jeffery," Rubin Silk added, his address supporting the closeness that seemed to be spreading like wildfire.

"I'm speechless, Jeff, but stoked," Peter Hubbard tagged.

"Love you guys," Sarah Petra said, then added, "Great team, Jeffery."

Jeffery Linus smiled as he boarded the NASA GFS flight with his team in nautical twilight, leaving the Bahamas. Cape Canaveral bound. Jeffery had been functioning on very little sleep since arriving in Florida three weeks ago. Still, there wasn't one minute of investigating possible portal sites that he would trade for a couple of extra hours of shut-eye. Walking in mud-soaked fields, standing under endless rain, swatting mosquitos the size of houseflies, and even missing Allison, wasn't enough to keep him away from finding and recording data at new EMP locations. He thoroughly enjoyed figuring out how they worked and loved estimating the opportune time to arrive at a portal before the show. The thought of capturing and studying dark matter caused the deepest part of his core to experience *Orgasmus*, as the Greeks would put it.

Still, he missed Dr. Allison Starr, and before his head hit the pillow in his furnished Cape Canaveral, ocean view condo, he dialed Allison, forgetting Seattle was three hours ahead of him. There it was only 5-a.m.

"Hello," Allison answered, sounding half asleep, but all business.

"Gosh, I'm sorry," Jeffery quickly calculated the time difference and knew he had stolen her last hour of sleep. "I didn't mean to wake…" his voice promptly trailed off as he interrupted himself. His scientific side was interpreting the way Allison had said hello. *Too formal.* His gut was sending up flares, shot by the male voice he heard in the background. It was authoritative, directing Pumpkin to get off the kitchen island. *She has company.* He quickly processed before speaking. "I didn't realize the time," Jeffery turned off all emotions. "I'll talk to you later." His last words were just a formality. He had no intention of ever calling back or taking her calls. Ever. A part of him had always known – the way she talked about Northern California, the way her eyes lit up, and the way she avoided the details of a relationship he knew still connected every fiber of her heart.

Red threads, Jeffery thought, before turning off his iPhone XXXVII and going to sleep. Alone.

Thirty-five

A lot had happened in the three weeks since Dr. Jeffery Linus had jetted off to Florida. A crazy series of events unfolded.

First, Dr. Allison Starr had stood frozen in the small hospital room. The chamber, functioning as a multipurpose area, a combo, if you will, to both examinations and operations, is where her mind slowly processed the patient's name on the illuminated wall-chart – Reese Kabula.

It was the same room where Allison's feet kept her glued to the shiny linoleum floor. Her anxious body swayed less than a yard away from the oxygen chamber, where her knees fought for stability. The 10-minute oxygen session seemed to last forever, just like the fatigue that had overcome her patient. The soot-covered face encouraged Reese's eyelids to remain shut, adding to his charred appearance. Meanwhile, questions flowed through Allison's head. *Will he recognize me when he opens his eyes? Will he still have feelings for me? Will I be someone he barely recognizes?* She tried to answer the series of questions but was suddenly interrupted from behind.

"Dr. Starr, this folder was left for you by Dr. Linus. I'm so sorry for the late delivery," Phil fumbled for an explanation, something he had done too much lately since coming to terms with his sexuality a week before graduation. Since reintroducing the man, his parents assumed was his college roommate as his intended life partner. "I've been so busy running the lab since Dr. Linus left, and it must have gotten shuffled under a stack of paperwork." He handed Allison a manila folder.

Allison smiled in his direction as she reached for it. "You worry too much, Phil," she softened his worried eyes. "You're stressing yourself out over nothing. I couldn't ask for a better lunch friend," she said, thinking of the last three weeks. She had eaten lunch in the lab at least a dozen times, probably just to feel closer to Jeffery but also to enjoy the company of Phil, someone she had learned was an excellent listener. He was sweet. Non-threatening. And, he had even rearranged his lunch to accommodate hers. The fact that he was gay made things that much better, in Allison's opinion, something she had suspected from the first day she met him, something Jeffery never mentioned and perhaps never even knew. The last two decades had finally put an end to homosexual and heterosexual stereotypes. Finally.

The world had embraced all-loving unions, just like Phil's parents had. Allison thought about his smile following his evening reveal with his parents at a local eatery, one that still offered a wraparound porch with limited outside dining. *They will love him.* She recalled saying, and later crossing her fingers, hoping his parents would accept Tim, a thirty-year-old who had just received his law degree. They did, with open arms. "Hell, I couldn't ask for a better friend." He had spent just as many lunch hours listening to Allison – about dark matter, about her mother, about Anastasia, her old relationships, and Jeffery. Now, one of the topics they had discussed was sharing the same space. She held the manilla envelope in hand, making it wait a little longer, then opened it slowly while her lips tried to share the name of her latest discovery. "Guess who's in the –

BEEP. BEEP. BEEP. The loud sound startled Allison and filled the small room with reemerging occupants. Dr. Ben Gerhart and Dr. Steven Holm were the first to arrive, followed by two HOC doctors who had been monitoring the patient's intake and lung performance on the other side of the wall. Unfortunately, the Hyperbaric Oxygen Chamber had malfunctioned, pulling HOC doctors away from monitors and sent them scurrying to the patient's side.

Allison stood, unable to move, something she never did in an emergency and something that sent a giant red flag in Phil Hoffmann's direction, prompting him to hold her steady. He knew he was the only thing interrupting her fall after the weight of her body leaned into him, her knees no longer helpful and her eyes swelling with tears.

"Who is he?"

"Reese," she couldn't get out his last name, but Phil didn't need it. He remembered the way her eyes looked when she spoke of

Reese Kabula over lunch. It was only one lunch, but more than enough to know she still loved him.

"Let's move out of the way." His body mimicked a crutch, which Allison relied upon with each step. Phil reassured her, "They are doing everything they can, Allison." He looked back before the door shut behind them. Four medical professionals swarmed over the rural firefighter. Minutes seemed like hours in the hallway at Swedish Medical. Allison wept uncontrollably. Paul's shoulder soaked up Allison's emotions which seemed to amplify each passing minute. It was the sound Phil Hoffmann didn't hear that prompted him to move Allison down the hallway to a private waiting room. The HOC stopped beeping. Dead silence.

Allison was lost. Her world felt complicated, and she felt sick to her stomach. But Phil Hoffmann wasn't about to leave her side. He would make sure she got home safely after closing up the lab and after making certain Allison's team knew she was going. Then, they would let her know the outcome; although, he could tell by Allison's trembling demeanor that she already knew.

Still clutching the manilla envelope, Allison's tears puddled loosely on the center of the envelope, weakening the golden-brown paper and exposing the photo inside. Even though Allison's eyes were saturated, she could make out the EMP's shapes and colors that peeked from the belly of the top photograph tucked inside. *Were you there, Mom? Was I supposed to be in that exact spot and at that very moment to say goodbye? Are you telling me this is another passing I shouldn't miss?* Allison could feel her mother's strength directing her.

Dr. Allison Starr wouldn't miss another goodbye.

Thirty-six

Stubborn doesn't cover it. Outright refusal looked Phil Hoffmann in the face. Allison didn't want to leave Swedish Medical. She wanted to see Reese Kabula, wanted to sit beside his lifeless body so he wouldn't be alone while waiting for the PTP to wheel him to the hospital's morgue. Allison wondered who would take responsibility for his lifeless remains. She imagined his parents, pieces of a marriage she knew had dissolved when he was a young child, now parents that had grown older. *A lifetime has passed,* Allison thought, before she speculated about why Reese had never married. *Neither one of us did,* Allison admitted, realizing her own love life was a mess. *Jeffery is somewhere in the Bahamas chasing his dream, a reality that doesn't include me.* Phil reluctantly walked Allison and her thoughts back to the small room, its most recent job description – death chamber.

It wasn't until Allison pushed on the door that she felt her knees nearly give out – again.

"You gave us quite a scare." She heard Dr. Ben Gerhart say. "False alarm," Ben followed up as Allison's eyes focused on the muscular figure sitting upright on the exam table. "Great vitals, Mr. Kabula." And then, "We'll have you out of here within the hour." Ben Gerhart smiled at the steel-blue eyes that had worked their way open, eyes that were now looking directly at Dr. Allison Starr.

Phil Hoffmann held Allison's body steady while words she didn't realize she was speaking escaped her. "Reese. You're alive. Do you remember –

His eyes interrupted her. Of course, he remembered her. Before taking over the conversation, Reese studied Allison's dark brown eyes, a soothing pecan effortlessly floating in caramel syrup.

"Allison, you look beautiful." It wasn't the reaction she expected—no passive-aggressive communication. No sarcasm. No mumbling. *Maybe he changed,* Allison thought, as she waited for the animosity to start, but it didn't. Instead, his tone didn't reveal the slightest possibility of a hidden agenda. The Reese Kabula standing in front of Allison had body language that said quite the opposite as he effortlessly regained his strength to stand and quickly made his way to her. Reese's arms pulled her against his fire-retardant jacket, which smelled like an out-of-control campfire. "I've missed you," he didn't play games. "There's not been a day that I haven't wondered how your life ended up." Finally, he pulled back enough to let a smile pass between them.

Phil was a spectator now, watching the embers heat between his new lunchtime friend and the firefighter that had taken over the job of supporting Allison's shaky knees. Phil embraced his inner self as he revealed the much-accepted 2037 masculine norm, wiping several tears. It was a world where people didn't label intense emotions as feminine or masculine, only human. Nevertheless, Allison could still feel Phil's emotional support and quickly turned, introducing her friend to her past.

"Phil, this is Reese Kabula." She wanted to say more, *the man I told you about, the love of my life that I abandoned in California, the man I saw in my dreams, and the man who will always have part of my heart,* but she didn't. "He's the firefighter who pulled the seven-year-old out the window, then returned to the inferno, carrying the father to safety." Then, quickly, she returned a smile in Reese's direction.

"Nice to meet you, Reese," Phil said. "The waiting room is still buzzing with chit-chat about your heroism. Because of you, that family is alive." He extended his hand, shaking Reese's hand, then smiled at Allison, letting her know he wasn't forming an opinion on her heart's decision. "I'm going to head home," he backed up his smile. "Allison, I'll see you tomorrow."

Reese and Allison wished Phil a good evening and stood like lifelong friends in a room that birthed a new label. But, as awkward as the moment should have been, it wasn't. It wasn't a death chamber. Not tonight. Tonight, the small OR transformed into a chrysalis.

There wasn't any finger-pointing over a relationship that had ended. No expectations. No comparisons. No would-haves. No should-haves. They stayed in the present, exchanging smiles and glances that were long overdue until Allison heard the overhead page – Gerhart's team report to OR three. At first, Allison thought about ignoring the page; after all, her team knew she was leaving, but Allison imagined a life needing her assistance and felt compelled to help.

"That's me," Allison stated. "I have to go."

Reese stared into her, long enough to notice that she was fighting deep emotions, just like he was, as they struggled to depart. Quickly, he wiped a tear from Allison's cheek, one he swore looked like a glistening ball of amber working its way down an Oregon pine.

"I have to get going, too," he said. "I'm staying at the Holiday Inn tonight. Then back to my hideaway in Northern Cali tomorrow," he added, subconsciously revealing his home location, something he didn't know she already knew. He leaned in, kissing her on the cheek. "Take care, Allison."

He watched her turn away, but not before she gave his upper bicep a farewell squeeze and sent words in his direction that exposed her vulnerability.

"I'm glad fate brought us back together," she said. Reese couldn't see Allison's eyes steam like a small pot of coco as she hurried off, leaving him standing there. He remained still, breathing in the cinnamon-colored pixie dust that Dr. Allison Starr had stirred in his soul.

That was three weeks ago, and in that time, Reese Kabula called Swedish Medical at least a half-dozen times, two of which he was able to speak directly with Allison. Still, she refused his advances to meetup, an attempt to rekindle lost love. Instead, thinking of Jeffery, she waited for a phone call she had been expecting from the Bahamas.

Now, on the eighth of October, Allison's phone vibrated during her last round at Swedish.

"Are you still at the hospital?" The voice asked Allison, who had politely pulled herself away from a recovering sixty-year-old, long enough to answer the vibrating phone. It was Phil Hoffmann. Not Jeffery. Not Reese.

"Yes," she answered. "I'm leaving within the hour." She exhaled, releasing a bit of relief. A part of her was glad it wasn't

Jeffery or Reese. She needed friendship right now. No complications.

"Can I meet you at your apartment when you leave Swedish Medical?" During the last three weeks, Phil had been over for dinner twice, had bonded with Pumpkin, and felt comfortable sharing his lows and highs with Allison. He needed friendship right now too.

"Let yourself in." "I will be there within the hour, Phil," she answered, detecting a slight emotional quiver in her friend's tone. She had leaned on his friendship many times recently since Dr. Jeffery Linus had taken on the role of ghost-hunter, and now, it was her turn to be there for Phil. She had programmed Phil Hoffmann's print in her security system, an old habit, and a backup plan for Pumpkin's care, in case she had to work a double at Swedish, something that had happened several times since the recent devastation caused by the fires in Oregon.

Allison's whiskey-colored eyes grew tired on the monorail ride home. Still, they managed to stay open until just after one-a.m., first talking to Phil about walking in on Tim, the love of his life, having sex with another man, a visual that would take years to undo. "The two of them completed a lot of the same law classes together,"

Phil shared with Allison. "Tim didn't know I closed the lab early today, and he certainly didn't expect me to come home two hours earlier than normal."

"I'm sorry, Phil." Allison held his hand in hers. She wanted to tell him he'd find someone else or that he could do better, but those words were overused when it came to the death of a relationship. "Red threads," she said instead, "will lead you to the person you're supposed to be with." It was the only thing that made sense to Allison and the only thing she felt would offer some comfort to her friend besides a few hours of sleep. There was no point in letting Phil Hoffmann travel home so late. Jeffery Linus had unknowingly left a new razor and toothbrush in the bathroom nearly a month ago, purchases by Allison. And a clean lab coat was hanging in the bedroom closet, embossed with Swedish Medical's logo, an item Jeffery no longer needed. "You're welcome to stay here tonight. Pumpkin will share the sofa with you," she smiled.

"Thanks, Allison," and then, "have you heard from Jeffery?"

"Red threads," Allison repeated before sufficiently answering. "No, I haven't, but things will work out the way they're supposed to."

By four in the morning, Allison's body was soaring over the mountains of Northern California, floating effortlessly over tall pines and hidden cabins. Her eyes searched for Reese Kabula, but he wasn't there. Not until her phone rang was her memory jolted back to the here-and-now. It was an action reminding her that Reese Kabula had informed her a week ago on the phone that he would be visiting the Oregon coast during the second weekend in October. An open invitation that Allison hadn't accepted.

Half-asleep, Allison Starr answered her phone. "Hello." Okay, so it was formal, compared to the normal – *hello sweetie, miss you, any luck in the Bahamas?* – but she didn't expect the abrupt responses on the other end of her phone. She didn't expect dismissal from Dr. Jeffery Linus, and Allison most certainly didn't expect the good doctor to forward her subsequent attempts to get ahold of him. There had been numerous failed attempts before Phil left Allison's apartment for his shift at Swedish and again on the long monorail ride that Allison made toward the coast of Oregon.

That's right – Oregon. The decision to accept a weekend getaway came after Jeffery finally picked up the phone. A quick and stern announcement met Allison: "I need a break," Jeffery shouted, dismissing the love of his life without allowing her to get a word in edgewise. The stringent treatment changed Allison's world, but not in the way you might expect. Dr. Allison Starr didn't crumble; instead, she simply made two phone calls. The first call was to Swedish Medical to inform them she was taking her remaining days off. The second to Reese Kabula to accept his open invitation to spend time together on the Oregon coast.

Dr. Allison Starr would no longer settle for being the first mate in their relationship or *any* relationship. Deep in her gut, Allison suspected history was attempting to repeat itself.

Not this time, Allison thought.

Thirty-seven

The color of October flooded the silky flesh covering Allison's high cheekbones. Strands of long brown hair matched her warm hue, a golden honey brown, courtesy of the Seattle sun. Soaking it in, Allison felt alive, more than she ever had in her entire life. She remembered her mother's journal, recalled how her mother compared herself to a caterpillar, encased in a pupa, gently rocking on the end of a twig, waiting for rebirth, waiting to begin life as a butterfly.

Now, Allison understood. She had experienced her metamorphosis. It had started after Dr. Jeffery Linus had repeatedly forwarded her calls to voicemail. Then, finally, Jeffery cut her out of his life, keeping his NASA discoveries to himself, until he had no choice but to contact Phil Hoffmann, his replacement, in an unrelated matter.

"I left a file in the bottom drawer of the gray file cabinet labeled WIMP," Jeffery said. "Would you scan the contents and send it to me immediately?" *Weak Interacting Massive Particles*, Jeffery thought to himself, hoping the graphs he had spent hours perfecting would be of some interest in his team's next mission, a chance to study an area of low-threshold energy on the coast of Italy.

"Absolutely," Phil answered. "By the way, Allison didn't deserve the cold-blooded treatment she got from you on the phone the other morning," Phil announced sternly, sticking up for his friend. "I felt bad leaving her alone in her apartment as I caught a monorail to Swedish right after you hung up on her, and even worse when I heard you finally answered a return call and dismissed her altogether." Phil was on fire. "That's uncool, man."

Fuck, Jeffery thought. *It wasn't Reese. It was Phil.* Then, *Unfucking believable.* "You slept with Allison?" The question came out before Jeffery could stop it.

"I slept *at* Allison's," Phil chuckled. "I guess you never picked up on the fact that I'm gay." The announcement stopped Jeffery's heart, not because he had just discovered that his replacement was gay. That was not something he cared about one way or another. What had stopped his heart, what had just become apparent, and what had suddenly become evident is the fact that he dismissed the woman he loved out of his life because he thought she had rekindled her relationship with Reese. Call it separation jealousy. Call it stupidity. Call it just being an asshole. "We stayed up half the night talking about my broken heart after a man I loved crushed it," Phil continued. "She's a good friend."

"Have you seen her today?" It was a question with a purpose. Maybe he could set the record straight. Apologize. Beg. Whatever it took.

"No, she took a couple of personal days," Phil added, leaving out the why and where details. Jeffery had screwed up royally. There was no point in telling him how bad. There was no point in reminding him that Allison wasn't the type to cheat on someone she loved. There was no point in telling him that Allison had decided to meet with Reese Kabula. Privately. The rural firefighter had driven his GFS truck to Olympia, Washington, rendezvousing with Allison at a central monorail station.

There, with his smile, he whisked Allison away, taking her to the coast of Oregon. It was a familiar playground the two of them had shared long ago. Now, it was for an extended weekend. One Dr. Ben Gerhart had no problem approving spur of the moment with pay, reimbursement for donating extra time to Swedish, and working long work hours during Oregon's most devastating fire season – ever.

Everything about Seaside felt familiar, just like the chemistry they felt between each other. Almost two decades had passed, and time had touched both Seaside and their physical bodies, but the fall air seemed to molt layers of skin and years of separation, giving them both glimpses of their younger selves. Allison's hand still fit in Reese's. They meandered miles of the Oregon coast, their grip tight until they stopped to sit on a weathered swing-set, then the old lovers gently released tangled fingers. They directed concentration to other limbs that pumped consistently, building momentum and allowing

the air's friction to moved them like caterpillars. The movement on

an old swing-set mocked them as they reached forward in an old

relationship. Grasping.

By ten-p.m., walls crumbled as they fell onto a queen bed at

the Seaside Lanai, soaking in lost time, succumbing to the red

threads that tied two bodies into one. It was supposed to happen.

Everything that had ever happened between Allison and Reese

needed to occur. Predestined. Fate. Life's path. For nearly thirty-six

hours, they stayed tangled in ivory-colored bed sheets. The couple

came out for an occasional stab of roasted chicken and truffles, a

spoon of rich chocolate souffle, or a sip of tropical fruit juice –

benefits of having well-paid room service. By 10-a.m. Saturday, they

had caught up on seventeen years of missed passion.

Yet, something was off. Allison Starr felt a disconnect deep

in her gut. It was a feeling that kept her from a whole night's sleep

Saturday night. With the minuscule amount of moonlight peeking in

through the curtains, Allison watched Reese sleep. Reese's pineal

gland released melatonin with each breath, which Allison jokingly imagined was doused in dopamine, causing her to plant a giddy-girlish kiss on Reese's forehead just as daylight woke him.

By mid-afternoon, they were walking around the ruins of Seaside Aquarium. Shattered windows faced the Pacific. The high-pitched roar of harbor seals couldn't be heard, at least not from the inside of the buildings' decay. Perhaps, miles out, underwater, they were singing in a chorus of barks, moans, and grunts.

Allison noticed the faded red lettering on the Seaside Aquarium sign – *touch the stars* – making her think of Jeffery Linus' love of the cosmos, but only for a moment. Her thoughts quickly went to her mother as she spotted an empty glass tank through a lower window. Both the tank and window were cracked and hardened with sea-salt residue, but her memory of being in the aquarium twenty years earlier vividly played in her thoughts. Even though it was only in her memory, she could still see the giant sea star maneuvering up the glass tank. She watched it hover over its intended victim – a tiny snail – and her thoughts processed the creature's actions as she watched it emit its deadly enzyme, instantly turning the snail into a tasty liquid, leaving its shell empty. It was a relationship where the tiny snail felt protected and loved, unaware that the sea star didn't share the same unconditional feelings. Has Reese always been the sea star? Her thought was private, but her observation was becoming apparent.

The flashback to an empty shell was an accurate comparison to their relationship. That recollection, combined with the way Reese had directed their every movement on the Oregon coastal visit, set off a series of alarm bells in Allison's head. Privately, she admitted that his soul bled love for her when she did as he desired. Alarm bell number one – *he loves me if I walk miles of coastline until he is tired.* Alarm bell number two – *he adores me when my child-like spirit prompts my legs into action on the old swing-set until he wants to move on.* Alarm bell number three – *he expects me to spend an evening at a hotel he selected and eat what he orders through room service.* Alarm bell number four – *he shows no interest in my desire to stare at the Seaside Aquarium.*

Reliving the sea star visual and Reese's actions over the weekend were trivial examples. What wasn't insignificant was the years of similar relationship history that they shared. By Sunday evening, Allison's heart released Reese Kabula.

Allison suddenly realized she had spent too many years chasing and loving men that didn't love her the way she needed – unconditionally. She finally understood that red threads not only take us back to people we need to learn from, but the invisible fibers connect us to other possibilities, other faces, and strangers that are supposed to become friends. Clarity had taken over. The pain in her gut had dispersed. No cannonballs. It was a realization that changed her. She smiled at Reese Kabula. She would always have love for him, but she loved herself more for the first time.

She took a monorail back from the coast of Oregon to Olympia, then picked up a different monorail to Seattle after kissing Reese Kabula goodbye. Both tracks totaled two hundred miles, plenty of time to breathe in the world around her – deep breaths that made her feel new from the inside out. She smiled at the October sun that thinned her chrysalis skin, revealing her hidden wings. Hemolymph pumped into her veins like a raging river.

Her heart finally learned she didn't *need* Dr. Jeffery Linus or Rural Firefighter Reese Kabula to survive. More importantly, she didn't *want* either one of them. She wanted her freedom. She wanted to bathe in her strength. *Now, I know why you loved that Dalton Highway so much, Mom.*

Pumpkin, who had been visited twice by Phil Hoffmann for fresh food and water, greeted Allison at the door. Pumpkin purred as he followed Allison to the bedroom, where catching up on sleep was her priority. Closing her eyes, she pictured her mother's red Jeep kicking up dirt on the Dalton Highway in Alaska. She smiled after realizing how alive that road made her mother feel. As Allison drifted further and further into a deep sleep, she allowed her mother's tenacity to grease every fiber inside her sleeping body. The feeling intensified as each breath welcomed the impenetrable, delicate light-catchers that sprouted from her soul. Finally, in a night of deep sleep, she watched herself floating over the belly of Canyon de Chelly. Alone. No angel held her as she weaved between Spider Rock's massive rock legs. But, inside her inner being, she felt the life force of her mother, Enola May Starks, felt the spirit of her Aunt Dixie, and even sensed her biological grandfather, Grover Howard Starks, whose birth surname was and will always be Starr. The psyches slowly and deliberately settled inside Allison, wrapping permanent red threads around the tiny galaxy in her soul.

From the Arizona canyon, Dr. Allison Starr conceded to the final stage of REM sleep as she grabbed the bright red thread dangling before her. The force pulled Allison into the 1700s.

Thirty-eight

Allison could see the handsome buccaneer had chosen wisely, capturing a large ship that appeared seaworthy, quick, and armed with eight cannons. The act of mutiny on the open sea was second-hand for Rack and his men, who had taken the vessel by force. Unfortunately, the battle that seemed to be more challenging was the storm that mercilessly tossed them around on the Caribbean Sea as they made their escape.

Allison watched, as a non-participant, from her Seattle queen-sized bed, one that currently served as a small watercraft, tossing alongside Calico Jack Rackham and Anne Bonny. Allison watched, her eyes in REM, her heart standing close to Rack, a nickname his men had given him, and one Annie, the love of his life, often used. Allison's body twitched, her restless arms wishing she could touch Rackham, like the cursing female pirate currently standing near his muscular build. But, instead, Allison satisfyingly absorbed their strong connection. The passion between the courageous woman who stood by his side and Rackham was familiar. Pumpkin purred loudly; he was a stand-in, an unpaid actor, staged on the water's surface – a queen-size comforter – while Allison watched the movie from over 300 years ago unfold.

Just weeks earlier, Anne Bonny had left her husband, a sailor and a somewhat predictable man. Her heart wanted the dangerous pirate, a feral man who sought adventure. Infidelity spread like a disease in the 1700s, a time when lifespans were almost always cut short. The promiscuity happened after a routine sailing trip to the Bahamas. Anne Bonny felt her soul wrap around Jack Rackham's. It was as if a bright red thread violently and suddenly tightened, wrapping itself from Rack's heart to Annie's soul, pulling their worlds off-balance, like the sea was doing to the ship in Allison's dream.

"Save the loot, you fucking scurvies," Rack yelled loudly over the unforgiving waves that tried to topple his newly acquired ship. His men quickly obliged, knowing Anne Bonny, or Annie, as Rack called her, wouldn't miss if she decided to aim a pistol in the face of an uncooperative crew member.

"All hands hoay!" Anne Bonny reiterated.

"Batten down the hatches," bellowed Mary Read, a pear-shaped female who dressed like a man and carried a sword that had killed nearly fifty men during the last ten years. Annie recognized her bravery and passion for life and quickly succumbed to a friendship with the only female pirate she had ever met. The best friends spent a summer raiding fishing boats off the coast of Africa and taking what they needed – what they wanted.

Anne Bonny often thought of her sailor husband, the man she left behind in the Bahamas. He stood there, emotionless, his eyes sorrowful, his heart pleading with the cosmos for intervention. But it wasn't enough to keep her. Anne knew her place was with Rackham on the high seas.

Dr. Allison Starr's closed eyes watched men dressed in baggy trousers and skull caps tie down a crate of animal skins, a cask of rice, and several piles of wood as Mary Read had instructed. They also worked to unload cannons, pulling weight away from the ship's starboard, the target of giant waves.

"Save the booty," Mary bellowed. No one dared to question her authority. She was Anne Bonny's best friend and wouldn't hesitate to use her good-standing to send any disobedient man to Davy Jones' Locker. She had done so before and would again.

The Jolly Roger blew fiercely in the wind as Jack Rackham fought to keep the vessel upright in the unforgiving waves. Allison noticed the white skull and crossbones on the black flag, adding detail to her dream that gave it authenticity. She took in every feature, studying Jack's muscular build and the smile he maintained as he faced danger. Rackham was called Old Salt in pirate-circles. Men from all parts of the sea boasted that Jack Rackham's experience made him more seaworthy than any vessel.

Black Bart, barely eighteen and somewhat of a scallywag, approached the side of Mary Read with Old Red on his right shoulder, a reddish-yellow monkey with a patch of unruly gray hair that resembled an old mop on the top of the primate's head. The monkey's small black hands held an unripe banana, which he rapidly gnawed.

Old Red went everywhere with Black Bart and even watched over him during his drunken episodes, like a guard dog watches over a sleeping child. Maybe it was the monkey's way of repayment for being rescued. Black Bart took the monkey from a western African ship, which held the primate captive in a rusty, barred metal cage. Since then, Old Red spent his days as Black Bart's helper.

That was nearly five years earlier. Then, the thirteen-year-old boy, his newly rescued monkey, and Mary Read allied with Calico Jack Rackham. They boarded his ship-of-the-month to escape an angry crew of Barbary pirates off the coast of Tanzania.

Members of Rackham's crew questioned the teenage boy's connection with Mary Read; many wondered if she hadn't birthed the young lad, especially after noticing how he always received Mary's rare amount of special privilege. As a result, black Bart was often three sheets to the wind and unable to function on deck. Mary had forced several pirates to walk the plank after being caught in the same condition, but not Black Bart. She had a special bond with the young man, despite his alcoholism. But today, Black Bart was fully functional and was on a mission to deliver urgent news to Mary, Rack, and Annie.

"Ahoy, mates. Avast ye, a band of pirate-hunters head in our direction." Old Red seemed to understand the urgency, dropping the remainder of his half-peeled banana on deck as his monkey eyes widened. Black Bart stood in front of the three with his crooked-tailed monkey, nearly blocking Rack's view.

Typically, Rack didn't give the carouser too much attention, but this time, he ordered his men to reload the cannons and listen for further instructions. He, too, noticed the giant ship as he glanced around Black Bart's unoccupied left shoulder blade. It was coming fast and gaining momentum.

"Fire in the hole," Jack ordered as he directed his ship to keep course, head-on, without flinching. The storm was now at his back, and a new storm, one he found more exciting, lie straight ahead. Cannons fired at the pirate-hunters on his demand.

For Allison, the loud boom sounded like an alarm. It was 5:30-a.m. Pumpkin looked at her dark seaweed eyes the moment they opened. She stared back at him, noticing how the shape of his eyes matched those of the monkey in her dream. Even his hair resembled the primate's rusty-melon-toned coat. She smiled, shaking off her vivid imagination, before speaking to Pumpkin, who had been at her side for hours.

"Good morning, my little monkey." For a half-of-an-instant, she let her imagination run wild, then stood, making her way to the bathroom mirror. There she gave into her vivid imagination, looking past herself and into the imagined face of Black Bart as he stood in front of Annie, Rack, and Mary. She studied every detail she could remember, a crooked smile, squinty-eyes, a doppelgänger for her brother Mitch. Turning her back to the mirror, she looked into her bedroom long enough to let her eyes study the bed that had served as a ship throughout the night. Allowing her mind to wander, she imagined Mary Read, a sword in her right hand, deep-set eyes, long wavy hair that fought for direction, lips that didn't seek invite, and a heart and soul that seemed endless like her mother – Enola. Two spots over stood Calico Jack Rackham. His stance welcomed confrontation, a chance to devour a fierce component. He reminded her of Reese – rugged, seeking danger, unpredictable. A tease. Then, she thought of Jeffery, his persona composed of short attributes she sometimes yearned for – stability, predictability, dependability. *In my dream, Jeffery is somewhat like Annie's abandoned sailor husband*, Allison thought before she felt her blood run cold. The frigid reality took her eyes to the woman in the middle, Anne Bonny. Annie's brow line sat lower than most, framing the lowest part of her forehead and eyes that craved life. Long hair fell in wild strands to the bend in her elbows, which rested at a tapered waistline. But it was the look on Annie's face that shook Allison's core, one that shouted – I will not coincide with the norm. I will die for my beliefs. I will use my anger to keep you at bay. I will never surrender. I will live –

At that precise moment, Dr. Allison Starr wondered – *how many lives have I already lived?*

Thirty-nine

My life as Mary Read was short-lived, but my passion for having

been Annie's close friend is forever undying. I can't remember every

detail of every life I've experienced—just bits and pieces. Every cell

in my soul's dark matter holds thousands of memories, and when

manipulated, an intricate image appears. Each window to the past is

unique – never repeated. What repeats is the never-ending feeling of

déjà vu for places. That feeling occurs often. But – what happens

more often is my magnetic pull to other souls, those I've known

before.

My last host died in a small room at Swedish Medical. Her short lifetime was magical, not sad. The death of her tiny body was a process, one where an intense warmth multiplied inside each cell, protecting my consciousness. My soul, swaddled like a baby, and housed in a nonluminous cradle, was saved deep within Anastasia Elpis' small body until it reached the portal. There I was set free. For a short instance, my soul mingled with one of my past lives. I saw myself in the body of an elderly Indian woman – my thoughts soaking up a vision where I skinned and cooked the buffalo killed by our tribe's great warrior. You know him best as Dr. Jeffery Linus, once spared a cruel death by his angel – the soul I love by the name of Allie.

The memory prompted me to look in on him quickly as I floated in the cosmos. I watched Dr. Jeffery Linus and his team witnessing dark matter. I knew Jeffery and his EMP team had seen a tremendous universal secret in the Bahamas, learning information from the colorful arrangements of resilient cells that had danced in the dark skies. Still, I knew his team of scientists had no idea what the brilliant display of various colors represented.

I did.

That's because the universe is kind to the dying, allowing each person to revisit their human existence and even permitting an up-close and personal examination of each cell. As a result, I felt some comfort in my consciousness, embracing parts of me that were hard to accept as a human. My life with Dacey and Melantha Fears painted permanent peach dots of color inside my soul. Each brush stroke left me exposed, unprotected, and naked during my human childhood years with them. But the representation of my colors kindly reversed during my six short years with Karen Elpis. With her as my mother, those ominous peach dots metamorphosed into spots of warmth, love, and security. Even the crimson red, a sign of anger in my earlier life, become a raging fire inside my soul. It lit my way back to Allie so I could love her once again, in a different type of relationship. My Allison was right about the dandelion yellow. It represented my favorite flower, but only my second choice. Dr. Allison Starr was my first favorite wildflower – my joy, my happiness, and my hope.

Now, as an angel, I hover over my daughter, Allison Starr, watching her body toss and turn, spying into her dreams. I study her reaction to a previous existence, knowing her scientific mind processed bits and pieces of my past. Her past. Our past.

In future years, she'll watch other movies in her dreams. Perhaps a part of her will figure out that Enola May Starks' soul lived before Mary. She'll analyze. She'll imagine. And, somewhere between her research-based principles and her faith-based spirituality, she'll know I'm there. Our love will continue to grow as it has in the past. It doesn't matter whether we coexist in the same culture, as fellow-pirates, as mother-daughter, or as patient-doctor. We will always find each other, on land or sea.

This, I know. My many lives have given me the wisdom that the new breed of pirates in 2037 seek. Pirates like Dr. Jeffery Linus search for portals. Perhaps, he too will watch the same movie unfold, his mind taking notes on how his sailor's heart conceded to a pirate, leaving the love of his life in the care of Calico Jack Rackham, the rural firefighter in today's space and time. Perhaps, he'll understand that's why his angel saved him from the sudden death of a bloody buffalo stampede. Maybe, he'll figure out the angel was Dr. Allison Starr during a period of transition.

It was those same angelic actions that saved me during that time. As an elderly Indian woman, I sensed her presence, believing she spared the buffalo hunter's life, which allowed him to hunt food throughout several more winters so our tribe could survive.

Most recently, I encountered the time to thank her when I allowed my tiny eyes to peer into hers from the body of Anastasia. Now, that part of me dances in the galaxy as a bright sherbet orange, waiting for its next host. Last night, its glow brightened as it watched Allison Starr's soul absorb details from her life as a pirate. Like a child processing information, Allison was beginning to figure out the most sought-after universal secret. From the deepest spot in her core, Allison suspected she had loved both Dr. Jeffery Linus and rural firefighter Reese Kabula in previous lives, just as she knew she had loved me in many lifetimes.

In her Seattle apartment, Allison recognized pieces of Mitch, her long-lost brother, in Black Bart. *My brother,* thought Allison. And, even after waking, Allison couldn't help but look at Pumpkin differently. *A monkey? A dog? And now, a cat? Maybe Pumpkin has been all three,* Allison concluded. She was right.

Watching her study herself in the bathroom mirror, I felt the gamma-compressed red and yellow catalyze my soul and the cosmos. Anne Bonny starred back at me from the high seas, both as my friend and now, as my daughter. Our eyes locked, long enough for both of us to gain confidence in the fact that we would see each other again. And, again.

An orange haze surrounded me. Another transformation was beginning. It was time for me to go. *Forward*, I heard Dixie say. I didn't fight the process. I thought about my most recent human body and how bravely it surrendered. Anastasia and I orchestrated the where and when, making sure the scientific side of Dr. Allison Starr had a front-row seat, even though the soul I loved most as my daughter was over a thousand miles away. I felt her watching my dark matter as it was magnetically pulled from the desert floor and into the universe. Of course, I predicted Dr. Allison Starr's disbelief, knowing she believed many of the same things that I did. Like me, she required cold hard proof; otherwise, she would search the universe for a scientific reason—*The Kaleidoscope-Effect. Good one, Allie.* It still makes me laugh. *Funny.* Now, suspended between lifetimes, I was cold hard proof.

Now, I linger close to the cosmos near a bright star, willing and ready to answer the question put forth. I'm familiar with the process, knowing the most crucial after-death question waits for each passerby –

"Where is Heaven?" The universe silently asked me.

"On Earth," I remembered promptly answering, even after learning that my answer would instantly forfeit my chance to spend time with Dixie, my lifelong friend, or my biological father, Grover Howard Starks. Their souls existed in a different dimension. Heaven on earth wasn't a reality for them. For Dixie and Grover, it was a magical place where souls remained in angelic form. I captured glimpses of Dixie, my best friend, and Grover, my favorite father, during brief moments between my soul's reincarnation. They were often my angels in transport from one human existence to another. To live in their realm, I needed faith—more than I had.

My faith was in an earthly heaven. *Dixie would want me to keep going – forward;* I rationalized my decision in my consciousness. I even felt Grover's spirit nudging me – *keep going.*

"On Earth," I repeated. This time every cell inside my dark matter shouted my answer. It was the same answer I gave after

leaving the body of Mary Reed, leaving the body of an elderly tribal woman, leaving the body of Enola May Starks, and leaving the body of Anastasia Elpis. It would be the same answer I would give in lifetimes to come. I wasn't ready to reside in the Heaven that Dixie and Grover found satisfying. I needed another chance to find Mitch. I mourned for another opportunity to see Allie's smile. No matter how many lifetimes it took, I would find them both.

Forty

The sky matched the tall green grass. Allison's friend and ex-lover, the late Dr. Jeffery Linus, would have proudly labeled it a pear green. The greenery's untamed strands blew non-stop in the unforgiving summer wind that tickled the belly of America. Even though erosion resulting in land loss had changed the precise center in what used to be called the lower forty-eight, people still gave Lebanon, Kansas the title. Dr. Allison Starr, and others in the world of science, knew Cheyenne, Wyoming took center-stage. Still, at age fifty-seven, Allison considered Lebanon the center of her universe.

Nearly a decade earlier, Allison spent endless hours in downtown Seattle promoting President Pearl Thornburg via website or email every day after leaving Swedish Medical. Like most Americans, Allison wanted Thornburg to serve a second ten-year term and was happy when Pearl was re-elected POTUS, sworn in on January 2043. Most Americans wanted to implement more environmental laws and agreed to enact population control on islands and peninsulas to avoid America's most pressing problem – significant erosion and ocean pollution. Most. Not everyone.

Sometimes it's a sole human being that can change the direction of the world. In this case, the single round fired from a Ruger American Rifle destroyed America's strides to protect the environment. One man's ammo not only ended the life of Pearl Thornburg; it opened a wound that had scabbed over. Global warming crept back like a mountain lion with unforgiving jaws. The newly elected POTUS, Barron-T, dismantled the free health care system. Most Americans called the new POTUS a radical thirty-six-year-old. America was shocked when he eliminated free college. They cringed when he stopped funding the existing ACZ areas. But it didn't stop there. Barron-T eradicated the GFS automobile program. Like a progressive disease, pollution and erosion nipped at the edges of every continent.

By 2045, twenty percent of the earth's atmosphere became the new home for minuscule-sized phytoplankton that once lived underwater. The plankton transitioned to the earth's atmosphere after the ocean turned a stale metallic color, and sea life quickly disappeared. No longer did humans make a distinction between the Arctic, Atlantic, Pacific, or Southern Oceans. Now, people referred to the dark silvered body of water as the Global Ocean. The GO had covered eighty percent of the earth's surface by the time Barron-T reached half-term. That was 2048.

That was the same year Starr watched the last bit of sky-blue fade from her skyrise in Seattle. The creature comforts that Allison had worked hard for seemed to wash out to the Global Ocean slowly. Bits of the coastline sank day by day. It was a reality that the entire nation faced.

The first landmass to *completely* disappear was the Baja Peninsula in California. Allison absorbed the details in horror on her Wall-T.V., the newest LG model, during the fall of 2048. She watched as a rescue crew sifted through mounds of grey ash for survivors after a second explosion on the sinking peninsula. Major news stations panned left, then right, before settling on a snowy screen. Hours passed before the world knew what Allison suspected – the enormous mass of the Baja Peninsula sank into the Global Ocean, leaving crumbs for what used to be called the Gulf of California.

Dr. Allison Starr had signed off on sending a medical team to Baja from Swedish Hospital. Every fiber of Allison's body quivered in pain after realizing her signature aided and abetted the death of Dr. Ben Gerhart, Dr. Steven Holm, and their leading molecular scientist and her best friend, Dr. Phil Hoffmann. Tears streamed down the inside of Allison's heart. Her lungs deflated as she collapsed on her living room floor, where Pumpkin's worried eyes met hers.

"Reese was there too." Pumpkin didn't understand her strained announcement but sensed by her unbearable sorrow that she had lost the first love of Allison's life. Her most recent life, anyhow. "Reese is gone," Allison yelled in anguish. "Everyone is gone." There were no survivors—dangerous gases in the deep-water killed anyone that remained afloat.

The nation mourned. Even though evacuations should have been mandatory, Barron-T ordered the California governor to stand down. It was a decision that cost nearly six million people their lives. The massive loss reached around the globe.

Allison's mind replayed her most recent FaceTime with Reese a week earlier. She watched him smile into his Apple watch, a series XX and blushed when she realized her right index finger curled a strand of long brown hair during their chat, a gesture that seemed out of place in their monthly friends-only conversations. Yet, she could still see the video's backdrop – a fourth-floor corner office at Swedish Medical Center. Allison's name and title were in bold letters on the door – **Dr. Allison Starr, VP of Clinical Operations** – and there was a large picture window overlooking the Seattle gray sky and chrome-tinted Global Ocean.

A year after the Baja Peninsula sank, she lost Jeffery Linus in a 2049 plane crash somewhere over the Bermuda Triangle. His EMP team made world news after the same sizeable magnetic field that had pulled their plane from the sky also served as the portal for their deceased bodies. NASA's live recordings leaked to the entire universe. The footage exposed the existence of dark matter. Sunkist orange, burnt golden sugar, deep-sea blues, bright strawberry red, highlighter yellow, and crisp sapphire danced on news stations worldwide. The sky exploded in colors against the leaden sky.

Jeffery would be proud, Allison imagined, then permitted her mind to witness him as a young boy. Under a crisp Maryland blue sky, Allison saw him playing with a red race car, Lightning McQueen, in the front yard of his boyhood home. She watched his fingers, the same ones that had once wiped a mixture of potting soil and volcanic glass from her brow-line on the Seattle monorail. Then she imagined his soul, wrapped in Lightning McQueen's bumblebee yellow and candy red decals as it floated into the abyss.

In April of 2050, Pumpkin curled up next to Allison during one of Seattle's rainstorms. He didn't suffer as he took his last breath. Instead, a gentle purr vibrated into the side of Allison's thigh. She knew before her rust-colored brown eyes could look down that her furry friend was gone.

People handle loss differently. For Dr. Starr, death meant moving forward. That's what her Aunt Dixie would have wanted, and that's what her mother, Enola May, would have expected. Allison granted them both their wish by fighting the decay that spread throughout the world. First, Dr. Starr interacted with local businesses, providing free food and apartment stays for patients' family members. Then Allison Starr created home health care plans for residents in the ACZ areas that no longer received subsidized funding. Next, Allison formed a team to assist with infection control. And, finally, the good doctor founded a support system for grieving family members called *Anastasia's Angels,* whose principles revolved around the existence of dark matter.

Allison's fight for services and truth lasted almost two years. Unfortunately, and simultaneously, most of Italy, the Somalian Peninsula, parts of Japan, eighty percent of Hawaii, half of Costa Rica, the southern cone of South America, Florida, Michigan, Maryland, and New York disappeared. The GO's dark lifeless silver ate the world without swallowing between bites. Even Barron-T's mask mandates couldn't save the people trying to survive in the coastal regions. Allison had no choice, abandoning a city that once thrived; she chased the chance to extend her life, hightailing it to the center of America.

Allison was more fortunate than some people and reached Lebanon, Kansas before parts of the United States were unbearable for travel – extreme heat, and in other areas, extreme cold. She lived another twenty years after making her way to Kansas.

Allie died during the winter of 2073 in America's belly, at age seventy-eight, but not before witnessing the miraculous changes that occurred outside and inside humanity. She lived long enough to watch Barron-T's impeachment (in 2058, halfway through his second term), to witness both the executive and legislative branches in the presidential system completely dismantle (2059), and to see state lines and borders disappear (by the summer of 2060).

Some changes weren't so noticeable unless you were part of the scientific research community like Allison. Human beings born after 2054 had lungs that functioned without any difficulty in the newly developing atmosphere. As most labeled the new generation, *the beginners* discovered advanced ways to control the earth's surface temperature and atmospheric gases.

Allison stared down at her weathered hands on her last morning. Her hands had touched every human emotion; the most poignant memories including wiping the watery salt-filled liquid from heartaches and holding the hand of her mother, Enola May. Her fingers had squeezed the trigger on a Flintlock pistol in another life, causing a disobeying pirate to meet his early death. And, during an angelic transition, her talons managed to catch an Indian brave in midair. By evening, she rested her lifeless hands at her side, in a world where the new generation no longer kept track of months, weeks, or days. Time no longer mattered. Only people.

A tiny patch of metal reflected the bright red sun from its cemented position in a garden walkway. The coroner had the plaque engraved with the words: **Starr – 2073.** There were no other details. No one would remember the deceased person's sex, race, date of birth. The new generation chose not to. They understood what Dr. Allison Starr understood – life is a continuous cycle.

The beginners were right about life continuing. Seventeen hundred miles away from Lebanon, Kansas, and at the turn of the century, deep inside an Othello Tunnel, just east of a town once known as Hope, a twenty-year-old warrior princess breathed rapidly, first inhaling, then exhaling. The new mother, a leader for the beginners in British Columbia, had already picked out the names for her twins. One boy. One girl. Derick and Zyah, respectively. They would grow to become warriors in the new world.

The midwife looked on fondly, analyzing the young mother's words after her newborn son, Derek, was placed in the cradle of her left arm, and her newborn daughter, Zyah, was established in the crook of her right. Princess Sontee knew the crying babies were hers to raise and love.

"Don't cry. The world's not ending," the young princess reassured her newborns. "It's beginning all over again." *Remember,* the mother whispered into Zyah's tiny ear. *I told you that before.*

THE END

Sherie L. Howard currently lives in Washington state with her dog, Miles. **Portal 37: One, One, Seven** is the fourth novel in Howard's *Enola May* series. Howard considers herself an autobiographical fiction novelist, a controversial label.

Howard gives her readers a passenger seat in her own life while incorporating relevant topics. The *Enola May* series takes readers through the backroads of America as colorful characters maneuver issues like mental illness, addiction, infidelity, physical abuse, sexual abuse, criminal homicide, parent-child relationships, adult relationships, and spiritual battles.

Howard's most recent work – **Portal 37: One, One, Seven** – allows her readers to explore reincarnation in a fiction setting.